Penguin Crime Fiction
Editor: Julian Symons
Rogue Eagle

James McClure was born in Johannesburg and lived
in South Africa until he was twenty-five. He worked
on several newspapers in South Africa and became
a successful journalist, specializing in crime. Then he
came to England and became the deputy editor of the
Oxford Times Group of weekly newspapers before
resigning to write full-time. He has written a full-
length television play, the screen-play of *The Steam
Pig* (his first book which won the Gold Dagger
award in 1971), two other novels featuring Kramer
and Zondi – *The Caterpillar Cop* and *The Gooseberry
Fool* – as well as a black comedy set in England,
Four and Twenty Virgins, and *Snake*. *Rogue Eagle*
won the Silver Dagger Award in 1977.

James McClure is married and has three children.

James McClure

Rogue Eagle

Penguin Books

Penguin Books Ltd,
Harmondsworth, Middlesex, England
Penguin Books, 625 Madison Avenue,
New York, New York 10022, U.S.A.
Penguin Books Australia Ltd,
Ringwood, Victoria, Australia
Penguin Books Canada Ltd,
2801 John Street, Markham, Ontario, Canada L3R 1B4
Penguin Books (N.Z.) Ltd,
182–190 Wairau Road, Auckland 10, New Zealand

First published by Macmillan 1976
Published in Penguin Books 1978

Made and printed in Great Britain by
Hazell Watson & Viney Ltd, Aylesbury, Bucks
Set in Linotype Times

For Lalage

Lesotho is an African state; Sesotho is its language, and its people are the Basotho. But in the interests of clarity, the singular of Basotho – Masotho – has been avoided.

SOUTH AFRICA

AREA: 471,445 square miles – *1,221,037 square kilometres*
– or larger than France, Germany, Italy
and Portugal put together.

POPULATION: 23,724,000
For every 100 people, there are about:
70 Blacks
 9 Coloureds – *mixed descent*
 3 Asians
18 Whites – *more than half of them Afrikaners*

LESOTHO

AREA: 11,720 square miles – *30,355 square kilometres*
– or two thirds the size of Switzerland

POPULATION: 1,155,700

Chapter One

Wolraad Steyn, his palms sweating, clasped and unclasped the hand which would plunge the dagger. His father noticed this and frowned.

They were standing apart from the other dark-suited and solemn men gathered there in that farmhouse parlour. It was mid-afternoon and the sun, slanting in through the bay window behind them, burned into their backs as they waited for the minister to arrive. With the heat came discomfort, but the pair of them stayed where they were, knowing it was proper to show deference in this way, and to add to it their silence.

The others now and again spoke among themselves, yet in voices hushed almost to a whisper.

His hands hardened into fists. It was impossible not to anticipate what lay in store for him.

He tried to concentrate on the commonplace detail of the parlour. He noted its heavy furniture, the game trophies on the walls, a lizard peering from a crack near the ceiling, homely touches like the knitting set aside on a small table made from an elephant's foot. He glanced at the gunrack, identifying the calibre and make of each firearm all too quickly, and then at the portraits of forefathers and party leaders, staring from their oval frames in constant condemnation of any weakness.

But even as he did so, he failed to keep his thoughts within the confines of the room. They shifted to another room which he knew had to be in that house somewhere. A dimly-lit room, stripped and stark, containing only a form beneath a black shroud, resting on a table. The dagger would be there, too.

Abruptly, he brought his attention back to what he could actually see before him.

So this was the cell.

These were the men whose secrets his father had shared down the long, bitter years. And these were the men who had subjected him in turn to a cold and careful scrutiny before deciding he also belonged with them.

They were not the men he had imagined.

The shock of this discovery, made as Wolraad had entered the room, was still with him.

His hand clasped and unclasped.

One of the men caught his eye.

It was old G. K. Kroen, the absent-minded and much-teased teacher of English at the local high school; notorious for insisting that no Afrikaans should be spoken during his lessons, and for the pyjama top occasionally visible between his shirt buttons. His benign presence was perhaps the most unnerving.

There was a murmur. Watches were consulted and compared. Oupa Nel, their host, left through the far door.

Kroen came across to them.

'We're getting a bit worried about the time,' he explained. 'The Dominee is usually so punctual, especially when he's acting as chaplain. His only other engagement this Saturday was a wedding at eleven. Oupa has gone to give his house a ring to make sure nothing's wrong.'

Pa nodded.

There was something else Kroen wanted to say. He looked at the black mourning armbands they were both wearing, and then at the floor.

'Oh ja, but what use are words in the face of such a tragedy,' he sighed, then brought his head up. 'But still, you must be proud, Dirk. A brave son who died for the Fatherland.'

'Very proud,' Pa said.

This seemed absurd to Wolraad. He felt nothing. His younger brother's death had no reality for him. Boet had been killed by a terrorist mortar while on patrol with the South African Police along Rhodesia's northern border. Boet had been returned to them in a weighted coffin for a military funeral. Boet could not really be dead; not three whole days. Never.

'And yet,' Kroen added softly, 'a man should take care not to ask too much of himself.'

Pa bristled.

'What do you mean?' he snapped.

'As you know, I only got back from the Cape this morning.'

'And so?'

'Wish I'd been here to talk about today. Frankly, I was surprised to hear that these arrangements had not been postponed in view of the circumstances.'

'Don't we also serve?' Pa demanded.

There was a long pause. Then Kroen smiled very slightly, and said: 'True, quite true. And we're very pleased with our new recruit.'

He gave Wolraad's arm a friendly squeeze above the elbow.

'I'm going to see what Oupa's found out,' Pa said, striding away.

Kroen stared after him.

'You must keep an eye on your pa,' he murmured.

'Why's that?' Wolraad asked sharply.

'Hmmm?'

'I said: why? And why say it in that funny way?'

'Tell me,' Kroen said, with the briskness of a man forcing a change of subject, 'how does it feel to be on the brink? To know that within the hour you will be on equal terms with the highest in the land, from the State President down?'

Wolraad did not want to be side-tracked. He replied gruffly: 'You should know, sir – you've been through it yourself.'

'Ah, but when? A long time ago, Steyntjie, and we had no Presidents or Prime Ministers in our ranks then. The whole struggle lay before us.'

Some triggered memory made Kroen chuckle.

'Sir?'

'Talking of Prime Ministers, this will show you how different it was in 1944, the year I joined. General Smuts was still in power, and do you know how he described us? He said we were a "dangerous, cunning, political, fascist organization" – and all public servants were banned from belonging!'

'Huh! Fat lot he knew.'

'But tell me, Steyntjie,' Kroen said, again using the affectionate diminutive of Wolraad's surname, 'how are things with you really? You have Boet on your mind, I know, but also you seem very nervous.'

He sounded concerned, but not nearly as concerned as he had done about Pa.

'Why should I keep my eye –'

'Hey, wait a minute; I'm asking the questions.'

'It scares me,' Wolraad heard himself say.

'In what way?'

Wolraad shrugged. His involuntary admission had shamed and sickened him.

'Come on . . .'

'Ach, maybe it's the responsibility.'

'You don't think you're up to it?'

Again Wolraad shrugged.

Kroen looked very angry for an instant, and then said: 'Only a fool would judge himself fit for membership. To doubt your own worthiness is an excellent thing. Somebody should have pointed this out to you.'

'Sorry?'

'Should have pointed out that you didn't choose us, we chose you. And we did it without fear or favour, my lad; not for your sake, nor even your father's, but for the sake of our race and its Divine mission. Understand that?'

'I know but –'

'Still some doubts?'

'Maybe I'll –'

'Does that mean you also doubt the Brotherhood knows what it's doing?'

'Ach, no!' Wolraad protested.

'So why doubt at all then? Why should you have any doubts about yourself when we have none? You will meet any demand made upon you – we are sure of it.'

As this sank in, it gave Wolraad a sense of freedom and power which was quite extraordinary.

'Good,' said Kroen, who must have noticed a change, 'that's more the spirit in which to come before us. Can you hear the car?'

The Dominee's Volkswagen was whining across the open veld towards them.

This was it. Because he knew what was about to happen would affect the rest of his life, Wolraad wanted nothing to

12

escape him. He determined to imprint on his mind everything he saw and heard and even smelled. But it all blurred.

He barely noticed the car drawing up, or the muttered apologies in the passageway. He just felt the tug on his jacket and stepped forward.

He had an impression of bedroom furniture stacked aside in a corridor, and then of a darkened room sharp with the camphor of mothballs. There were men all around him. And voices.

Rising and falling, reciting and beseeching.

While his eyes remained fixed on what lay before him: on the form draped with a black shroud on which had been embroidered in red the single, terrible word. *Treason.*

The dagger was pressed into his hand.

He grasped it eagerly, raising the long blade high above his head. A light, contrived to give the effect of lightning on the high veld, flickered and flashed.

Then, as the chaplain began to intone, Wolraad plunged the dagger down through the shroud, deep into whatever lay packed there.

Again and again he stabbed, exulted by the final lines of the oath.

'He who betrays the Brotherhood will be destroyed by the Brotherhood!

'The Brotherhood never forgets!

'Its vengeance is swift and sure!

'Never has a traitor escaped his just punishment!

'The Brotherhood!'

'The Brotherhood!' he cried.

With that, it was done. The ritual of initiation into the Afrikaner Brotherhood, South Africa's most powerful and élite secret organization, was over.

At the small celebration which followed shortly afterwards in the parlour, the new member found himself never more at peace. Even Kroen's curious warning no longer perturbed him.

'God is good,' Wolraad declared.

And Dominee Swart, who was standing at his side, eating a doughnut, nodded gravely.

'Good – and just,' the minister added. 'But we, the guardians of the Chosen, must never allow ourselves to forget He is also a God of Wrath, who will visit upon any transgressor among us His most terrible punishments. The native who rapes his own mother will be judged less harshly than the man who betrays, even in his thoughts, our glorious Afrikanerdom. The ones He loves the most must be prepared for the full rigour of such love.'

'Of course, Dominee,' said Wolraad.

'These doughnuts are very good – have you tried one?'

'Not yet.'

'You'll excuse me while I fetch another?'

Wolraad watched him go over to where the womenfolk had placed coffee and eats on the sideboard before withdrawing again. Everyone had stayed on, and a very pleasant little party had developed. The peach brandy he and his father had brought across from their own farm was going down well, too. He knew that soon, when the Dominee had finished talking to him, the others would come up and offer their hands in comradeship. He looked forward to that.

An angry note jarred in the hum of genial conversation. Wolraad, recognizing his father's voice, jerked round to face the corner. But, a moment later, he was reassured by a light patter of laughter from the group of old die-hards standing there. It must have been hatred and not anger he had heard.

Relieved, he turned to take his glass from the mantelshelf. Noticing, as he did so, that beside it lay a souvenir from the little Free State town of Heilbron. He picked up the souvenir, a glazed model of an ox-waggon, and read the inscription: *Mass Rally of Federated Afrikaner Cultural Organizations, October 1964*. How apt – that had been the other milestone in his life.

He stared at the thing and, for the first time, felt grief catch him by the throat.

Boet had also been there, and with him that night as the great family gathered in their thousands around the open-air stage in the pitch dark. He and Boet, just youngsters then, worming their way to the front of the crowd, excited by the mystery of what was to take place. No grown-up seeming to know, just waiting patiently. Then, out of the darkness, like in the Bible, a voice saying: 'In times of storm winds He has provided the Chosen

14

Leader . . .' And quite suddenly, there, not three yards from them, the Prime Minister himself, revealed in the light of two blazing torches. While on either side of Dr Verwoerd, two big signs in luminous paint said *Chosen Leader* and *Chosen People* – sending shivers down his spine. Boet whispering the words aloud, as if he had never heard them before. Then the two of them, joining in the hymn together, singing for all they were worth, feeling ten feet tall. Two kids in bare feet. Him and Boet. His –

'The Dominee,' said Oupa Nel, 'has stopped for a chat with your pa, so I'd thought I'd come over meantime.'

Wolraad, startled from his reverie, reached out to shake hands, still holding the souvenir. Oupa Nel chuckled and took it from him.

'Ja, we were all there, weren't we? The Steyns, the Nels, the Van Heerdens – must've been half the district. And what a time of it you young ones had when all the cars and trucks outspanned and the tents went up!'

Wolraad swallowed hard, trying to clear a hoarseness.

But, before he could reply, Oupa Nel turned solemn and added: 'Look, I don't want you to think – well, it's this way, Steyntjie.'

The old farmer's hesitancy, and the awkward pause which he tried to cover by replacing the ornament, alerted Wolraad to the fact that something was badly wrong. He looked again into the corner: Pa was speaking in a low, relentless rumble; the others were listening, tight-faced and uneasy.

'What's up, Oupa?' Wolraad said.

'Please, it's nothing personal. We all want you to understand that. Nothing to do with yourself. Only would it be possible for you to leave now?'

Stunned, Wolraad just stood there.

'We realize it's a hard thing to ask of you, but – ach, y'know.'

'Why?'

'Let us say – ja, let's put it this way, your pa is not himself this afternoon.'

'Why?'

'He is – under severe strain. He is unwell.'

'Why?'

15

'Will you do this for us, Steyntjie?'

'But *why*? What's happening?'

Pa was still talking. Kroen had raised his hands, palms outward, as if to stop what was being said. The others were shaking their heads.

'I think you had better take him and go without delay, Wolraad,' the Member of Parliament urged, slipping over to them.

'Dirk is unwell,' said Oupa Nel.

'Distraught,' agreed the M P. 'Go now, young man – he is beginning to say things he will never forgive himself for.'

This was inconceivable to Wolraad. So utterly unthinkable that his mind gave a nightmare lurch, and he was left incapable of any response. He just went on standing there.

'Ah, but some do!' he heard Pa say, pointing to the picture of Prime Minister Vorster on the wall. 'Some of us need reminding of many things!'

Appalled, the circle froze.

Then Kroen said lightly: 'Quite so, some of us do need reminding – yourself included, Dirk. Why are we here today? To welcome into our midst a young man for whom we have high hopes – and who has been, in my opinion, sorely neglected so far!'

After a long moment, Pa smiled.

And the smile spread. Taken up gratefully in the hope that a comrade, beside himself in his bereavement, would be comforted and brought to his senses.

Wolraad knew every allowance was being made. He also knew that Pa's smile had been totally misunderstood. It chilled him to the bone.

The only military funeral Wolraad had seen was one held for two prison warders who were killed in a road accident after a party.

This had been some years before and his memory of it, as a casual bystander, had dimmed. So he was ill-prepared for the ponderous ceremony of such an occasion, and in particular for the leading role he was expected to play.

It seemed to last for ever. An hour beforehand, the chief mourners had assembled in the police vehicle yard, where a long line of black limousines, specially brought down from Pretoria, stood waiting. He and his family had met the high-ranking officers, also from Pretoria, and several others from different branches of the Defence Force. Then Wolraad had been taken aside and introduced to the five constables from Boet's last station who were going to act as the other pallbearers. They exchanged names and couldn't think of anything else to say. Although one gave him twenty cents he owed Boet. Finally they had reached the church, watched by an enormous crowd of all races, and Wolraad managed, without making the mistakes he'd feared, to carry his corner of the coffin inside. One of the press photographers had had a shaven head. There had been two figures on the roof of the Sanlam skyscraper with binoculars. The service had been words; kind words, good words, wise words, but words his mind could not string together. His mother had been comforted though. While Wolraad had stayed remote from any feeling, picking the dirt out from under his bad thumbnail, until the police had begun the death march, then he had been very pleased to take his place in the second car. His sisters didn't mind who saw their tears; they seemed to wear them like their black gloves.

But now they were on the farm, down in the corner of the pasture by the river where he had dug the grave with his own hands, the funeral had meaning for him. He followed everything the Dominee read out, and was very moved by a text from Joshua which seemed to state what was in his own mind exactly; Boet had not died for nothing. He heard his father grunt, and saw, out of the corner of his eye, his mother taking hold of his hand.

Then the guard of honour fired a salute and, with ears ringing, Wolraad tossed a handful of earth and walked away.

Down to the willow tree which overhung the clay pit; he didn't much want to talk to anyone for a while.

'You used to play here?' asked Kroen, having followed him. 'Ja.'

'Did the *umfaans* teach you to make oxen with it?'

'Ja. Then, when we were bigger, we used to put balls of it on the end of willow sticks and shoot it at each other. Boet was good at that. I was better at making oxen.'

17

Wolraad discovered he was actually pleased that Kroen had come with him, and smiled to show this.

Kroen nodded companionably and took out his old pipe. It was the same one he used to always place carefully on the desk before beginning a lesson, as though promising himself a small treat if he taught well. The knurled bowl was grey with chalk dust.

'And how is the family? Your mother?'

'This will be a good memory for her. She liked the General. Everything. She was counting the people.'

'Lot of them; never seen more. Strangers as well.'

'It can mean more, having them.'

'True, very true. And your father?'

'Pa? You saw him.'

'He hasn't –?'

'No. He is proud. That is all he will say.'

The third match got the pipe going, and Wolraad could hear the crackle of its dry tobacco from where he stood; old G. K. loved his trading store mixture.

'And the idea of a holiday, Steyntjie?'

'I put it to him.'

'Good.'

'He said there wasn't anywhere he wanted to go. Ma tried, too, even said she'd write to her family in South West, but he said that was just another Bantustan these days. Since détente.'

Kroen shook his head.

'Your pa must get up-to-date in his thinking! Best I have a word with him, like I promised. On the other matter, have you suggested a game reserve to him? There's plenty in Natal if he's already seen the Kruger. Rhino in Zululand, or –'

'Ja, it's best you talk to him.'

The hasty interruption was not lost on Kroen, who turned to see Pa ducking in under the willow branches.

'Your ma is asking after you,' Pa said. 'She wants you to show the high-ups your scribbles.'

'Ach, no!'

'You're still doing your paintings then?' Kroen asked Wolraad with interest. 'Dirk, man, you've never said! And here am

18

I, ready to pay good money for one! If ever there was a light kept under a bushel.'

'We sell mealies and milk on this farm,' Pa replied irritably. 'You come too, because there's a bloke from Rhodesia you should meet.'

All three of them began the trudge up to the house, which was still surrounded by scores of vehicles – Wolraad's mother had organized a wake under the gum trees.

'Ja, he's English-speaking, mind,' Pa went on, 'but I know him from somewhere, maybe an agricultural show. He can tell you a thing or two. That's why he came today; to show gratitude, he says. Not a bad bloke. He's with Pik.'

Kroen was looking as he'd done after the initiation, when Pa had forgotten himself in his grief and talked a lot of nonsense about Mr Vorster.

So Wolraad said the first thing that came into his head : 'Did you notice, Pa? When the guns went off? What the cattle did when they heard the big bang – and the kaffirs on the land? It was as if they suddenly knew also what had happened to Boet.'

This only made the tension worse.

Once again he had said the wrong thing; once again his father was somehow ashamed of him, as he was when painting or playing the concertina were mentioned. Wolraad was sure then that Boet's death had not done him the good he'd secretly hoped it would : the gap between him and his father hadn't closed – if anything, it was greater than before. Still, by remaining true to Afrikanerdom, by being a good Nationalist, and by striving to distinguish himself among the Brotherhood, there was always the chance this gap might some day be bridged.

That would at least lessen the curious feeling of dread their separateness gave him. Dread of what, he couldn't say, but it was growing stronger week by week now.

Chapter Two

Even at night, when darkness had obliterated most of the folksy, frontier touches of the tiny Lesotho capital (population: 18,000), Maseru did not look its part as the Las Vegas of South Africa. One Holiday Inn could do only so much to sophisticate a village skyline, and the neon work on the other tourist traps, such as they were, was unimaginative. But then, like a market stall, and in particular one offering forbidden fruit, Maseru had no need of the hard sell. Which meant, along certain approaches to the main centre, there was plenty left to please the eye.

Finbar Buchanan slowed his stride to consider the horse droppings under the stop sign at the next intersection. It was this sort of thing, and not just the way the stone buildings seemed to grow from the ground, so unlike the transient ticky-tacky of those latitudes, that endeared the place to him.

He walked on glumly aware that endearment was as far as the relationship would go. People saw Maseru in a variety of ways. Most of the white South Africans, teeming in over the border barely a mile away, regarded it simply as a geographical loophole, allowing them the best of what was banned in their land: gambling, strippers, black sex even – and blasphemy: *Jesus Christ Superstar* always played to packed houses. Then there were the cynics. Two immediately came to mind: a bitter black politician with a weakness for romantic imagery, and a Roman Catholic mission priest from Ontario. The politician had likened Lesotho to a mountainous desert island, poking up out of the cruel sea Apartheid, and saw Maseru as its port, pandering to the debauched tastes of visiting pirates. They bought with stolen gold, he said. While the missionary had made a wry joke of it, by pretending that the map of South Africa on his classroom wall was, in fact, a diagram of the Calvinist brain, and that Lesotho – the small, shaded area – represented the inevitable repository of repressions, with Maseru as their outlet. Both had something there, but Buchanan's own view was at once more sentimental and more pragmatic. On the one hand, he saw Maseru as a reluctant tart, doing the only thing she could to keep at least some of her million hungry dependants fed and the landlord happy – which was, of course, what had put any thought of an affair out of the question. And on the other hand, he agreed with his masters in London that Maseru was ideally situated for maintaining a check on the temperature of the body politic, south of the Limpopo.

However, on nights when Buchanan was low, and this was one of them, the pragmatic lost out to become a parody of the anatomical allegory. Or was it perhaps an analogy, he asked himself, for the effects were to leave him feeling not so much as an agent of DI6 as a bloody rectal thermometer.

Now given over entirely to this mood, which had its own curious comfort, he slammed his way in through the side entrance to Mackenzie's Hardware Ltd, and then into his so-called suite of rooms. There were two of them: the first he used as an office, the second as a darkroom and a place for making coffee.

The ceiling strip jittered and came on. Its hesitation was understandable, for what the bright light revealed proved instantly depressing. The walls seemed to take a pace forward, crowding the cheap desk, tube-frame chairs and dented filing cabinet. With them came the maps, time-tables, trade calendars and once-comic headlines that gave the room its feel of a real press office – which indeed it was, for most of the time. As was further suggested by the lists of official phone numbers on yellowing paper, the bent spike stacked fat with handouts, and the half written story sticking out of the Olivetti. For sheer suffocating familiarity, Buchanan doubted Dracula had a worse deal, and at least the bastard got out nights. It was almost a relief to step through into the other room, and have the light there emphasize its impersonal orderliness.

He always made this check.

Then it was story time. He lit a Texan, flicked back two pages in his notebook, and began again to transfer the details on to Telex forms for handing in at the Post Office later.

'This was not t first time otters hd struck at t fish farm,' he typed. 'Soon after it opened, they took 1,000 (thousand) carp in a single night raid. In a country so desperately short of protein tt Oxfam has described Lesotho's schoolchildren as quote noticeably listless unquote, these losses can be reckoned almost in terms of human life.

'However, t SA Govt hs again come to t rescue, and is sending a Natal Parks Board fisheries expert to help w this and other problems. Fish Raiders Ends.'

Buchanan read it over, deleted the sentence beginning 'In a country', and stuffed the forms into the breast pocket of his safari suit. Then he checked his news diary, and found the feature on Rupert's flying circus was still outstanding. Some discovery: it'd been nagging him for a week.

So he started right away on the intro, hoping to gather momentum: 'Every weekend a team of top-flight South African surgeons flies in to Maseru to perform intricate and costly operations – for free. Thanks to the generosity of Afrikaner multi-millionaire Anton Rupert, whose worldwide cigarette companies include Rothmans of Pall Mall, Dunhill, Peter Stuyvesant and other household names carrying a public health warningghjk.'

Some other time, perhaps. From Stuyvesant.

'Oh, bugger,' he said, having second thoughts.

And he went to make coffee.

Buchanan forced himself into a decision to complete the horrible thing. It was either this or have the rot finally set in, making him incapable of banging out the banalities his cover job demanded. What irony existed here: Maseru was stiff with agents who styled themselves journalists, and then flagrantly never wrote a line; while he was kept slogging away at trivia, with surely no time for anything else, seven days a week. And yet, when all was said and done, his industry did reward him with a strong position as the one hidden pebble on a very pebbly beach.

Then, just as the kettle – which did a quick job at that altitude – brought the water to the boil, the telephone rang in the other room. He was half-way there when the Ansaphone answered it.

A minute later, Buchanan put down his cup where the type-

22

writer carriage wouldn't bump into it, seated himself heavily, and slipped a carbon between two sheets of copy paper.

That was a start.

He tapped out the name of his freelance agency and the slugline.

That was even more of a start.

He looked to see if the carbon was the right way round, and it was.

Adding the date did no harm.

He wondered idly who had rung him, and what dreary snippet of news they wanted to impart.

'Every weekend a team of,' the keys spelled out slowly, almost on their own.

Buchanan stopped there, and ran back the tape on his Ansaphone.

'If this is Monday,' an American accent said, 'then I'll be in the bar at Fritz's. If it isn't, then you're a slob and I'll be calling you pronto. Say you still love me.'

Whose voice this was then caught up with the other Buchanan, and he knew his first guess had been only partly correct. True, the call wasn't personal; but wrong, it wasn't about newspapers either.

The girl Maseru knew as Nancy Kitson was a goofy blonde. There had been a cheesecake picture of her in the local paper. Popular Nancy, 27, 36-24-36, the caption had explained, was making light of the sprained ankle which forced her to drop out of an American roadshow. It had also said that she'd fallen in love with Lesotho and was applying for a resident's permit from her hospital bed.

Naturally, Nancy had got it – and a job with the Lesotho Airways Corporation. She became a receptionist to give the somewhat hickey airport something of an international flavour. She also became the girl every male wanted to be seen with, as often and as publicly as possible. Even one of the two resident BOSS agents was known to expend a good deal of waggish charm on her, while keeping the other eye on incoming flights. Once, it was strongly rumoured, he'd winked the wrong one and unwittingly turned a secret courier, confident of evading detection,

23

grey overnight. But this was really a mild example of the bar tales that had gone into circulation with Nancy as their pivotal point. Most had their fascination in the fact that while she always remained serenely accessible, her virtue – to all appearances – remained intact. And in this hotbed of fantasy, her reality had rapidly dwindled, as she must have calculated it would.

Because the girl Buchanan knew as Nancy Kitson was, to put it crudely, a minor CIA agent. One of the doughty band still active in southern Africa after the collapse of the Rhodesian network in March 1970, when Smith's heavies arrested two operatives, and the Consulate, having lost its only useful function post-UDI, was finally closed. Although, of course, Nancy's move to Maseru had been much more recent than that, and she had not worked in Africa before.

Buchanan found her a sweetly-determined bitch with a nature nowhere as beguiling as the one she pretended to have. After the standard chatting-up procedure at the airport, watched with amusement by The Winker, they had taken dinner together at the Holiday Inn and exchanged a few professional confidences. As far as anyone could make out, one thing had then led to another – but predictably no further, and the couple had parted friends. This little pantomime, which gave neither party much pleasure, did mean, however, that they could meet occasionally without arousing suspicion. On the contrary, every observer was always quite certain of Buchanan's intentions, and often expressed such insight with a very dry wit.

Sod them for a start. Right then he was preoccupied with what *her* intentions might be, and this kept his step brisk. A youthful arrogance ensured that she wouldn't be calling for his assistance unless the matter was tolerably important to them both. This was the limit of his expectancy: crisis-mongering was not, in the words of his otherwise urbane superior, Buchanan's bag. Not in poor wee Lesotho anyway, where all they needed was an adaptable sensoring device to pass back what information it gathered. At the time, of course, the job had sounded like a sinecure after Saigon.

Nancy was not in Fritz's when he arrived. This was no surprise as a cheerful tardiness was all part of her act, so he sat

24

down on a stool at the counter and asked the Basotho barman for a whisky.

But Harry didn't hear him – he was having his patience tried, too. Buchanan looked at the customer responsible and instantly recognized the type. There was a trendy poster down in the arcade which said it all. Proclaimed it in mock-Gothic lettering around a drawing of a glowering hulk: Yea, though I walk in the Shadow of the Valley of Death, I will fear no Evil – 'cos I'm the meanest son-of-a-bitch in the valley ... Something like that.

And Hulk's Aertex shirt and ridiculous rugby shorts did little to offset the general effect.

'Okay, okay, so I've been in bloody Lesotho since only lunch time,' he confided peevishly to Buchanan, as one white man to another, 'but already I can see these black buggers think they own the place.'

'We do,' said Harry, very darkly.

'Rubbish!'

The Basotho barman raised his hand and pointed it like a pistol.

'Go! Fly to the United Nations and see for yourself! We got a seat there like any other independent Afro state.'

'Independent?' echoed Hulk, his eyebrows arching high. 'Since when? You lot couldn't do a bloody thing without us! Be honest with me. Just try. Christ, even your Chief Justice and your Attorney-General are two whites from the Republic, speci- ally brought in when you went *independent*, as you calls it! Two honest-to-God Afrikaners who –'

'Man, are you out of date,' Harry began.

'Two honest-to-God –'

'Citizens of Lesotho,' Harry countered, abandoning the finer points of the argument.

'Ja? And what colour are they now? Tell me that!'

Delighted with himself, Hulk turned eagerly for his applause.

Buchanan was going to have to disappoint him. He had more than enough of clichés during the day to welcome any he found walking about at night.

'Piss off,' he sighed, standing up.

That brought a pause. His height seemed to surprise Hulk as much as his direct manner. Both were noted, thought about and then the man thankfully went on his way – straight back across the border, with any luck.

'Thanks, Jock,' said Harry, grinning.

'My pleasure, Sambo,' replied Buchanan, returning the subtle flattery. 'I'll chance anything for a bloody drink.'

Harry served a double and hung around.

'Sometimes these pigs really get at you,' he murmured conversationally. 'I mean the answer's there on your tongue, but not in your heart. You dig? Like there was some truth –'

But before this could get any further, Nancy Kitson arrived breathless.

She looked the same as ever: straight out of the shower and into just the clothes she needed to answer the door in – knotted blouse, blue jeans and slip-slop sandals. So fresh and perky you always wondered what the time was.

'Hi!' she said, and then specifically to Harry: 'Make it a steelworks, huh? I'm bushed.'

'I still love you,' Buchanan grunted.

'Me too. Let's find us a seat and you can tell me all about it. All right, Harry?'

'Fine, Miss Kitson – coming up in a minute.'

Nancy chose a good table, close enough to the regulars to give them plenty to watch, but out of earshot. The few tourists around on a Monday night were mostly bunched in the other corner.

When Buchanan had seen to her chair and then sat down again, she leaned over and whispered in his ear.

'Right, lover: the way I've been spreading this story around, you'd better at least hold my hand, for Chrissake. Only Finbar, sweetest, please be gentle.'

Her smirk had a prettiness all of its own.

He obliged, whispering back: 'What am I all of a sudden? The best goddam lay south of the border?'

Nancy laughed the lovable dirty laugh that contrasted so well with her two flaxen plaits, and that had them all staring. She relaxed.

'No way. But as we might have some conferring to do over

the next couple of days, I've been letting slip a few – gees, Harry, that's great!'

Buchanan waited until the barman retired.

'Oh aye? Letting slip a few what?'

'Screw the details, Buchanan: we've got business to discuss. Something's come up that maybe isn't anything, but right now seems kooky enough to justify bringing you in.'

'Thanks,' he said.

Nancy Kitson seemed to need a little time to arrange her thoughts. Buchanan let her, being reasonably content to keep hold of her hand and take a long, covert look around the bar. The Bureau of State Security was nowhere to be seen, nor were any of the local lads – he wondered what they might be missing.

'The day before yesterday,' Nancy said softly, 'that's on Saturday, I had a listed Rhodesian come through on a South African Airways flight.'

'Daring stuff. ZANU or ZAPU?'

'Neither. He's white and he belongs way the other side of the ball park. Want to guess?'

He shrugged.

'His name's Johnny Tagg.'

Buchanan's grip tightened involuntarily.

'Good God,' he said, 'the master megalomaniac himself, and founder of the RNCP. Well, I'll be buggered.'

'Not in my time, honey. Make with those initials.'

'The Rhodesian National Caucasian Party, but don't try to remember them – it was never allowed out of its cage. The Right-wing themselves saw to that, so no more need be said really. The man's mad.'

'That much I'd gathered. And potentially dangerous.'

'In a very limited sense, like a nasty kid. He has cooked up some diabolical schemes in his time, only they've been too grandiose – and horrible – to get off the ground. His excesses are, in fact, his saving grace.'

'But what,' said Nancy, 'if someone took him seriously, modi-field his ideas, and gave him the money and support he needed?'

'We might be right in the poo – except I doubt very much if that could ever happen.'

She took her hand away and used it to lift her glass, frosting over herself as she sipped slowly, ignoring him.

'Well, what's Johnny been doing lately – and what's he up to here?' Buchanan asked. 'The last I heard of him, he was going off in a huff to be a Gulf mercenary. But then we tend to rely on you lot to watch that end of things – bigger budgets, smaller fry.'

It wasn't that easy to get a rise out of her. Nancy was down to crunching on the ice before she replied.

'Tagg left Rhodesia all right – to move south and take out SA citizenship. We expected him to get mixed up in one of those neo-Nazi organizations the *Sunday Express* is so hot on exposing. Nothing doing. Instead he got himself a job with an irrigation firm, and started going round the farming districts, selling sprinklers and windmills and all that.'

'And the catch?'

'On the quiet, he was also doing his best to keep up sympathy for the Rhodesian cause.'

'Officially?'

'We doubt it. But Smith needs all the help he can get, so as sure as hell he wasn't being discouraged. A creep like that can blow up quite a storm at –'

'Oh aye, but Vorster isn't going to be pushed into anything he doesn't like, lassie. He's already made it plain Rhodesia's not going to be his Vietnam, and pulled his cops out. When Angola –'

'Even so, every little helps.'

Buchanan lit a cigarette. There were legions of pro-Smith propagandists in the world, both paid and unpaid, all doing their damnedest for what it was worth. Seen in this context, Tagg – for all his personal peculiarity – presented no special threat, and doubtless this was why the man had been allowed to pass into partial obscurity. Nor was a weekend visit to Maseru anything to write home about: thousands made the journey every year. There had to be a lot more to this, or else the CIA was cracking.

'Ah,' said Buchanan, trying to enter into the spirit of the game, 'then Tagg's still here?'

'Check,' Nancy replied smugly.

'Maseru?'

'No.'

'Where exactly?'

'Somewhere that doesn't gell. A trading store in the mountains, one of the remotest. The only whites for sixty kilometres in any direction are two old guys who run the place – a couple of screwball recluses.'

'But –'

'Don't "but" till I'm finished. According to the pilot who does the weekly mail drop, Tagg isn't the only guest at Mapapeng right now. Within the last two weeks, Stoffel says he's flown in two others. Both of them complete strangers as well.'

'Strangers to whom?'

'To the trader, Koos Brandsma, for a start. Stoffel stuck around for lunch – you know what a hog he is – and says things were pretty uptight. They got even uptighter on Saturday when Tagg arrived. I couldn't push my idle curiosity any further than that.'

Mapapeng: Buchanan had guessed as much from her opening description. And, as he'd tried to tell her, he had once stayed there while doing a series on all the mountain stores for a trade supplement – a crafty dodge to familiarize himself with the territory. Mapapeng wasn't only remote, it just wasn't of this world – and nor were Brandsma, the store manager, and his sidekick Willie Potgieter. They had made his brief visit memorable by arguing plaintively over which of them should put a bullet through the grizzled head of the dog at their feet; this argument had gone on every evening, from sundowner to nightcap, and he'd often wished he knew who had finally done the deed. Even setting that aside, they were about the last people he'd expect to actually invite guests to stay, and – from what he knew of Tagg – they were hardly the sort of company that idiot would seek.

'It's a trifle odd,' he conceded.

'Odd? There's either a simple answer or it stinks! And logically, it can't be simple because, logically, Tagg *has* to be connected in some way with the traders to be able to barge in like that.'

'Could be through one of the other two – or both.'

29

'That comes down to the same thing. So a link must exist – agreed?'

'Hmmmm.'

'Try pondering the one other fact I've been able to find out: there's no record of any previous private charters to Mapapeng in our books – and they go to-hell-and-gone back.'

So Buchanan had been right in his assumption: this sudden influx of visitors at Mapapeng was indeed something quite out of the ordinary. He began to take a more personal – and critical – interest.

'That bloody well isn't all you know,' he told her. 'The first two to arrive must have had names. Surely you've had them checked out by now?'

She smiled to show she'd really been the one doing the angling, and said: 'Hooked? They had names all right, but we've not come up with anything yet, so they could be aliases. That's why we were hoping you might be able to give us some background on the traders – any chance of that?'

Buchanan had already started to work on the problem. His own acquaintanceship with the traders had been, largely because of the ailing dog, rather sketchy. But thinking about the article he'd written gave him a sudden idea: one which wouldn't waste more than an hour of his time should all this be a no-no, and one that was worth a try anyway. His imagination had also begun to race a little.

'It's just gone eight,' he said, looking at the cuckoo clock above Harry's head. 'I suggest we have a slight tiff now, and meet up again at your place around half nine.'

Nancy's idea of a slight tiff was to exclaim in ringing tones: 'I will if you want me to, *but not in the nude.*'

Buchanan had to wait until they'd run the gauntlet of an ecstatic silence, and gained the pavement outside, before he could warn her he wasn't going to take any more buggering around. For example, she still hadn't given him the names of Mapapeng's two other mystery guests.

'Hadn't I?' said Nancy. 'Allegedly, they're a certain Pik Oeloefse and a Meneer Dirk Steyn.'

There were ashtrays everywhere in the Convent of the Sacred

Heart. Buchanan took them to be a sign of the nuns' true charity, and tried to forgive the heavy reek of cabbage water.

'Poor old Father Waldo,' the Mother Superior said, as she switched on the fan in the visitors' parlour, 'his leg isn't any better, you know. But he will insist on being so self-sufficient, and there's not much we can do about that – he'll be along in his wheelchair, just you wait.'

Buchanan waited and, some five minutes later, Father Waldo, looking like a bear doing a circus turn, rolled in through the doorway, triumphant.

'Finbar,' he said, 'it's a pleasure to see you, my boy. Now get this door shut behind me to keep those bloody women out.'

After eight years of it, he had as yet to adjust to his retirement, and in particular to an almost exclusively female environment. The more the kind nuns fussed over him, the more he muttered dark texts from St Paul's views on womenfolk. And never, he claimed, had he believed more firmly in the wisdom of priestly celibacy – although he was damned if he knew why he couldn't have grandchildren.

None of this had, of course, crept into the piece Buchanan had written to celebrate the old priest's jubilee; that had been a properly dull chronicle of a life's work based on the mission at Peray, all place names and dates. He'd done a quick check on them at the office.

'You had a bone to pick with me,' Buchanan murmured, closing the door and then perching on the table.

'Good. When was that?'

'The last time I went up into the mountains without telling you first. There's just a possibility I may do a follow-up for Oxfam on their school feeding programme, so here I am if there are any messages.'

'Peray?'

'Sorry. The school they're interested in is nearer to Mapapeng.

'Dumela?' Father Waldo asked, with the sharpness of someone whose knowledge of a subject verged on the encyclopaedic. 'Don't forget that was in my district too!'

'Aye, Dumela. Anyone you know there?'

It was crude and it was cynical, but Buchanan knew no other

way of getting the ball rolling. And once that had been achieved, all it took were a couple of slight deflections to direct it towards the goal.

In under ten minutes, Father Waldo, possibly as shaggy, but without white hair then, was back in the saddle doing the wandering friar bit along the range which linked Dumela and Mapapeng and other points east.

'Koos Brandsma?' he said. 'Bless him, I've known the poor soul many a year. Oh, long before his wife died in her riding accident. I used to stop the night twice a month and we'd chew the fat over a bottle of Scotch. His father had the store before him, you know.'

'Aye, I had that in my story on the place. And Willie? Another old friend?'

Father Waldo laughed, a little strangely.

'I suppose one could say that now,' he said, 'but at first I'm afraid he regarded me with the gravest mistrust!'

There was no need to urge the priest to go on; he leaned forward to continue his reminiscence with the gusto of a gossip, immunized by time against any feelings of irresponsibility.

'One of the lesser mysteries is our Willie Potgieter,' Father Waldo disclosed. 'Just suddenly appeared there during the war, quite out of the blue! Koos didn't offer any explanation, apart from once mumbling something about someone to keep him company. Which I found unremarkable until my people down in the village told me something else. They said Willie had been seen arriving at Mapapeng on foot, all sunburned and ragged. That was during the war – early '42, before the snows came.'

'Didn't you say something about this to Koos?'

The great head shook.

'But surely –'

'Never got around to it, Finbar. You know how it is in the mountains, the way people mind their own business. Besides, it was a month before I was back – I'd been sent on a retreat – and by then Willie had settled in. Soon it was as if he'd been there all the time. I was pleased for Koos's sake, he'd been very lonely since the wife died, and well . . . Willie and I got on all right, too. I used to take letters for him to Peray, to be forwarded with our mail to Maseru. There wasn't a plane service then, of course. No radio, either. The big changes came after the war.'

Father Waldo cracked his knuckles.

'Does Willie still play his fiddle?' he asked, a shade too brightly. 'Always had a fine ear. Taught him a few airs myself.'

'Could do.'

Buchanan slid off the table and confronted the old man. Something had happened to his story, smack in the middle. It'd turned suddenly feeble as though he had decided against going through with it after all. As if it might only cause someone unnecessary trouble.

Professional Christians were, however, always at a disadvantage should you want to put a direct question to them.

'Strictly off the record,' Buchanan said to Father Waldo, 'is there any particular reason why you seem to stress all this took place during war-time?'

'I've got it!' boasted Nancy, taking her foot down off the verandah railing.

The time was a little after ten, and they were seated in deck chairs outside her room at the Hunter's Moon boarding house, an extremely respectable establishment on one of Maseru's better streets. Legend had it that the wife of the original proprietor had once taken an elephant gun to a mouse in the larder, because the name hardly made sense otherwise.

'Oh aye?' coaxed Buchanan.

'Willie Potgieter was a draft-dodger – right?'

'South Africa didn't have a draft, they were all volunteers. But you're warm. Volunteering went into a second stage, with those willing to fight beyond their borders wearing a red flash on the shoulder.'

'How's that?'

'The red flashes made them a prime target for the Ossewa-brandwag. You must have heard of them: the Oxwaggon Sentinels, best known as the OB.'

She scowled into the embroidery she was affecting.

'That pro-Nazi Afrikaner group?'

'*Group?* Jesus, woman, the OB ran to just under half a bloody million! Smuts had to hold back troops to contain the situation – riots, bombings, sabotage, the whole shooting match. Over three hundred cops arrested; charges of high treason; a pitched battle with the army in Jo'burg that lasted two days!'

Nancy tossed the embroidery aside.

'Don't exhaust yourself for my sake,' she said primly. 'I'm with you up to the point where Father Waldo probably suspected Willie was an O B man on the run.'

'Would you like to finish it?'

'Father Waldo, being a charitable old bastard, couldn't see what harm little Willie was doing at Mapapeng, so he let sleeping dogs lie.'

Buchanan took it from there: 'And, as the years went on, he was vindicated. Willie never left the place.'

A horse clopped by, carrying its half-asleep rider home.

'So where has this got us?' Nancy asked. 'Was Willie Potgieter an O B fugitive?'

'I'd say it was a strong possibility, but Father Waldo never asked. It gives us a vague tie-in with the world of Johnny Tagg, of course.'

'And that's all?'

'No,' replied Buchanan, who could be a tease himself when goaded. 'I asked Father Waldo if he'd ever come across any of their friends. He hadn't, said he'd never known them to have visitors, but there were the letters he used to take down to Peray for Willie. They were always addressed to the same person, so the name – if not the address – has stuck in his mind ever since: D. J. J. Steyn.'

A short silence was only natural.

Buchanan broke it by saying 'Which could, I'm afraid, indicate that simple answer – something along the lines of an overdue reunion, perhaps.'

'Very convincing,' replied Nancy, staring hard into the night. 'Only it stinks even worse now. What Stoffel described sure didn't sound like a sentimental journey – and, if it was, then how come Tagg was invited to join the party?'

True; even when the circumstances were taken at their most innocuous, his presence at Mapapeng was a little like a baker's thumb in a meat pie.

'To get back to first principles, Buchanan, we still *know*

34

nothing. It's still all ifs and buts and maybes, with a listed maniac hovering in the background. My boss is going to want something better than that. Any suggestions?'

'Willie Potgieter seems the key figure, whichever way you look at this thing. Get some fact on him – verify this O B connection, for instance – and the rest might start making sense.'

'A great idea, but how? I thought the S A Military Intelligence files had been "lost in transit" when the Nats set up a new security system in '47? No inside man is going to help you there.'

'Your gracious approval is all that really matters, Miss Kitson,' said Buchanan, rising and making her a small bow. 'Just you lie back and leave the rest to an old hand.'

'You fight dirty!'

'Oh aye, since a very small boy.'

An hour later, after going through the usual rigmarole to contact field headquarters, Buchanan had stated the bare bones of his problem and received a reply. All that was on offer, however, was a tentative suggestion.

It would mean driving north into the Orange Free State and then east, skirting the whole northern border of Lesotho, to Ladysmith, Natal. With no guarantee that the gentleman he sought hadn't turned senile.

This seemed to give the matter an urgency all of its own.

Chapter Three

Every British schoolboy with a coarse streak in him had made witticisms about the Relief of Ladysmith, Buchanan among them. So he knew a little about the famous siege there. He also knew that Lady Smith's maiden name had been Juanita Maria de los Dolores de Leon, which a great many more hotel clerks would have believed in.

He did not know the exact location of 21 Bandolier Road but, with the day to himself, was content to potter about along the dirt of the back streets for a while. The encircling hills, from which the Boers had lobbed in their artillery fire, were slightly oppressive – although, in effect, they served only to heighten his usual response to being in the Republic.

Peace and order certainly reigned, as its champions claimed. There was probably no peace and order to match it in the world, let alone in Africa, that messy, happy-go-lucky, violent continent. And the white suburb through which he was passing typified what was meant. The colourful gardens, bright with bougainvillaea and Barberton daisies, were trim down to the last blade; watered, weeded and tended for ten hours a day. While the pretty bungalows of varied design, with their gay awnings and ornate burglar guards, had windows that glittered and verandahs polished to shine like fresh paint. Even the toddlers were kept neat and tidy, as they wandered about in their sunhats, toting toy pistols and bullying big dogs. Here and there, those who saw to all this, the servant boy in his canvas tunic and the nanny in her nurse's overall, hummed and sang away the day until their return, with the cook, to the precise rows of dinky two-room dwellings provided outside town. And yet, underneath it all, in a literal if trite sense, was still the substance of Africa. Which gave Buchanan that same feeling of unease he sometimes had when confronted by a quiet child with clean fingernails, perfect manners and a reputation for always doing what it was told.

Number 21 Bandolier Road was a maverick, a disgrace. High fences of split poles had been erected on either side of it by Numbers 19 and 23, as though to signal their fervent wish not to be associated with it.

The tin-roofed bungalow was itself set back about fifteen yards from the pavement, although it seemed more distant because of what stood in between: a hedge of cactus, plum trees, and the tallest weed Buchanan had seen outside a cemetery.

He picked his way up the path, scattering bantams caught unawares by his approach, and went up on to the step. The peeling front door was wide open, and the long cluttered passageway leading down to the back porch empty. He tried the knocker.

An aged Zulu retainer appeared from a side room. He was jauntily clad, as though for the Edwardian seaside, in tennis shoes, cricket flannels and the red-and-white striped blazer of Sandhurst Military College. His expression was distrustful.

'Is Major Munro in?' Buchanan asked.

But first he had to be sized up. The shrewd, somewhat bloodshot eyes went carefully over every detail, dwelling for a time on the camera.

'*Yebo*,' the manservant confirmed.

'I'd like to see him, please. Tell him I'm a reporter — Buchanan.'

'You in Brigade of Guards?'

'No, never.'

'You big enough.'

'I had an uncle in the Seaforths.'

'*Hau*, splendid!' the Zulu exclaimed, beaming and trundling off.

It had been an inspired guess. In seconds, the man was back to conduct Buchanan through to where Major Andrew Munro, late of the South African Military Intelligence Corps, by way of a previous commission in the Gordon Highlanders, sat at a desk in his study, mending watches.

'Shan't keep you long,' apologized the Major, exchanging his monocle for a jeweller's eye-piece. 'What will you have?'

'Well, a beer if possible.'

'Stoup of ale for our guest, Joshua, and I'll have my usual, if you'd be so kind. You may dismiss.'

Joshua stamped his turn, then skipped away to do his master's bidding.

'Seems a good chap,' murmured Buchanan.

'Oh, magnificent! Damn shame his sort were never permitted to bear arms. Now I really must get this perishing balance wheel right.'

Biting on a smile, Buchanan wedged himself into an armchair stacked with newspapers, and looked around.

The floor of the study was like the front garden. Piles of books had been allowed to grow as they pleased, and there was actually a broody hen, muttering away to itself in an undergrowth of screwed-up sheets of note-paper. More books, ranging from Homer to Low's war-time cartoons, took up most of the walls, which were otherwise hung with edge weapons and pictures of various kinds. Jousef Karsh's portrait of Churchill had pride of place, above a small bust of Smuts, and there, beside a delicate Highland water-colour, was a vivid Karoo sunset in oils.

While the Major was, like the best of old soldiers, fading away. The colour had almost totally gone from his patrician features, now the flesh was thinning and the skull had begun to show through. His hair had greyed to near-white on either side of the careful central parting. His moustache, however, had been tinted by tobacco fumes to the gold of an old tiger's whiskers, and still had something of a bristle to go with the steady green eyes.

It wasn't until the Major had replaced his monocle and turned round, that Buchanan registered what he had on – fresh laundering and sharp creases had been factors to take for granted.

The Major's trousers were, in point of fact, a pair of worn tartan trews, held up by a ceremonial belt, and the thin shirt had patches of darker khaki where badges must have been sewn until quite recently. Hardly much insight was then required to see that here sat a more gallant Crusoe, insistent that his Friday should have the pick of their resources from the rusty attic trunk. Nor was this, with such proud men, depressing.

'You look like a Buchanan,' the Major declared dogmatically, having made his own careful appraisal. 'Great ugly, heathen buggers you all are, too. Not related to Jack Buchanan, by any chance?'

'No, sir.'

'Frightful man. Seaforths; your uncle?'

He was reaching for his *Army List* when Joshua returned with the drinks, happily breaking that line of thought.

'Bung-ho!' said the Major, relishing his first gulp.

Buchanan replied with a Gaelic toast, and instantly won the man's heart. After that, equally satisfied he was in reliable company, it was much simpler to come – almost – to the point.

'Steady the Buffs!' Major Munro rebuked him, when it seemed Buchanan might be about to disclose his true credentials. 'Good God, man, there's no need to compromise us both! If it's the lowdown on the Ossewabrandwag you're after, I'm only too happy to oblige. I blether on about it to anyone with the goodness to listen, and have done so for the best part of forty years.'

Then he nodded at the note-paper on the floor, and said: 'You're actually knee-deep in the stuff. I know it's a trifle over-done perhaps, but I'm taking a stab at my memoirs.'

'But what if –'

'Who? BOSS? The Security Branch wallahs? They've nothing to fear from me and they know it. After all, most of this guff has been published before, if not in such detail – a lot of old hat.'

'That still says a lot about the strength of the State,' Buchanan observed wryly.

'Undoubtedly! But the worst of it is, Buchanan, that they may very well be right: nobody's the least bit bloody interested in the OB today, except possibly as part of our colourful past.'

The Major prised off the back of a wristwatch, handling the pieces clumsily in his agitation. A shaken conviction would, of course, explain so many false starts.

'It could retain some relevance, sir.'

The long fingers became slow and sure again.

'As I said though,' growled the Major, glancing up with a twinkle, 'a lot of old hat. Perfectly ordinary history books, even ones available in this God-forsaken country, record the activities of the O B.'

'Major?'

'Additional footnotes are really more my line – and are, unless I'm grossly mistaken, what you're really after. Let's not shilly-shally, Buchanan.'

And that was an order.

'You're right. I've come across an individual we have reason to believe was once a member of the O B, and possibly one involved in something fairly unpleasant. Or at least drastic enough to make him a marked man.'

'Have you indeed!' the Major chuckled. 'But my dear chap, the Republic is lousy with former stormtroopers who now lead respectable lives – most influential ones, in many cases.'

'But not on barren mountain tops.'

A very odd look crossed the Major's face, as he put down the watch and stood up.

'So Joshua was right in thinking your car had a Lesotho number-plate?'

'Aye, that's true.'

'And Mapapeng comes into this?'

Buchanan nodded.

'Then I take it you must be here about wee Willie Potgieter?'

'The same.'

'*Wrong,*' contradicted the Major, gleefully. 'Not his name at all. It's Steyn – Willem Hendrik Jacobus Steyn.'

He allowed that to sink in while he beat on a small gong to summon Joshua. His manner had become jittery with suppressed excitement, as though he was about to tell some devastating joke, and yet he was anything but senile.

The name did not have to sink very far.

'Any relation to D. J. J. or Dirk Steyn?' Buchanan asked, handing over his tankard to be replenished.

The Major cocked an eyebrow.

'We have been doing our homework,' he said approvingly.

'That's quite correct: they're half-brothers. Same father, different mothers.'

'Oh, Christ,' said Buchanan.

He wanted to kick himself. He wanted to quietly strangle Miss Nancy Kitson. And he resolved that in future he would faithfully obey the dictates of his own sound common sense, while ignoring completely the allure of more beguiling fancies. It'd been a long way to come to hear what he had himself said, in effect, the night before in Maseru: the half-brothers were simply staging a reunion.

'Why the "Oh, Christ"?' inquired the Major.

'Because it would suddenly seem – well, that we're wasting your time, sir. Unless Johnny Tagg means anything to you in connection with the Steyns?'

'It doesn't, but please explain.'

'Or Pik Oeloefse?'

'Yes, I do know a bit about him: big-game hunter turned wild-life photographer, and all that rot. A neighbour of Dirk's – he farms as well – and a friend of long standing.'

That only made it worse; taking an old friend along on a junket like that was a very natural thing to do. And no doubt Tagg was there to flog windmills.

Self-disgust made Buchanan overlook the nuances provided by Stoffel the pilot, and keep his reply short: 'Dirk Steyn arrived for a holiday at Mapapeng two weeks ago, only our attention was drawn to this because of this other –'

'The Devil he did!' exclaimed the Major, taking his turn at looking very surprised. 'Dirk? At Mapapeng with Willie?'

'Aye, a family get-together one supposes.'

The Major's expression then became one of intense suspicion, and he stalked over to the window to stare out of it for a while, leaving Buchanan bewildered by this unexpected response. And cautiously pleased with it: there might have been some point to his journey after all.

'You're quite right, Buchanan,' said the Major finally, coming about with his shoulders set square. 'This is very definitely a matter which requires investigation. Those with a greater faith in human nature than I have, and particularly those who believe it can undergo radical change, might well feel otherwise. But

41

I view this "get-together", as you call it, with the gravest misgiving.'

'Why, sir?'

'That's rather a long story.'

'But perhaps I should hear it, Major Munro – if you're willing to spare the time.'

He was; on condition the telling was left until lunch was over. He had first to complete his morning's quota of work, as his pension didn't run to much jollity, and then he'd need a short while in which to recover. Buchanan agreed readily, certain now that he was earning his own keep.

Lunch was scrambled eggs on spinach, both out of the garden, and a pie made from apples off a neighbour's tree which overhung the high fence. Joshua served in white parade gloves.

Then the Major produced a broached bottle of cheap port and they sat themselves in cane chairs on the back porch. Despite the informal comfort of the situation, it had the air of a pre-battle briefing about it which Buchanan also found reassuring.

'How well acquainted are you with Brother Boer?' the Major began. 'The Great Trek inland of 1836 and all that?'

The quirky detail of history was all that ever imprinted itself on Buchanan's mind, but he replied as best he could: 'I know about the shoddy tricks on the part of the British which drove them to it – and that one of its leaders was a dandified waggon-builder called Maritz, who probably got hoist on the petard of his own sales talk.'

'Excellent! And later than that? Concentration camps?'

'The term was actually coined by the British during the Boer War to mean the concentration of the population of a rural area in the interests of their own safety. Many came voluntarily, and security was such that Boer commandos sometimes spent the night in them. They were run badly and disease –'

He stopped at the Major's impatient nod.

'Quite so, but you should have started with the main point: the British losses during the war were 22,000, while the Boers lost 32,000 – but of those, 26,000 died in concentration camps, poor devils. Most were women and children.'

'And that is where the story begins?'

'It must do; like the Irish, who have also suffered under Pax Britannica, so much of what the Afrikaner does today is based on strong race memories of the past.'

Buchanan would have felt he was in for something of an ordeal then, if he hadn't noticed a gleam in the other's eye which seemed to promise a punchline.

'Among those 26,000 victims of sheer bloody ineptitude,' the Major went on, settling back, 'were the offspring of a certain Karel Steyn, who was what one called a "bitter-ender", or a chap who wanted to fight to the finish. Steyn lost all his four children in a camp in the Transvaal, and it wasn't until his good lady had recovered sufficiently from her own deprivations, that they were able to begin another family. The effort, I fear, killed her; she was by then nearing her forties. But it was a drawn-out affair, and she lasted long enough to fill little Dirk – who was born in 1910, the year of the Union – with a good deal of worthy polemic.'

'How long was that?'

'The first Mrs Steyn passed away in 1917; overcome, it was said, by the excitement of a small party held to celebrate the Russian Revolution.'

'Oh aye?' said Buchanan, struck by the quirkiness.

'The Great War had seemed to men of Steyn's outlook to offer them a chance to escape the British yoke once again. By 1917 such hopes had begun to flag, and so the rise of the Bolshies brought renewed comfort. Malan assured his followers that "Bolshevism stands for freedom, just like the National Party".'

'The same Malan who became Prime Minister of South Africa in '48 and introduced the Suppression of Communism Act – plus apartheid?'

'Always, I regret, the same Malan – although never *quite* the same, either. But we digress.'

'The first Mrs Steyn had just died.'

'Ah, yes; leaving Karel with young Dirk, and a farm that wasn't doing at all well because of his political preoccupations – the Afrikaner Broederbond, or Brotherhood, had just got under way. So he did what seemed then a most expeditious thing: he married the very capable Maria, whose land adjoined his own. She was a widow, and had no children, and was an excellent farm manager. This was still in 1917.'

'Quick work!'

'It was. Without wishing to be unduly indelicate, young man, hers were indeed fertile if fallow fields – and very shortly afterwards Willie, Dirk's half-brother, arrived.'

The Major broke off to shoo away a chameleon attracted by the flies on the rim of his glass. When he returned to his story, the tempo picked up.

'All was set for a new dynasty to begin. Dozens of little Steyns threatened to appear on the High Veld. Then Maria Steyn thoughtlessly declared an interest in a party started by the Boer general and folk hero Smuts. This we know. We don't know why further children weren't born to her. But we can surmise that this caused a certain rift between her and her fanatical spouse, who looked on Smuts as a traitor for doing deals with the British. The important thing is that this rift transferred itself, in due course, to the two boys, Dirk and Willie.'

'The eight years between them must have already made things difficult,' Buchanan observed.

'Absolutely. And then there were the physical and temperamental differences to contend with as well, from young Willie's point of view. Have you seen either of them? Runt of the litter, we'd have called Willie in our day. Stunted, slow-witted and plagued by weak eye-sight – his only asset being a good ear for music as he was, in his odd way, a sensitive wee lad as well. He certainly made a very poor showing against Dirk, who had taken after his father and was the epitome of the breed: tall, strapping and resplendent in native intelligence. As the years went on, one can imagine the rivalry that existed, especially as the father favoured Dirk and treated Willie with the scorn he dared not show his mother. Without Maria Steyn's supervision, of course, the farm – now twice the size – would have meant time away from his politicking. Not too much for you, I hope?'

Taking this to mean that the Major was now poised to get at the meat of the matter, Buchanan muttered a polite denial. There was nothing too complicated about it so far: a marriage of convenience had given Dirk Steyn a stepmother he despised for her political beliefs, and a half-brother he despised for his identity with her, and his puniness.

'Very well, Buchanan, here's the rub. Fresh hope came again to the Steyns and their ilk with the rise of National Socialism in Germany. Diederichs and Van Rensburg, later to become national figures, went over to study its methods. Nazi organizations of various kinds sprang up all over the shop. Dirk, already of voting age, and a militant idealist, joined the Brownshirts.'

'And wee Willie?'

'Ah, this was his chance at last to show he was no mother's milksop, but also a true son of his father. In 1933, at fifteen, he entered the local branch of Hitler Youth. The music-maker, as Dirk contemptuously called him, was doing his bit.'

'But didn't Hertzog's government throw the Hun organizers out in '34, Major?'

'That wasn't the reverse one might suppose. Young Willie soldiered on, and Dirk, then twenty-four, rose to even higher things by following Malan into his new Purified Nationalist Party – as opposed, by awful implication, to its rival. The following year saw the start of the real conflict between them. Dirk was then eligible, as an Afrikaner Protestant of superior character, for the élitist Brotherhood – recently reorganized with help from Germany. Its rules allow anyone to divulge their own membership – although nobody else's – and you can be sure the first person Dirk informed was Willie.'

'He was still getting at him?'

'Even his own mother did, as he was so unlike her canny, robust self.'

'Poor little bastard . . .'

The Major poured a drop more port.

'Willie's fortunes went from bad to worse. In 1936 the Hitler Youth and kindred organizations were banned. Although substitute bodies took their place, Willie could never regard them in the same light. Nor could he vote, still being too young. He tried to make a name for himself in the general outcry against Jewish refugees being allowed into the country. But his unprovoked attack on one Solly Brokenshaw went down exceedingly badly, as Mr Brokenshaw was a pedlar upon whom every farmer's wife in the district relied for her buttons and hairpins. Dirk was ordered to bring him to heel.'

'What was Willie doing for a living – farming, too?'

'Odd-jobbing on local construction work, building dam walls and so forth. He had a gang of blacks and a lorry.'

'I interrupted.'

'Not at all; very relevant, actually. Then came an apparent turn in his fortunes. Another Great Trek was held as a centenary celebration, with ox-waggons lumbering in from all directions. It was so successful that a Bloemfontein devil-dodger, Dominee Kotze, decided to form the O B to perpetuate the spiritual boost this had given Afrikaners, and to realize their aim of national independence. Dirk dutifully joined – but Willie was in it like a shot, able finally to claim parity with his half-brother. That happy situation was, however, short-lived: relationships beween the Purified and the O B cooled off. Malan, who'd at first helped recruitment, told his followers they might resign.'

'Cooled off?' echoed Buchanan.

'These factions believed implicitly that Herr Hitler would win the war.'

'I'd gathered that, Major – but why the split?'

'Because Malan wanted to do the negotiating when the time came. He'd already had a messenger from Ribbentrop, assuring him all the Germans would want was their old colony back in South West. The Purified were welcome to Lesotho, Botswana, Swaziland *and* Rhodesia, by God!'

'Oh aye? And the O B wanted in at the table, too?'

'You've got the drift, but again we digress. Dirk then naturally ordered Willie to follow him from the ranks of the O B, but the little runt defied him. Willie had become a stormtrooper and a self-styled explosives expert, having handled dynamite building his dams.'

'That can't have pleased Dirk,' said Buchanan, getting up to stretch.

'No, but it did no end of good to Willie's morale, and he assumed an air of enormous self-importance. That lasted until the well known affair of the trio who tried to blow up a trainload of army dependants.'

Buchanan sat down again.

'They were blasted to sweet buggery themselves – and Willie was suspected of having supplied them with unstable material. His denials were to no avail and the OB chucked him out. So he went to Dirk, cap in hand, and asked for a place among the Purified as he was now old enough to vote. Dirk, fearful of his flourishing reputation as a party stalwart, threw him out as well.'

'So he –'

'No, but we're nearly done,' said the Major, trying not to smile at whatever he had up his sleeve. 'Remember Leibbrandt? The South African boxer who joined the German army and then came back to be dropped off secretly on the coast?'

'Vorster accepted his offer of fighting Communism not long ago,' Buchanan said after a pause.

'Should have been shot. Came armed with a fistful of dollars and a shortwave radio to lend Van Rensburg a hand in running his stormtroopers. Van Rensburg didn't take to him, so he wandered off and set up his own band of worthies, the Boerenasie. And –'

'Willie was back in business?'

'He was indeed. Like a flash. Until two Boerenasie worthies, presumably handling unstable dynamite, blew themselves up in the privacy of their rural retreat.'

Buchanan laughed – but, as he discovered, prematurely.

Because the Major went straight on, unmoved: 'That's when things went completely haywire for our hero. According to Dirk, who visited him shortly afterwards in great secrecy under cover of darkness, Willie had become a marked man. He was told that the OB had decided he was a fifth-columnist, bent on deliberate liquidation, and – in Mafia parlance – there was a contract out for him. The full details of this conversation are not known, but one can imagine Willie's response to this unexpected display of brotherly concern. It is a fact, though, that within the hour Dirk was driving him down to the Lesotho border, and that he was advised to make for the remotest part of the Maluti mountains.'

That couldn't be all, surely. How flat. How unfunny.

After a moment or two, Buchanan said: 'And? What was

the follow-up? To know as much as this, you must have been reading those letters passing to and fro through Maseru.'

'Of course, dear boy. We felt we had to keep tabs for the duration. What long, nostalgic collections of balderdash they were too; strident with pathetic denials. Very tiresome.'

'He must have also asked when it would be safe to return.'

'Invariably. Mapapeng bored him stiff, and so did Koos Brandsma – they were very different types. But Dirk always wrote back saying he was sorry, it wasn't safe.'

'And this correspondence lasted until the end of the war, I gather?'

'Far longer than that I would think. In fact, from what you've told me today, it must have lasted until very recently.'

'What?' Buchanan boggled. 'Dirk saying it *still* wasn't safe?'

'His exact words, in all probability. Or would you encourage Willie to return to a land now run largely by his former OB comrades, all lusting for revenge?'

'Hold on a –'

'Especially,' the Major cut in, 'with formidable fellows like Vorster, ex-stormtrooper general, at the very top?'

Then he got up and turned his face away while he examined a wasps' nest in the rafters, just as a mischievous child might have done to hide a grin.

'Poppycock,' said Buchanan, choosing the word with care. 'I don't bloody believe it. Vorster and his cronies left that world when the war ended and the Nats got into power.'

'Nonetheless, I'm sure I'm right.'

'Poppycock. If the contract still existed, they could have winkled Willie out years ago – a simple check on the mail by Security and that would have been it. Three ANCs were kidnapped from Lesotho – why not Willie? It doesn't wash.'

'You must agree, however, how much better off we've all been without our small friend these few decades,' the Major replied, turning to show that grin.

It stretched unevenly from ear to ear.

And Buchanan realized he had fallen into the very same trap which had kept Willie Steyn in needless exile for more than thirty years.

'There never was a contract,' he said, grinning too.

'Nor the slightest suspicion on the OB's part that he was a Smuts fifth-columnist – just an infernal bloody idiot. Dirk had simply been lying his leathery arse off, and we were very happy to let him.'

That was when the big laugh should have come. But Buchanan didn't laugh and neither did the Major; the implications weighed too heavily, now their minds had turned to the present day.

'Jesus, what a ruthless sod!'

'Politicians are apt to be, Buchanan, if they fear their careers may be jeopardized – even more so, if they believe they have a Divine Calling. But what Dirk did went further than that.'

'Must have hated Willie's guts.'

'Now you're overstating the case. It's a lot colder and cruder than that: Willie – like a black – just didn't mean a thing to Dirk.'

'Then why the hell has he . . .' began Buchanan.

Suddenly seeing the purpose of the fine detail in Major Munro's story. The plethora of facts hadn't been provided so that each might be remembered individually. But rather that they might, like the tiny dots of a print-maker's screen, blur together and reproduce one stark picture of the two half-brothers. The picture of them which the Major carried in his own mind's eye – and into which it was impossible to fit the idea of a happy reunion.

Convinced of this now, as he would never have been by a thumb-nail sketch, Buchanan got to his feet.

'Give me a reason Dirk's there, sir,' he said.

'I can't, laddie,' the old man replied. 'I can, however, suggest that only one power on God's Earth could have persuaded him to make the journey.'

'Oh aye?'

'And I am not at all sure *that* bodes well for any of us! You'll have to tread very carefully.'

Chapter Four

Nancy had news for him. While Buchanan had been in Lady-smith the day before, seeing Major Munro, she'd received a telephoned inquiry from South Africa. The customer had wanted to know how difficult it would be to get by air to a place called Mapapeng; he believed a Meneer Steyn had recently made such a journey.

'That's a curious bit of fishing,' Buchanan remarked, indicating that she should adopt her first pose.

They had only just met up again, ostensibly to do some glamour shots on the edge of a hotel pool at one, when most of the guests would be inside stuffing themselves. It was a ploy so charged with ulterior motivation of a mundane sort that any sub-activity of a clandestine nature would hardly suggest itself. Less theoretically, it would also help towards the rent.

'Maybe it was fishing, although I don't really think so,' said Nancy, simpering. 'Seemed so unsure of himself and went in for long silences. You know how it is when people aren't used to handling things like that? Top of which, he sounded young and very Afrikaans. Twice I had to ask for a repeat.'

'No name? A little more to the left, please.'

'I told him there'd be a mail plane going that way on Friday at ten, and was asking his name in case he wanted a reservation, when he rang off with a quick *dankie*.'

'Hmmm.'

'But how did you do yesterday? The other goodie I've got for you can keep.'

Buchanan moved in to do some closer-ups, and to give her the basic situation. To the list of known reprobates at Mapa-peng, begun with Johnny Tagg, had been added the lethal, if latent, Willem Hendrik Jacobus Steyn – who she knew as Willie Potgieter. But in baffling association with them both was

50

the half-brother Dirk Steyn; a man for whom any voluntary contact with an 'Englisher' like Tagg was as unthinkable as with the aforesaid Willie. Dirk was, moreover, zealously law-abiding within the framework of his own beliefs, and a loyal party member to boot. This element of decided incongruity had the overtones of a bishop in a brothel, while making the church elder's intentions – as opposed to those of His Grace – appear unhealthily devious.

'I'll say!' agreed Nancy, forgetting and letting her tummy bulge.

'Very fetching,' muttered Buchanan, who'd released the shutter on his Rollei at that very instant. 'And with your phone call on top of it, that makes Dirk the real centre of attention.'

'I'm taking five while you tell me the rest,' she said, and retreated beneath the big beach umbrella that shaded her table.

Buchanan cranked off the remaining exposures and began a change to colour stock. His fill-in flash, reflectors and tilt-head tripod were all doing a grand job of keeping the few onlookers impressed, all of whom sat at a respectful distance and pretended to read salacious magazines. One basking banker, with two-way mirrors in his spectacle frames, was about to light his cigarette at the filter end, so taken was he with the scene before him.

Nancy slipped on a robe which did as much to dampen casual lust as a bucket of warm water, and Buchanan felt – for the first time – a little sorry for her. He set down his Rollei and picked up the Pentax.

'The rest's informed conjecture,' he said softly. 'According to my sources of information, the one thing that could make Dirk act so uncharacteristically would be *an order from above.*'

The 135mm lens filled the viewfinder with the quick lift of Nancy's dainty brows – and the frown that followed it.

'Meaning?'

'Take your pick. There's the Brotherhood or, if you see this as something a whole lot bigger, the ruling party itself. It's the only answer that fits all the other conditions.'

Buchanan did a slow pan and picked up Louis Fouché, the younger BOSS agent. He was standing languidly against the wall of the men's changing hut, very tall and dark and graceful, like a matador in his Monday clothes. Rings flashed on every finger.

'Can Louis lip-read?' Buchanan murmured.

'Huh! That you should worry when you're talking through your ass.'

'Am I?'

'Just a minute,' she said, 'give me a chance to adjust.'

He understood how Nancy felt. The whole thing did take some adjustment once the first shock had passed. It wasn't so much the idea of Dirk being on official business, which was perplexing enough in its own right, as what followed from there: that Tagg had to be on official business, too. And if this was true, it made her warning about the danger of his finding the right sponsorship twice as alarming. None of Tagg's schemes would have been too grandiose for a national budget.

'That sure as hell ties in,' she admitted finally.

'With what?'

'My other goodie, which wasn't doing so well on its own. Or did you get anything on Pik Oeloefse as well?'

'Not one of my informant's strong points. He's a big-game photographer, and a long-standing buddy of Dirk's. They have farms next door to each other.'

'That I didn't know, but it doesn't contradict. The boss came through first thing today to say that for Pik Oeloefse read P. K. Hattingh, who gets his stuff into the same lousy magazines as you do. I can see the bells ringing. Articles on the ways of the warthog, and on how the Bushman makes his poisoned arrows – all fully illustrated.'

'And pretty expert,' observed Buchanan, who had read the Bushman one and been impressed by the toxicology.

'We're really more interested in *where* he's been picking this stuff up. It seems Meneer Oeloefse has been spending a lot of time lately in the Caprivi Strip, doing his thing with a very long lens. Which wouldn't be so interesting if the Strip wasn't South Africa's only access to the Zambian border.'

'Christ, I thought it was off limits to the ordinary citizen.'

'Think about it.'

Buchanan did just that. But not for long, however, because

the obvious innuendo of Nancy's disclosure had placed the man now at the top of the Mapapeng league.

'He could be using Dirk as an excuse to set himself up in the mountains with that very long lens,' he said, just as Louis Fouché started towards them.

'But why?' asked Nancy quickly. 'What would he want to use it *on*? There's nothing going on up there.'

Buchanan didn't have time to give an answer, even if he'd been able to think of one.

The BOSS agent ducked in under the brolly and stood over them with elegant nonchalance.

'The power of the mighty press,' he joked.

'We do seem irresistible to some,' agreed Buchanan.

'Ja, so I can see. Only you must be careful, Miss Kitson, this man you're with has a bad reputation. The Customs tell me he was away chasing his "bits of fluff" again yesterday – came back at midnight worn out.'

'A girl in every *dorp*.'

'That could be very true, Finbar. You've certainly put some mileage on your clock.'

A deliberate give-away: Louis had been on his prowl round the car parks again, noting down the figures on the speedo and subtracting them from the sum he'd done the last time. The boy was a tireless and subtle worker.

'You're still interested in buying my old VW then?' Buchanan inquired innocently.

'You know me, I'm always interested.'

'Oh aye.'

Louis had a fondness for creating awkward pauses; it was best to let them last and spoil his fun.

'Pin-ups?' he asked after about a minute.

'That's right. Does a chap good to vary his diet.'

'So what's next on the menu?'

'The usual, Louis; I'm away to the mountains for a couple of days to follow-up on a school feeding scheme, then I'm –'

'That's all right then,' Louis interrupted, leering at Nancy. 'Just as long as it wasn't *you* – hey, Miss Kitson?'

She did her dirty laugh and then said: 'Look, you two, I'm supposed to be back on duty at five-to.'

'Hell! You mustn't let me keep you! Nice to see you again, Finbar man. Okay Nancy?'

'Fine,' she said, and waved.

Louis Fouché withdrew with his innate grace, moving far more rapidly than it looked. He disappeared through the glass doors into the cocktail lounge.

'Jesus, what was that all about, Buchanan? I've had him at my counter often enough, but he's never tried that sort of crap before.'

'Just a wee reminder who's BOSS.'

'Oh, for Chrissake! What was he getting at?'

'Pure ritual. All us legitimate newshounds get it once in a while, just to show he's not a man to discriminate. And, like he says, he's always interested.'

'Blatantly!'

'Why hide under a bushel?' Buchanan sighed. 'BOSS helped set up the government here, and it's going to see it sticks to promises like Lesotho will never be a terrorist springboard. God help us all if that ever happened. Have you thought how just a suggestion of –'

'Look, it *is* getting late,' Nancy said sharply.

And went straight out into the sun and slumped sensuously up against a palm with her eyes screwed shut.

'Will this do?'

'Chin up a fraction – that breast's squashed – better – get rid of the creases – hold it . . .'

Buchanan banged his way through the film, cranking the Rollei like a Model-T on a cold morning. The gawpers behind him were right, he conceded: dwelling on firm flesh in a land of noticeably listless kids was somewhat obscene. But he did it rather well for all that.

'I can talk?' asked Nancy, through smile-clenched teeth.

'It's in the can.'

'Then what was the big idea in telling Fouché about a trip into the mountains?'

'Oh, that; it's just a lie I made up the other night for Father Waldo. Did you notice? I got a totally nil reaction off him.'

'My boss'll go bananas. He's said no –'

'Sod your boss. Mine says he's mildly intrigued, and would like what information I can lay hands on. That little probe said that either we're totally wrong, or this Mapapeng thing is out of Louis's class. I tend to favour the latter.'

'It'll go on his report, you stupid bastard!'

'The consequences of which could be instructive.'

Now the sun had nothing to do with the way Miss Kitson was keeping that adorable jaw clamped tight. She was possibly very angry indeed.

'Aren't you a smart . . .' she snapped, before invective failed her. 'Now, when you don't go, Louis will want to know exactly why!'

She stalked off to get changed.

While she was away, Buchanan packed everything back into the gadget bags, strapped up the legs of the tripod, and dealt indulgently with the inquisitive who idled their way over.

'Er, *ektually* what is the idea behind this?' asked an obese sunbather, mouthing a cigar.

'Advertising job,' Buchanan confided.

'Man, that's interesting, hey? Advertising what ektually?'

'Navel oranges.'

'Ah,' said the obese sunbather, and went away to think about it.

Buchanan had a bit of a ponder himself.

Then emancipated Nancy, still suffering for her art, gave him her bag to carry – although it weighed next to nothing – and they went out to the car park. Louis was not there to improve her mood, so they threw everything in the back and started for the airport.

'Well?' she said, after a sombre half-smile. 'Let's hear how an "old hand" is going to handle the next stage.'

'He's restless.'

'I see.'

'And he thinks he may have given himself a rather brilliant notion.'

'Which is?'

'To make it seem the most natural thing in the world that *he* should pay a call at Mapapeng.'

'Jesus!' exploded Nancy.

Buchanan braked to avoid an elderly South African, who was only there for the craftwork, and then steered round one who had come for the beer. He listened to breathing noises.

'You can't risk blowing this until you're sure you know what we're dealing with,' Nancy said in the sensible voice of a first-grade teacher. 'It might not be like anything you imagine – which is why Louis didn't react. Or seem to. I mean it could be something even *he* would want to know about.'

'Suggestions?'

'What about this new opposition party to Vorster on the far Right? The Reconstituted Nats – Herstigde, HNP.'

'No way, Miss Kitson.'

'Why not? Dirk's a real hardliner, you say. So are they: they're against détente with Black Africa, fraternizing with the depraved Englishers – you name it, they're his people. He's up at Mapapeng to run a secret conference where the Security won't be around. Why should he trust them?'

'No reason he should,' agreed Buchanan. 'But, for starters, Vorster has effectively crushed Hertzog's HNP *verkramptes* and –'

'All the more reason they should –'

'Let me finish, lassie. We went over this theory yesterday ourselves. Firstly, what is Tagg doing on HNP business? He's Johnny, not Jannie. Secondly, Dirk Steyn wouldn't be seen dead hobnobbing with a Hertzog, not after the old man took sides with Smuts during the war. Dirk's a common or garden Nat or nothing.'

That kept Nancy quiet until a place could be found to park the VW at the airport.

Then she said: 'We've got nothing on Dirk – and just how fresh is your data?'

'Not very, but it's reliable.'

'Reliable enough to go crashing in on this old eagles' nest?' Nancy scoffed. 'Or are you just hoping for the best, with God-knows-what at stake?'

'We'll have to see. The chief wants more dope before he hits the crisis button – and I'm a terrible man for discretion, as you know.'

56

'How are you on risking your neck?'

'Below average.'

'Then let's hope that my boss can talk your chief into firing you first!' she said unkindly, flinging her door open.

'He'll have to hop to it,' replied Buchanan, 'because I think I'm just in time to catch that plane over there.'

Stoffel Hoogte was a gluttonous, habitually cheerful expatriate Afrikaner with the head of a cherub and the body of a one-legged buddha. He took every other step on an artificial limb he called Cassidy and treated abominably. He could, he claimed, fly anything.

And his mountain passengers, whether missionary, doctor, or Basotho on his way to the mines, placed their lives in his hands quite confident this was so. Stoffel had, for instance, safely landed on a bare slope after losing both his propeller and part of his undercarriage to two vultures in a mid-air collision. He had also survived having several pints of porridge regurgitated over him and his instruments by the infamous Aunt Tannie, sister of the trader at Siwewe, while flying blind in the middle of a hailstorm. And once he had touched down with his rudder control gone.

On the ground, however, his vast appetite and overwhelming coarse jocosity made less of an impression, and priests were known to lock up their nuns when he dropped by. The Protestants of the Parish Evangelical Missionary Society took similar measures, with more emphasis on their scantily-stocked larders. But, for all that, no pilot enjoyed a better reputation – nor had more prayers said for him – in the Maluti.

That afternoon he didn't seem the same Stoffel. His take-off from Maseru was hurried and clumsy, and before the climb was completed, a moody silence had filled every cranny of the Piper's cramped four-seater cockpit. A silence which, if anything, intensified after a course had been set due east for the mountainous half of Lesotho.

This aroused Buchanan's curiosity but he said nothing, and gave his attention instead to the landscape sliding away beneath the port wing.

The fact of being able to see the border of Lesotho, defined by the contrast of its arid bleakness against the prosperous, expertly-cultivated farm land of the Republic, was something he'd never grown used to. Every adult knew that true frontiers were not drawn on the ground, but in invisible ink about six feet above it where men did their thinking. But here, as a child would suppose, was a clear demarcation line across which one stepped into a very different world.

A depressing world too, for all its stark grandeur. The lowlands were everywhere striated by the deep, sharp-edged gullies called *dongas*, as if some monstrous predator had wantonly ripped its talons this way and that, leaving the earth to bleed dry of its moisture and turn to dust – which, in many places, it had. There were more *dongas* in the foothills, starting on the slopes and penetrating deep into the arable and grazing land of the valleys. And still more *dongas* in the highlands, where the quality of the soil was even poorer.

His mind recoiled from trying to imagine an entire life spent in toil on that drear, ungiving surface, and lifted his gaze to the horizon: from a distance, the Maluti Mountains were often a pleasing and picturesque blue.

There they were already, the first range repeated again and again like a wodge of colour transparencies sandwiched together. Or, as the guide books said, set in serried rows like the seats in a gigantic amphitheatre that towered up to ten thousand feet – the back wall of which gave Natal its spectacular Drakensburg, and the inspiration for such names as Giant's Castle and Cathedral Peak.

Stoffel broke silence with a little wind and said: 'Cloud isn't bad today.'

'Oh aye.'

'It's a bugger.'

'What is?'

'Cloud.'

They flew on once again in silence, but it had lost its stifling weight and presently Stoffel began to mutter to himself.

'I'll tell you what else is a bugger,' he volunteered, snatching at a backsliding St Christopher, as turbulence made the plane judder and the saint's magnet lose its grip. 'My boss has been chewing me for chucking passengers out without a 'chute.'

'That sounds unreasonable.'

'Ach, no, Finbar man, this is serious, hey? Two days ago, a Basotho priest from the mission at Peray was going to be picked up at the old air strip over Medikane side. The boss had a radio message from Father Stephan for us to go there, and I was told to do the detour before hitting Gotsong. Okay, so I didn't put her down, but I could see there wasn't a bloody *grasshopper* waiting, and nobody on the bridle-paths for miles around. Now Father Stephan is kicking up hell. He says the priest was definitely at the landing strip two hours before my ETA: he'd been left there by a boy who pushed off with the horses to see some friends on the way home. He was at the strip and he had two heavy suitcases with him, plus a saddle. Now, because they don't know where this priest is – Stephan got the trader to tell the men to look–he wants to know what the hell I'm playing at.'

'You'd have seen him if he'd been lugging those cases around?' Buchanan asked.

'Too right! That bloody kid took him to the wrong place, I bet you!'

'Must have done.'

Buchanan lapsed into a moody silence of his own. This little mystery had reminded him of the ones he himself faced. The chief of these being the telephone call Nancy had had from the young Afrikaner: it implied a lack of secrecy and an innocence that wasn't in keeping with the rest. Nevertheless, he was confident that the decision to go to Mapapeng had been the right one, and so suspended any further conjecture pending his arrival there.

The plane was by now right in among the peaks, weaving a bumpy path between them through the up-currents of hot air. The blueness had gone to be replaced by a biscuity colour, hatched by the grey of heather and something that looked very like tumble weed. In fact, not a few of the American tourists who ventured into the Maluti on a pony trek, compared the landscape with that of Arizona and other points west.

'You're going to which village?' Stoffel asked.

'Dumela – a follow-up on the school feeding programme.'

'Hey? But that's much closer to Mapapeng, man! I'm only going to Gotsong with this stuff.'

'Nancy's idea. I'll nip across to Dumela on horseback to-morrow, pick up the story and then ride on to Mapapeng for the night. Then you pick me up there on Friday morning when you drop the post.'

'Bloody cheap-skate!'

'Oh, you think you're worth a special charter then?'

Stoffel grinned and tapped at his fuel gauge: the needle had stuck on full.

'Anyway,' said Buchanan, 'I've got to be back in Maseru on Friday, and so this does – in its way – save me time.'

It also gave him a perfectly reasonable excuse to approach Mapapeng in a way which would make the refusal of hospitality very difficult, if that was what the trader and his guests would have preferred.

Stoffel mumbled rudely about bums who took advantage of the cut rates when they travelled 'part load' on flights already chartered, and then fell to complaining about the missing priest again. He was still not yet anything like his usual self.

As always, Buchanan was finding flying very abstract and lacking in any real sense of movement – the plane bounced and jiggled on its string, and the world kept turning slowly beneath them. This was, as he'd tried to explain to Stoffel, why he'd never felt the slightest interest in becoming a pilot. An explanation offered both before and after Stoffel had once jokingly abandoned the controls to him and they'd gone into a very nasty stall and spin.

Then he saw something that made him touch Stoffel's arm and point.

Four horsemen with rifles slung across their backs were moving at a canter through the valley ahead. What was immediately noticeable about them was that none wore the brightly-coloured blanket every Basotho regarded as more essential than a pair of trousers.

Stoffel dipped the Piper's nose and went down in a shallow glide, cutting right back on engine noise.

They never stood a chance. Stoffel came at them from behind, dropping right down to fifty feet above the valley floor. He was almost upon them before the first could think to turn and look – a very startled Willie Potgieter, instantly identifiable by his moon face and the flash of his glasses. Then Stoffel opened throttle and zoomed up, wagging his wings in a mocking salute.

St Christopher went ace over apex.

'You'll be bloody popular,' said Buchanan, feeling the seat-belt bite as they tilted into a hard bank to the right.

The horses had bolted. Willie had been unseated, but the other three were still busy with their reins. They were all white, Buchanan noted – possibly even a little whiter than usual – but he couldn't see faces.

'Ach no, they must learn to take a joke,' chuckled Stoffel, as he swung back on course for Gotsong. 'The bloody Mapapeng commando ...'

'Favourites of yours then?' Buchanan asked, intrigued by the pilot's malice.

'Bastards.'

'Oh aye?'

'That's two times I've seen them out hunting. Hell, Willie knows the same as I do that the Basutes have bugger-all meat, so why must they hunt the buck, hey? There's about three left, they tell me.'

Then Stoffel clammed up, frowned, and looked very embarrassed he'd said anything at all.

That would normally have given Buchanan a fair wee ponder, but under the circumstances all he could think about was the aptness of the description: the four horsemen had looked like a commando – or, to be really corny, a real Boer commando straight out of a history book. A sight which was always stirring if ominous.

By the time Stoffel began his approach to Gotsong air strip, Buchanan had, however, dismissed his more fanciful impressions of the encounter. The four riders had looked like a commando because they wore broad-brimmed hats, had rifles on their backs, sat heavy in the saddle, and rode in tight formation, stirrup to stirrup. Any four hunters doing the same four unremarkable things would have looked like a commando. The logic of this was irrefutable, even if an undertaste did linger on.

This left him with the few facts which had been suggested: that Dirk Steyn, Johnny Tagg, Willie and the man Oeloefse found each other's company congenial; that they rode side by side across a single-track path so they could talk to each other; that no man actually interested in hunting would attempt it in Maluti, and therefore these expeditions were simply a ruse to achieve complete privacy. Which was a fair start, although it still didn't take him very far.

'Business is good,' said Stoffel, nodding ahead as the mission station came into view. 'You've never been here before, am I right?'

Gotsong lay uncomfortably in the lap of a great stern mountain; a small, untidy clump of stone buildings with thatched roofs. Not a tree grew on the barren, stony ground to give any shade from the sun, and the only green anywhere was the paint on the water tank round the back of the house, beside the windpump. But there was some colour in the long queue of patients, mostly womenfolk in their cheap blouses and ankle-length skirts, who waited on the bank of a stream trickling down past the surgery; the pinks and blues were as pleasing as shells on a beach.

'Aye – about how many does Doc Cousteau see in a day?'

'Hundred, one-fifty, it depends. Tuesdays I take him over to his clinic at the store at Mapapeng and there it can go higher. Takes so long he rides back after. Easy, my girlie.'

The Piper had begun to buck as they lost height and hit small, powerful thermals.

'Mapapeng?'

'Ja, once he bust his leg doing that, and it was three months before he'd bugger off and get a quack to fix it. A mad bastard, you'll see. Just a sec.'

The ground was coming up fast, with Stoffel apparently aiming for a narrow path cleared of boulders and anthills. The heat shimmer above the engine cowling turned the strip to a watery mirage that rippled towards them, as hard as all hell. Then, with a thud and a thump, they were down and taxiing towards a waiting group.

So Cousteau had been to Mapapeng only the day before yesterday – that could indeed be interesting, thought Buchanan, unbuckling his seat belt.

*

But several hours later he had still not met his host. The mission helpers who unloaded the plane had explained that the Doctor was operating on a man who'd been carried in on a door. And Matilda, the Basotho housekeeper with a face like a wizened sweet potato, had asked the visitor to wait in the living-room.

Buchanan went on browsing about. There was an ancient harmonium in one corner he kept coming back to. The brass pedal plate on the left read *Mouse*, while that on the right asserted *Proof* – which must have made it a bestseller in early evangelical circles; French missionaries having been established in Lesotho well before the Great Trek left the Cape, as he'd learned from a feature done on Marija.

He worked the pedals and tried a note, and was not persuaded by the maker's guarantee that he hadn't pinned a rodent under some moving part. Then he swung round on the stool.

Piles of very old magazines, mainly *Paris Match* and the defunct *Réalité*, were stacked along the east wall under a long window made up of panes small enough to fit in a Piper's cargo hold. A wall rack held a rifle, shotgun and hunting crop; there was .303 ammunition scattered on the homemade dresser, and beside it, in antipathetic mimicry, a spill of cartridge-shaped penicillin ampoules, all duds. No tracts, no hymn books, no weight of Old and New Testaments – just a sampler, embroidered by a child, which gave friendly warning that the Good Lord bugged every conversation within those four walls.

Perhaps one of the children in the faded snapshots above the fireplace, each mounted on card cut from food packets and given pencil embellishments to look more like frames. There were five of these, and a portrait of the woman who had borne them. This much superior picture had been taken in Bordeaux while she was still a ringless spinster; her expression was timid yet resolute, as if she had known then that although society had prepared her a comfortable corner among the petite bourgeoisie, Providence, the cunning bugger, probably had other plans. Her small grave lay just outside the window.

'My apologies, m'sieur,' said Cousteau, struggling out of a blood-stained white coat as he came in from the passage. 'The day has been long.'

63

The doctor was stocky and had a large head. His hair, although tonsured by age, was still a rich chestnut, and its ragged cut belied he was obliged to be his own barber. His eyes were brown, and his thick eyebrows forbidding, but his nose, which began Grecian and ended Durante, led to an affable mouth accented by the circumflex of a boulevardier's moustache.

Buchanan introduced himself and explained what he hoped to do at Dumela the following day.

'And then I'll go on to Mapapeng and catch the post plane back on Friday,' he added.

'Ah, an admirable plan!' said Cousteau, who dithered a moment and then went to rummage in the dresser.

'I wasn't so sure about that after talking to Stoffel this afternoon – he sends his regards, by the way.'

Cousteau held up a bottle and said: 'Cognac?'

'A wee drop would be grand.'

'Good! Then I have the perfect excuse. You know Koos and Willie at Mapapeng?'

'Oh aye, stayed with them once. But –'

Cousteau had left the room; he was back within seconds carrying two plastic mugs.

'Then why should you be shy?' he asked, pouring the drinks. 'Everyone is welcome in the mountains.'

'It's just I hear they've got rather a handful of guests at the moment.'

'Guests?' Cousteau repeated, holding the mugs to the failing light. 'Guests? Only two.'

'I thought Stoffel said three?'

'Three? Oh no, there is another man there, but he is not what you call a *guest*, M. Buchanan. He's a water engineer come to measure for new pipes, that's all. Excellent: the dosage is exactly equal – your glass.'

Buchanan took the mug, and said: 'Even so, I'd –'

'And then there is Willie's half-brother and a friend come for a reunion. Good health!'

They each took a sip and then moved round to the chairs beside the fireplace. Buchanan had the beginnings of an idea he'd need that drink.

'Dirk is the name of this half-brother,' Cousteau explained.

'It seems he recently lost his younger son, killed in Rhodesia. Koos Brandsma says this caused him to want to remove what was bad from his conscience. Death often makes a man look deep into his heart – not so?'

'Aye, very true,' Buchanan agreed. 'What was the problem?'

'An old family quarrel – about what, we don't know. Dirk brought this other man, Pik Something, along because he wasn't sure how it would turn out. I understand that: I'd wish for a companion myself if I undertook a similar journey. However, Koos says it has all gone very well, now the big surprise is over, and his only fear is that Willie will want to go home perhaps.'

'What are the chances of that?'

'Who knows, my friend? Koos wishes he knew more for his own sake. All that the men have told him is that they had different fathers, and that the quarrel arose from this.'

'Different fathers?' echoed Buchanan, brightening. 'You're sure it wasn't different mothers?'

'No, no! That is what they told me also. If their father had been the same, then wouldn't their surnames have been the same, too?'

And Cousteau giggled, making a surprisingly manly sound of it, because his visitor had overlooked something quite so obvious as this.

Buchanan hadn't. It was just he couldn't resist having it spelled out for him that things were not so above-board at Mapapeng after all. Willie would never lie to spare Koos Brandsma's feelings – nor would he, without some very special reason, be still denying himself the right to be known as a true son of Karel Steyn.

Chapter Five

Breakfast was at seven. Cousteau ladled some mealie meal into Buchanan's bowl, slid over the powdered milk, and went straight into the arrangements he'd made for the journey to Dumela. His stable boy was to take Buchanan as far as the village, see to the hiring of a guide and horses for the second leg to Mapapeng, and then return to Gotsong. Buchanan thanked him and then the two men ate in silence, each preoccupied with thoughts of the day ahead.

They were out of the house at eight minutes past to discover it was a beautiful morning. The sky was blue all the way to the moon – still just visible, pale above the surrounding peaks – and a light breeze was tousling the coarse blond grass on the slopes around them.

As they were making their way around to the stables, a woman broke from the line of waiting patients and ran towards them, holding out her baby. Cousteau took it, cradled it in his thick arms, and – after a glance down – spoke to her gently. She shook her head. He spoke again and again she shook her head.

'The child is dead,' he murmured to Buchanan. 'I think she cannot accept this as only one of her babies has survived.'

'Some sort of congenital defect?'

Cousteau nodded; 'She's poor,' he said.

And then he carried the baby to the dispensary where he found a Bayer's Aspirin carton for the mother to use as a coffin. It pleased her very much when he daubed a cross on the lid with some mercurichrome, and she left, keening softly. Cousteau looked around for somewhere else to store his dispensing notes, grew impatient and tossed them into a corner of the hut.

'*Merde!*' he said.

'I'll be off then,' said Buchanan.

'Hmm? No, no, my friend! You must forgive me – a moment's weakness is so good for the soul. Allow me to show the way – come!'

They left the dispensary – a rather grand name for a small selection of basic remedies, a large collection of old bottles and two measuring flasks, plus a funnel – and cut across in front of the hospital huts. There were three of them, each filled with a dim sprawl of the sick lying on straw mats. A gaunt mission helper, in a tattered white coat and pink beret, was sitting on the doorstep of the last one, sterilizing some instruments in a saucepan over a Primus stove. Cousteau said something to him, and the helper laughed, stirred his retractors vigorously and pretended to savour the smell of the steam.

'Reuben Motseki, a formidable man,' Cousteau confided, as they walked on. 'He was once a Karoo beauty cream salesman in the Transvaal.'

'Oh aye?'

'Really a South African Basotho – his home was in Sharpeville, where many of our people live. They locked him up in an asylum after that business there, but – thank Heavens! – he was made able to escape and come to me. I'd had no intelligent assistance since my wife died.'

Buchanan hid a half-smile: Cousteau had this way of talking as though he and the Almighty arranged quite a few destinies together, and yet he walked along kicking a stone, just like a kid.

'What were the bits and pieces in his pot for?'

'The case that came in yesterday as you landed. I fear Motseki and I may have to attempt surgery for his internal injuries. He's too badly beaten to call for the plane.'

'Who by?'

'Bandits, robbers who must have stolen his horse after tying him up. They broke his jaw, so I'm not sure. He was found by some children over to the west – about ten miles away. But don't worry, they will not be foolish enough to attack a European. Ah! Everything is prepared I see.'

A Basotho boy of about twelve was waiting in the stable yard, holding the reins of two horses which he'd saddled and made ready, even down to securing Buchanan's haversack and gadget bag to the pommel on the black stallion. Cousteau made a swift, expert adjustment to the length of the stirrup leathers, and Buchanan swung up.

The stir of brute strength beneath him felt good, and suited his mood exactly; the stallion clopped forward a few paces, eager to be off. Buchanan waited for the boy to mount the gelding, and then turned to offer his final words of thanks. But the doctor was too sly for him.

'God go with you, M. Buchanan,' Cousteau grinned, cracking the stallion on the rump with a hand like a roof tile.

Three hours later, under a drought-happy sun, Buchanan was again reminded of the trendy poster in the novelty shop. There were no hulks about, but it was much the same sort of valley: steep-walled, strewn with boulders, and so dry it parched the throat merely to look at. Parts of the mountains were, when he came to think of it, very Biblical. The same little caravans of donkeys, same goats, same thorns and sharp shadows, plenty of arid wilderness – it'd been a good while since they'd last seen another soul on the bridle-path.

And yet, when he looked round at the high cliff-faces, there was this feeling of being watched. The Maluti was very ancient and somehow knowing, as if it remembered not only the primitives who had made paintings on the walls of its caves, but even the dinosaur which had left tracks in the rockbed of some streams. And, of course, there were indeed eyes fixed on him: crows, rock rabbits, perhaps the occasional snake or lizard, would all make careful note of his passing. No low-key blarney was ever going to dissuade them that here was an intruder.

'Soon now,' said the boy, whose shyness had kept him quiet mile after mile. 'We go that side and you will see.'

Then he rode on slightly ahead, leaving Buchanan to check his watch and estimate how much time he could spare for the job at Dumela. The teacher there, Tims Ghoomie, was a good sort, and his attempts to feed his pupils deserved the full treatment. On the other hand, it might be important to reach Mapapeng early enough to catch Koos Brandsma on his own in the store, and get a few bearings. But so far, they weren't doing too badly, and Buchanan decided to play it by ear.

They climbed slowly out of the valley, took a left fork in the bridle-path, and continued along it until gaining a small plateau from where, as predicted, their destination came at last within sight.

The village of Dumela – some thirty huts on a bare patch surrounded by a spiky wall of tall candlebra aloe – was tucked behind the knee of a ridge that came back on itself, like a folded trouser leg in bleached khaki drill. And one pleat away, on the far side, was the school they were heading for.

And the last of the stepping stones.

Buchanan's idea of playing things by ear had lost out. He was sitting on the school's only chair watching Tims, whose resemblance to a black Groucho Marx seemed to have doubled, scuttle energetically about the yard, organizing the next act. The impromptu performance had already lasted the best part of fifty minutes.

'And finally in conclusion,' announced Tims, 'my students would like to present the Manure Song and Dance, which I had the honour to write myself. Thank you!'

Buchanan, determined to appear in the spirit of things, applauded as half a dozen children, solemn with self-importance, scattered dry cow pats on the ground in front of him, and then bustled back into line.

As manure song and dances go, this one was short and sweet. It gave Buchanan an excuse to leave his chair, which had made him feel like a cut-rate potentate, and use his Pentax to advantage. The dance began with the children doing their chore of collecting cow pats for fuel, and then came the twist when they told their parents that each day they'd be taking some cow pats to school; the parents' indignation – loudly and joyfully screeched by the older pupils – gave way, however, to gasps of amazement and delight when they saw the mimed goodies come shooting out of the school's garden.

'That was grand,' he said, as Tims came over.

'One moment, please, sir.'

Tims then proclaimed a half-holiday to celebrate the occasion, called for three hearty cheers, and allowed the children to go scampering off as soon as their slates were neatly in rows on the schoolroom floor.

'When will the article be produced?' Tims asked, taking charge of the haversack. 'We will receive a copy as per last time?'

'Oh aye, I'll see Father Boucherat gets one to pass on. Oxfam may run something in their paper, and I'm going to try a few others.'

They began the short walk down to the bridle-path, where a new guide and fresh horses were waiting.

'It is a shame Chief Rasumaati was not here to see you,' Tims said, stepping fiercely on a caterpillar. 'I know he will be most grievously disappointed.'

'Off boozing again, is he?'

Tims laughed and nodded.

'Gone since Sunday – that must have been truly a terrible wedding. The other men, they are all home – the last one yesterday. And look sir, you see there?'

'The black one? The mare?'

'That is his horse, back two days. The others see him ride out in the night – then nothing. I tell you, his wives will be very cross!'

Buchanan stopped and turned to Tims.

'Was this wedding over to the west of Gotsong, by any chance? There's a man at the mission –'

'Oh no, this was south he went,' the teacher said, and walked on, still grinning at the thought of the errant husband's homecoming.

Complete with his alibi and an air of guileless endeavour, Buchanan rode up the last slope and on to the turfed shelf of rock that was Mapapeng.

The trading store itself was hard against the mountain wall, with the stables and corrugated-iron warehouse giving the other two sides to the hitching yard. The trader's bungalow was a hundred yards farther on, enclosed in a dusty hedge, and backed by a couple of poplars. There was also a clump of blue gums shedding their strips of pink bark in between the two main buildings, and a stray willow near the spring. Koos Brandsma went to a lot of trouble to keep a little greenery around him, but then he had the leisure and Mapapeng was his own, as much as anything could be in a country where all the land belonged to the King. This was actually what set Koos apart from most other traders, who were really just managers of a chain of stores begun by Lord Fraser, a leading apologist for the South African Way of Life, and founder of the St Dunstan Schools for the Blind. It also explained how Koos had been able to work on past retirement age.

Four was later than Buchanan had hoped to arrive, but as he and his guide trotted towards the hitching yard, it became obvious that Thursday had brought a busy afternoon behind the counter. There were close to sixty horses, ponies and donkeys tethered to the rails, and at least as many Basotho were milling about, exchanging gossip and news of their harvests. Unable to store the bulk of their maize crop, they were there to sell it to the trader – who'd sell it back to them as flour later in the year, but not at glut prices. This was always grounds for fairly lively debate outside most stores, but some of these discussions appeared to have gone further than that.

There was no sign of Willie and the three guests anywhere.

Buchanan paid off the guide, shouldered his bags, and stepped on to the end of the store's long verandah. It was crowded with people buying titbits of cooked meat from the vendors, or having lengths of cloth stitched into simple garments by the man with the Singer. He picked his way through them, returning their greetings, and went in the door marked ENTRANCE ONLY.

A little girl, aged about six or seven, who limped from a long walk, was just ahead of him. She was carrying a small bowl of beans to be weighed by a clerk who'd give her a token before she went into the store proper; the strong-willed could have the token cashed at the till if they liked. He swung right and tried Koos's office – nobody there. Having dumped his baggage, he went back across the weighing room and into the store, catching up with the child again as she used her token to buy half a candle. Then, way over the other side, under a festoon of

71

saddlery, he spotted the trader arranging a display of three-legged cooking pots.

'Hell, where the dickens did you spring from?' asked Koos, turning at the mention of his name.

It was the same Koos Brandsma – at least, superficially. He still wore the short-sleeved shirt, pork-pie hat and short braces favoured by his generation of Afrikaner, and the smooth, almost glossy face, was quickly as bland as ever. But around his clear grey eyes and at the corners of his mouth, something new had been added. A wariness was the closest Buchanan could get to it, although worry came into the mixture as well. He'd seen the same thing in people who expected a crisis, like those with a lingering death in the family.

'Dumela,' Buchanan said lightly. 'Went back to do a follow-up on that feeding programme.'

'Oh ja? And?'

'They've worked bloody hard, but only the cabbages made it – and even they are having the hell knocked out of them now by insects. So relax, your business isn't in any danger.'

'Business, you calls it? Since when has six rand a head per month been business? I tell you, at today's prices, there's nowhere I can stick my profit!'

'Except . . .' added Buchanan suggestively.

Koos laughed and opened a flap in the counter for his visitor to pass through and join him.

'Any chance of me staying the night? Stoffel will be in to-morrow around lunch time and he can pick me up.'

'Ja, on the post plane,' Koos responded automatically.

'It's all right with you then?'

Koos licked the tip of a finger and began to polish the keys on his till. He looked troubled.

'I'd have radioed I was coming, Koos, only you said to drop in any –'

'Okay, okay, that's true, so don't make me feel bad, hey? It's just I've got a lot on my hands at the moment.'

'Oh aye?'

But there was an interruption. A tall Basotho with a beard strode up to the counter, and placed two pellets of rabbit dung and a quartz pebble on the rubber change mat. Koos swept them coin-fashion into his hand, and tipped them into the till. He flicked open a paper bag, half-filled it with a scoop of icing sugar from a dust-covered jar, and placed it on the counter.

'Anything else?' Koos asked, with a wink for Buchanan.

The bearded man picked up the bag, stowed it gravely in the folds of the threadbare blanket he wore, and made slowly, stiffly, out of the store, striking the floorboards with the tip of his staff.

'Who's the big spender?'

'Ach, that's Manfred,' Koose replied, taking the rubbish out of his cash drawer. 'Mad as a bloody *meerkat* – thinks he's a prophet and all that, I ask you.'

'And the sugar?'

The question went ignored.

'It's like this,' said Koos, absorbed in some inner conflict which brought with it another long pause. 'I've got three blokes up at the house besides me and Willie.'

'Doc Cousteau mentioned someone was staying.'

'He did?'

'Relations, I think he said. Would I be crashing some sort of family reunion?'

'Ach, no Finbar! You don't understand!'

'Too true, old son, but I'd like to.'

Koos looked up from the till as if words had been put into his mouth. He smiled faintly, and then went on with his polishing.

'Look, is something wrong?' Buchanan asked, knowing damn well there had to be. 'Would you rather I buggered off?'

The office was indeed a far better place to talk. And it promised to be quite a session when Koos sent across to the house for some lagers. Then they both put their feet up.

'You know, it's good to see you again,' Koos said, filling his pipe with dry leaf from a cloth bag. 'Let me say right at the start that there is no question of you not staying at Mapapeng tonight. Hell, how would it look if Koos Brandsma turned a friend away?'

And he laughed more comfortably, like a man who'd taken a decision that had settled something in his mind.

'I could always doss down in Doc's clinic.'

'That bloody shack? Never! The rats would take your toes off. We'll just put you in with the *Engelse* in his rondavel.'

'Oh, ta,' said Buchanan disdainfully, and won himself an appreciative chuckle.

Much of his friendship with Koos was based on a traditional sympathy between Boer and Scot, which in turn was based on their joint enmity for the English. One that had been shared in the Cape, when not a few Gaelic words had found their way into Afrikaans from Calvinist pulpits. This was something which Buchanan, who was required to be most things to all men, played on pretty hard – providing he was allowed to make the subtle distinction.

'Ja, I'm sorry, but there's no alternative. The only other room I've got is a storeroom and they're using it for a darkroom.'

'Oh aye?'

'Oeloefse. Pik Oeloefse. You've heard of him?'

'The big-game photographer?'

Koos nodded, and appeared curiously relieved that the name had meant something to Buchanan.

'But who's this Englishman you've got for me?'

'Johnny – he's a water engineer, stationed now somewhere in the Transvaal. Not really a bad bloke.'

The lagers arrived, stressing the fact that when Koos beat about a bush, there was very little left of it.

'Weren't you going to tell me something?' Buchanan said, keeping it light.

'Oh ja, but it seems the Doc has already put you in the picture. About this half-brother, Dirk, who has come here to make up with Willie?'

'He didn't say much more than that.'

Koos shrugged, and mumbled: 'There is not much more to say. Dirk came without warning because he said he was afraid a letter couldn't say what he wanted to say to make Willie see him again. You know Willie ran away from home over the stepfather.'

'No, I didn't.'

'And Dirk brought Pik with him to act as – what do you call it? A sort of referee, a go-between, but that wasn't necessary. And so, they have stayed on for a little holiday.'

'But where does the Englishman fit in?'

'Johnny? They – I mean Dirk – sent for him to come and see if a hydraulic ram down in the valley couldn't get me more water for my plants. It's funny, but they hit it off, and now he's here for the rest of the week, too. I've asked for a charter for him on Saturday.'

'When are the others leaving?'

'Saturday as well, maybe. But you see what I'm getting at? It's a strange atmosphere at times, old wounds – you understand? You have to be careful, not cause any upsets. Let me be frank with you, Finbar: there is a chance Willie won't be pleased if I ask someone else in tonight, but you go quietly and everything will be all right.'

So that was what was chiefly worrying Koos: he was still afraid that Willie might up and go, leaving him stranded after all those years. It was an interesting relationship that could bear some looking into – neither man had struck him as any queerer than Carruthers.

'You make me sound one hell of a troublemaker.'

'You mustn't take it that way, man!'

'The old rule: keep off politics and religion, you mean?'

'Ja! That will do nicely!'

'You know me then; anything for a square meal and a bed,' Buchanan promised, hoping this would gain him the trader's confidence.

Much happier, Koos settled down to enjoy his lager. Then he became slightly mischievous and leaned forward: 'Wait till you meet this Pik Oeloefse bloke. There is a real troublemaker! I mean, I prefer Johnny to him, and for me to say that, it's something. Oeloefse's been up in the Caprivi Strip for bloody years, and I think the sun has got him a little in the head. Vorster, Vorster, Vorster – that's all you get from him when he's in his drink.'

'Oh aye?'

'I admit; at first, I was interested. I never knew that everything Vorster has ever done – you know, what the world makes such a fuss about? I never knew it had already been done to him personally.'

Buchanan made his go-on noise.

75

'True. By old Slim Jannie – by Smuts. Vorster was put inside without trial; he was in solitary for forty-two days; he was under house arrest, too; and he had to have permits at one time to see his *vrou* Martini.'

'But how did this come up?'

'It doesn't "come up", man! Oeloefse just bloody goes on and on. Then he tries his tricks on you.'

'What sort?'

'He tries to make you say that Vorster's life history makes him too soft on the criminal.'

'You've lost me.'

Koos poured out his second lager and took a gulp.

'You can see he likes playing the fool with an old man who doesn't read newspapers. How am I supposed to know Vorster pardoned that *skelm* who was always breaking out of jail and shooting policemen?'

'Willem Goosens?'

'That's the one. And that one of his chessboards was made by a murderer in the cells? Plus the fact his *kaffir* servants is nearly all bloody ex-convicts? Is that fair? A fair question to ask?'

It was bizarre. Mad. But Buchanan smelled method in it, and he, too, leaned forward.

'Surely this doesn't just get on your nerves, Koos? What about the others?'

'They just laugh. They say no decent Nat could think such a thing, and they warn him he'll be thrown out. Even Willie laughs, man, and what does he know?'

The tension was back in Koos. It was around his eyes, and at the corners of his mouth. The trader was patently not party to whatever was happening at Mapapeng, but his intuition was very alive to it and this was gradually taking him apart. The ground force had to be considerable.

Or, more simply, things weren't adding up for him, and that was the line to pursue.

'This darkroom Pik's set up, what's it in aid of? Don't know of much big-game in these mountains.'

Koos lit his pipe before answering: 'He's doing scenes; says he'll probably make a book for tourists to buy. But he doesn't want to keep coming back, so he's trying out the pictures here to make sure they're all right. He's lucky I've got a lighting plant, or that enlarger *dinges* wouldn't work.'

'Aye – brought it with him, did he?'

'Of course,' Koos said, coughing on his smoke. 'He says he takes it everywhere.'

Buchanan used one of the trader's matches to light his Texan, and sat back. Koos had taken that tripe very calmly – probably didn't know a Baby Brownie from a bloody goblin. The guns might produce more.

'Talking of big-game, though, on the way up yesterday I saw some men with guns – was it them? Stoffel got it into his head to go down on them like a bloody Stuka, so I didn't –'

'*Yirrah!* That was Stoffel, hey? You better not tell Willie that! He wants to murder the *ou*!'

'Was he the one who fell off?'

'I don't know,' said Koos, shrugging again, 'they didn't say exactly what happened, but they were angry like you've never seen it. Ja, those are my guns. They like to take them even though I say it's pointless, there's no buck any more. Think it's big sport to shoot *dassies* – you know what they are?'

'Rock rabbits,' said Buchanan, wondering if he wasn't beginning to develop a bit of a twitch himself.

The conversation had just petered out; the only other piece of actual information being that the four holiday-makers were away from the trading post the best part of every day. Then Koos Brandsma had returned to the store to supervise the cashing-up, and Buchanan had gone across to the house.

He put his bags in the guest hut occupied by Johnny Tagg, and sat down on the man's bed. It was no time to feel bemused or befuddled, for that matter. His job was to get the facts, and that he wasn't going to achieve through any more talking. Action was what was needed.

The most immediate to suggest itself was a thorough search through Mr Tagg's possessions. After a quick check at the door, Buchanan began on a pair of silver-backed hair brushes, and worked his way through string vests to dirty hiking socks. He examined the small leather suitcase, the toilet bag, and turned over the bed. The most telling thing he came up with had been lying on the bedside locker from the start: an illustrated pamphlet distributed in May 1974 by the Rhodesian Ministry of Information, Immigration and Tourism: *Anatomy of Terror*.

Buchanan flicked through its familiar pages, dismayed as ever by the tasteless, if inadvertent, jokiness of its title. For the *Anatomy of Terror* was just that: fifteen photographs of the bodies of mutilated black Rhodesians who'd fallen victim to terrorists, plus another of some slaughtered cattle. Only two things detracted from its sickening impact – a cover drawing of such amateurishness it properly belonged in a school magazine, and the fact that at least one of the photographs had also appeared in propaganda underlining the folly of collaboration with the terrorists. He sighed and then returned the pamphlet, like everything else, to exactly the position it had previously occupied. The *Anatomy* was not everyone's idea of an ideal bedside book, but certainly the sort Tagg might favour. At least one leopard was sticking to his spots.

That left the hut next door, and the worldly goods Dirk Steyn and Pik Oeloefse had chosen to bring with them. But Buchanan was not persuaded they would yield any more than Tagg's had done, and the improvised darkroom, being so much less accessible, seemed by far the better bet.

No professional photographer worth a damn needed roll-by-roll assurances he was doing all right, however reasonable this might sound to a complete layman like Koos. At most, he might use a daylight tank to develop the odd film here and there, providing spring water could be properly filtered, but to actually employ an enlarger was nothing less than eccentric. Or, given the other circumstances, as ill-defined as they were, a great deal more than that.

Buchanan dug about for his black changing-bag. He had to make the most of his unexpected arrival while its benefits lasted, and among them was what might prove his only chance of getting into that darkroom alone. With the time factor now critical, a small improvisation of his own seemed in order.

He used the changing bag to remove roughly twenty frames from a fresh 35mm cassette, and then tore the sprocket holes along one edge. He rewound the film, put it into his Pentax, and kept flicking the advance lever until the thing jammed.

That done, he stuffed the bag into the bottom of the haver-sack, and started for the house, armed with his own very credible reason for wanting to use a darkroom.

The stone path took him through the rockery and round past the beehives to the back verandah where Solomon, the Basotho cook was plucking a chicken. They exchanged greetings and compliments, and then Buchanan asked the way to the room the other guests were using for pictures.

Solomon immediately took a quarter-plate enlargement of himself from his pocket, and Buchanan made all the right noises. The old chap's lined face was superbly printed.

'Yes, it is bally good,' said Solomon, putting it away again, 'but will the boss also make a card for me?'

'Oh aye, if I can get this camera unstuck.'

'It is all right for the boss to go in their place?'

'Don't see why not. Isn't locked, is it?'

'*Aikona*, but strict orders no go in there. Not just me, but the master also. There is medicine inside that does not like the sun.'

'I know about it, so I'll be careful.'

Solomon brushed the feathers off the front of his apron, and hobbled along the verandah to a small storeroom that had been tacked on at the far end. The door was locked, but Buchanan understood what Solomon had meant when the cook took a key from its customary hiding place on the lintel and did the necessary.

The sweet and sour smell of developer, acid bath and fixer caught at Buchanan's throat as he stepped into the storeroom and all but shut the door. The air, which had been trapped in there all day, was also stale and warm, like someone else's breath, and a few moments' ventilation were a must.

Buchanan did a quick survey.

On the left, along a shelf which had previously held cans of paint, to judge from the dried rings and drip marks, were the three plastic trays for the three basic stages of print-making. Beyond them was a larger tray, and beside it a container of expensive hypo-eliminator, which did away with the need for prolonged washing in water. On the floor under the shelf, was a chromed metal sheet, cleverly arranged in juxtaposition with a bottled-gas heater so that prints could be speedily dried and glazed. Already one thing was evident: no picture produced in that darkroom was necessarily ever seen outside it until the process was complete – whereas an overnight swill in the bath, and a few hours out in the sun, would have suited most purposes more than adequately.

On the right, on a wider shelf with cup hooks along its edge, was a small 35mm enlarger of the sort that can be taken to pieces easily and packed into a box no bigger than a gramophone. There was also an easel for giving prints white margins; a stack of different grades of single-weight paper, whole-plate size; two Nikon stainless steel developing tanks; a stirring rod and a thermometer. The easel struck an odd note: it was hardly an essential item for test printing.

What was odder still was the number of negatives left carelessly unprotected on the enlarger's base board.

It was time to close the door.

Buchanan slid the bolt, and turned to find the blackout – which Oeloefse had contrived with yards of cloth from the store – was absolute. What couldn't get in, couldn't get out either, so he flicked down the light switch to begin a proper examination in secrecy.

But, even as his fingers touched the toggle, he realized he'd made a boo-boo: the petrol generator wouldn't come on until nightfall.

For half a minute, he stood in total darkness being coarse in whispers, and then decided to make the best of things. He closed his eyes to focus his concentration on touch, and began to feel over the shelves. He didn't waste effort on the shelf with trays, which was treacherous with spilled chemicals and quite unsafe as a hiding place for anything, but began exploring every other surface minutely. There was nothing under the linoleum, and the floor was concrete, so he was soon back at the enlarger. The negatives were an enormous frustration.

Then he had an idea. By tweaking back a corner of the cloth over the window, and pulling against the drawing pins which held it there, he was able to admit a thin ray of light. Using this like the beam in an editing machine, he ran a strip of negative in front of it.

Chapter Six

There was Solomon, in all his glory: one three-quarter face, one in profile, outside the kitchen door. The other four exposures on the strip were of Mapapeng, which had been given grandeur by a magnificent cloud formation, expertly brought out by filters. Technically, the negatives were excellent, showing plenty of shadow detail even where the silver had clumped most densely. And the same standards applied to the three other strips Buchanan inspected. Two of them shared an almost unrepeatable sequence of galloping horsemen, their blankets flying like cloaks, which was worthy of any coffee-table publication. Oeloefse had to be doing exceptional work if these were his throw-outs.

Buchanan looked at the negatives again, but could find no scratches, holes or other blemishes to warrant their grubby state. Nor were there any indications of reticulation, which was always a danger under makeshift conditions in the tropics.

Perhaps he was trying to make something of nothing.

He replaced them and began poking about in the enlarger. There was nothing rolled up and slipped down its supporting column, and neither had the lamp house been used for a secret cache.

Then his fingers discovered another length of negatives, which had been left in the holder. This find was a little too easy to promise anything but disappointment, yet he took them over to the window and let the chink of light show.

The six frames were all of the same uninspiring slope, destitute of any living creature, and of the few nondescript mountains lying beyond it. Pictorially, there was nothing whatsoever to recommend them. Even the use of a 400mm lens in the last shot, which compressed everything into virtually the same vertical plane, had failed to pull off its usual cheap trick of making dullness less dull. And, from a technical point of view, the negatives were a mess: the first exposure being almost right, but the others tailing off in half-stop jumps. There was dust on them, too, embedded in the emulsion.

If paradox was the mother of mystery, then she'd just pupped right in Buchanan's hand.

Solomon came to the door and said: 'The master he is looking for you, sir.'

'Tell him I'm in here and I'll be out in a minute,' Buchanan replied, hastening to return the strip to the holder, and to get it back in the way it had been.

He closed his eyes again, squeezing the colour out of the red and green spots he was seeing, and slid his hands over to the boxes of paper. What he touched in the top one made him freeze – it was a 35mm cassette with the top off but the film still inside it.

'Jeeeeesus,' he sighed softly.

The annoying lack of electricity had saved him from making an irreparable and drastic mistake. If, as originally intended, he'd had the orange safe light turned on while examining the boxes, the paper would have remained quite unaffected – but the film would have fogged instantly.

No matter how quickly the lid had been slapped back, the damage would have been done and his goose well and truly cooked. No explanation or excuse could have got round the fact he must have taken time out from his running repairs to meddle, and that was an interpretation at the lowest end of the scale. After all, the safe-light would have destroyed his own material. Nor could he have replaced the film with another, because any film, however humble, becomes unique once it has passed through a camera.

'Aye, aye,' Buchanan said, more calmly.

He'd set films aside himself in similar fashion, when working in his own darkroom where he could be confident nobody would interfere with contingency arrangements. So there was that side to it. But he could also think of no better way of inhibiting unwelcome exploration.

The discovery of an open cassette in the next box he tried made him more certain he'd somehow hit pay-dirt.

But his fingers, which were feeling about under the wad of bromides, testing the smoothness of the composite edges, and otherwise trying their utmost for him, could find nothing to report. They kept at it though, box after box, through extra-hard to extra-soft. Five boxes, five films, and a big fat zero.

Buchanan paused, and thought again about that paper range. The different grades weren't something anyone could feel: he was remembering from a glance before the door had been closed. Extra-hard, hard, normal, soft, extra-soft; a perfectly conventional selection for dealing with a variety of tonal contrasts, as recommended in any manual of instruction, and therefore, in itself, quite unremarkable. On reflection, however, that was about three grades too many for a pro – and especially one whose negatives were of such consistent quality.

'Finbar? You're still in there, man?' Koos asked, tapping on the door.

'Sorry, having a bit of bother.'

'Want Pik to give you a hand? They're just coming up the path from the river.'

'I'll be out in a sec – don't . . .'

Buchanan had been stroking his fingers over the paper inside the extra-soft box – this being the one Oeloefse was least likely to ever need – to see if the man was using it to store a normal grade with a matt finish. And about half-way down the pile, the sensation of faint tackiness had suddenly given way to the smooth sheen of a glazed print.

'Don't what? Speak up, please.'

'Don't catch a panic!' Buchanan called out, feigning honest exasperation in the South African idiom.

He heard Koos laugh and move off.

There were seconds left.

Just three of the glazed sheets were going to have to be enough. He used the film to mark the level from which they'd been extracted, replaced the lid on the box, and stepped quickly to the window.

The ray of light played over the top sheet like the beam of a tiny torch.

It most certainly was a print.

Buchanan turned it the right way round and frowned. For

an instant, he was distracted by a surge of *déjà vu*; by the feeling all this had happened before, and that there was nothing novel or exceptional in what he saw.

The picture showed a black man in a white shirt lying with his hands tied and his head partly blown off. There had been a plate just like it in *Anatomy of Terror*, somewhere towards the back.

The second picture showed the same man, but no longer in close-up. In the background was a distinctive mountain peak and, in the foreground, a Basotho blanket.

There were four figures in the third and last print. Three of them wore dark hoods over their heads – and blankets pinned at the left shoulder. The other figure was that of a fat black priest in his clerical garb. He was kneeling in a shallow grave and, having had a bullet put into his brain, was going down slack into it. Two suitcases stood nearby.

This picture had been taken with a very long lens, and there was, given its terrible import, understandably some camera shake. Guerrillas were at work in Lesotho.

Buchanan just made it. The loud knock on the door came as he finished winding the film back into its cassette, and he was able to open up immediately.

Pik Oeloefse's eyes went straight to the base board of the enlarger, where the Pentax lay on its front with the back plate open.

The big-game photographer had a tan on him like a birthmark. He wore two studded leather wristlets and no wristwatch. He was big-boned, hairy, and all male – until one noted the soft, prim mouth above the grey goatee. This mother's touch was not, however, an uncommon characteristic among the butch heavies of his race.

'Koos sent me round,' he said, in a deep, guttural voice. 'I'm Pik Oeloefse; pleased to meet you.'

Buchanan introduced himself, crunched hands and then waved at the camera.

'Bloody thing's been really playing up,' he said.

'Let's have a look-see.'

Buchanan was hoping he would.

The camera was picked up and given a cursory inspection. Oeloefse removed a sliver of film from behind the wind-on spool, and rubbed his thumb over the sprocket wheel. Then, keeping his head inclined at the same angle, he had a damn good look round the room. The only thing he might have been able to fault was the previous position of the negatives, so Buchanan had swept these aside, apparently to give himself space to work in.

This check seemed to satisfy Oeloefse, who then gave his full attention to the Pentax. He worked the advance lever a few times, and listened to the clunk of the reflex mirror.

'Can't understand it,' said Buchanan. 'I'd feel less of a bloody fool if the thing was obviously broken, but this happens only off and on, and —'

'Ja, that's sometimes the way. It jams tight, hey?'

'Like a rock. I suppose I could've got some gubbins into the doings that floats about. You see, as you wind on, the sprocket sticks and rips the bloody —'

'Man, there's no sense in taking a chance till the thing's fixed,' Oeloefse broke in irritably, snapping the back shut. 'That's not the way I treat my equipment, I can tell you. These are delicate things, hey?'

'Sorry.'

Oeloefse smiled very briefly and motioned Buchanan out of the room ahead of him. He locked the door, put the key in his pocket, and led the way through the house.

Koos was pouring lagers into tall glasses he had arranged along the wall of the front verandah.

'All okay now?' he asked.

'Our friend here better get his camera looked at,' Oeloefse replied, the merest trace of contempt showing as he glanced down at Buchanan's pukka riding boots. 'I can give him the name of a workshop in Jo'burg that won't rook him flat.'

'Thanks very much,' said Buchanan

Oeloefse mumbled something in Afrikaans and sniggered, Koos smiled, but looked a little guilty for doing so.

'How lame is Johnny's horse?' Koos asked, switching pointedly back to English. 'That Dingaan has always had a bit of a weakness in the left front.'

'Ach, it can walk all right,' Oeloefse grunted, taking a lager and perching himself on the wall. 'He'll be back by and by. Where's Willie and Dirk got to?'

'Gone off to have a wash. How far did you get today?'

'We saw the falls.'

'Much water?'

'It was okay.'

Koos handed a glass to Buchanan, took one himself, and they settled into a couple of cane chairs.

From round the back of the house came the cough and splutter of the lighting plant being cranked over. The engine caught, doofed-doofed-doofed, and then resigned itself to a steady, even throbbing. The bulb in the verandah socket glowed, flickered and came on bright. Oeloefse looked up at it thoughtfully.

The safe-light would be working now.

'That could be Dingaan,' Koos remarked, cocking his head and listening.

They all listened: gradually the plod of an unequal gait and a jingle of harness grew louder.

Buchanan stood up, idly parted the granadilla vine which screened the verandah, and looked out over the garden to where the eastern bridle path skirted the hedge.

'Aye, it's him right enough,' he murmured.

Johnny Tagg was riding in, pink and porky against the sunset, with his hat tipped low and his rifle under one arm, like a clip from a salami Western.

'Finbar? I'd like you to meet Dirk, hey?'

Buchanan turned with a polite smile.

The man was very much as Major Munro had described him: six foot nothing; lean build; outdoor complexion; eyes blue; narrow face, high forehead, cleft in chin; general impression: belligerent patriarch, second class; not to be teased or fed cream buns.

'*Aangename kennis, meneer,*' Steyn said, his tone slightly mocking.

'And it's a pleasure to meet you too, sir,' Buchanan answered, who wasn't going to be fazed that easily. 'Had a good trip today then? Pik was saying something about a waterfall.'

'Ja, it wasn't bad. And what brings you to these parts?'

'Man, didn't I explain to you just now?' Koos broke in, giving Steyn his glass.

'Sorry – ja, you're the bloke who writes up on these aid programmes. Who for, may I ask?'

'*Panorama*,' said Buchanan, naming the Republic's biggest propaganda glossy, '*Personality*, different magazine sections of newspapers, both Afrikaans and English, anyone who'll buy the stuff – and of course, to any other country that's supplying aid, like the States and Finland. I also do light news and human interest for –'

'Hell, I know the name!' said Oeloefse, nodding at Steyn. 'This *ou* has been in *Panorama*, too, man! Those colour shots of the pottery?'

'Royal Lesotho Weavers, I think it was,' Buchanan said.

'Correct. The issue after my zebras.'

Buchanan felt like a tightrope walker who'd just stepped off on to his tiny platform for a short rest and the turnabout.

Then in came Willie, and the change in him was far less subtle or superficial than had been evident in his companion at Mapapeng. Buchanan's memory of Willie had been of a dumpy, dishevelled man with a moonface, who allowed the stubble to grow on his chin, and whose glasses were smeared and dirty; a sloppy devil who liked to shuffle about in his carpet slippers, dribbling shreds of tobacco from the cigarettes he was always rolling, and making promises that some time soon he'd get the books done. But here instead was a spruce, well-kept figure in his mid-fifties, with his hair trimmed short and his shirt tucked in, emitting the bright confidence of someone valued for their efficiency. Small wonder Koos felt perturbed: this was no longer little Willie, but Willem – the outcast who'd always wanted some day to win his half-brother's approval. And must have done, in some curious fashion, by the look of him.

As Buchanan greeted Willem, there was a gleam of excitement behind the clean lenses, and with it the decided impression that somehow his presence had heightened a secret pleasure.

'You write *kak*,' Willem said, lifting his glass. 'I read what you put in the papers about Mapapeng, and that's what it was, pure *kak*.'

Koos jolted with the shock of this gratuitous rudeness and opened his mouth to protest.

'Willie,' said Steyn softly. That was all.

Oeloefse scratched himself.

But it would have been unnatural for Buchanan not to respond, so he said: 'Sorry you felt that – sure it wasn't the way you read it?'

Surprisingly – or perhaps, it wasn't – Steyn laughed the loudest at that. Koos also laughed, and then Oeloefse, and finally Willem himself, who seemed eager not to be the odd man out.

'You've got to watch these Press boys,' Oeloefse warned jokingly. 'You should know by now they can twist a man's words!'

'And the camera can lie, too, for that matter,' Buchanan added.

'True, very true,' conceded Oeloefse, without missing a beat.

'Ja, that's true,' Willem said. 'But you can tell.'

Steyn exchanged a quick glance with Oeloefse which should not have meant anything to Buchanan. Nor did it, in its entirety, because the one thing he knew without any doubt was that he'd come across real pictures, not fakes, in that box of extra-soft.

'Tell how?' Koos asked.

'Ach, don't start Pik up now when it's nearly supper,' Steyn objected, smiling thinly.

'Are we quits then?' Buchanan asked.

'We're quits,' agreed Oeloefse, offering him a Rembrandt filter-tip.

'I'll stick to my own, if you don't mind – oh, bugger, I've left them in the hut. And my matches.'

'Solomon can go for them,' Koos offered.

'No, he's getting the grub – I'll just pop down there.'

Buchanan raised a thumb in friendly salute, and strode quickly down the steps and into the garden. Night had fallen and he walked cautiously until his eyes had adjusted. As he reached the rockery, his foot struck a watering can that had been left on the path.

The noise this made had an interesting effect. A shadow he could see on the curtain of his rondavel moved quickly across the light. He had been wondering what was keeping the gregarious Johnny Tagg so long at his toilette. In fact Oeloefse's cue had just saved him thinking up some other excuse to get away for a minute or two and check.

The sinister significance of the watering can itself was debatable, but it did seem a bloody silly place to leave one when the rockery was being replanted anyway.

Tagg, going at it two-handed with his hair brushes, turned and said: 'Hello, there; these your things are they? Your things?'

Repetition was his hallmark. His teeth, for example, were each the same size and shape as his bitten-down nails; while the pouches under each piggy, self-seeking eye, had their matching pair in the paps that sagged into the stretch of his soiled sports shirt. His short legs and arms bulged shapelessly and looked interchangeable; as did his eyebrows and the two halves of an out-of-date moustache.

He was going to have to repeat his hair brushing too, as his ginger locks would be messed up when that clean shirt was put on. What an odd way to go about things.

'Aye, that's my clobber,' Buchanan said. 'I hope you don't mind – I'll be out of here in the morning, being picked up by the post plane.'

'Ah! Ah, well then, not much time to get acquainted. You're from the U.K.?'

'Maseru.'

'So Koos said. But, y'know, before then? The U.K.?'

'By way of Hong Kong, when I was about five.'

'There's a thing.'

Buchanan got his Texans out of his haversack – they'd been hastily replaced in it by someone, upside down.

'Like a ciggy?'

'I never say no!' smiled Tagg, making his choice with the care of a man trying to avoid the long straw.

He tamped both ends of the cigarette against his watch face, flipped open a petrol lighter and set fire to his hand.

'Christ!'

'Aye, they do leak a bit in the heat.'

'No harm done. Here we go ...'

Buchanan took his light and stared down the long plume of smoke of his first exhalation. The discarded bush-jacket on the locker was either hiding the *Anatomy of Terror*, or the thing had gone.

'Well, I'll be off to join the motley again. Coming along for a noggin?'

'Soon as I've freshened up. Look, if you're wanting to –'

'Promised I'd only be away a minute. Nice meeting you.'

'Er, Fin – what was it?'

'Finbar, but I'll answer to anything if it's booze you're offering.'

It wasn't a bad exit line, as exit lines go.

Oeloefse was outside on the path, and may well have been eavesdropping.

'Hello again,' Buchanan said amiably.

Oeloefse smiled and nodded. But passing the man was like walking by the open door of a cold-room.

Buchanan reached the path and hesitated. A lot might be learned from a swift sneak round the back of the rondavels. But then again, a lot could be lost before anything had been made of it.

He carried on and climbed the steps back on to the verandah. Through the french doors, bracketed by the horns of two buck Koos had presumably shot long ago, he could see Solomon setting the food on the table. Koos was fussing over the carving at the sideboard, the way old men will, and Steyn was listening to the Afrikaans news on the portable radio.

So Buchanan took Oeloefse's perch on the wall, and helped himself to another lager. With any luck, he'd be able to get in a little thinking.

But Solomon came out to clear away the glasses.

'The boss has not been by Mapapeng in many months,' the cook chided, hoping for the familiarity a guest might extend to him. 'Has the boss not been well in himself?'

'Same as you, Solomon – I've been busy. But I suppose it has been quite a time. I see the old dog's finally copped it.'

'Boss?'

'Died.'

Solomon shook his head disapprovingly, and muttered:

'That a bad, bad business. You mustn't say anything for Boss Brandsma, or he will be very sad. A big mistake.'

'What was? Shooting the dog?'

'Not shoot.'

'But he did the – whatever, did he?'

The cook brought his tray up closer, took a careful look over his shoulder, and then dropped his voice low.

'You know Boss Brandsma and Boss Potgieter talk about who must shoot dog? Talk, talk, every night, talk-talk. They are old men. The dog is an old dog. They see his beard goes white same as their beard. One day soon they must go away from these mountains to a proper white man's place for them to be sick and go to hospital. But Boss Brandsma he does not want to go. So they talk, talk, who will shoot this dog. You remember?'

Buchanan nodded.

'Then these funny ones come here. The first night, the Boss starts to talk but they do not understand. That is the mistake. The Boss told me this in his own words, he –'

'Solomon?' Koos said from the french doors, 'where the hell's the gravy, man? What's he gassing about?'

'This boss asks where is the dog, so I tell him,' Solomon replied with sudden spitefulness.

Maybe he'd been hurt by the way Koos had addressed him, which was so different to the polite patronage Buchanan recalled vividly from his first visit.

'Ach, that,' Koos grunted.

Solomon slipped past him into the house and disappeared towards the kitchen. Steyn wandered out, arms folded.

'I gather it happened by mistake?'

'Not at all, Finbar. I was just saying to Willie we must put the old bugger out of his misery, and Dirk here just did it so simple.'

'Ja, I put my boot on its neck,' Steyn said.

There were footfalls on the path below and the two men from the rondavels came up the steps. Willem slipped out of the house through one of the bedroom doors.

'The gravy is on the table, boss,' Solomon announced sulkily.

'Good, then let's all go in, shall we?'

Buchanan was given a seat beside Oeloefse, and opposite Tagg and Steyn. Willem sat at the bottom of the table, and Koos presided over the top.

'*Laat ons bid,*' said Steyn, and dropped his head to say Grace.

Thank God for Amen, thought Buchanan, who didn't catch another word of it.

As Koos dished out, Steyn continued to speak in Afrikaans to the others. Tagg nodded a lot.

'He's telling them tonight's news on the radio,' Koos explained, handing Buchanan his plate. 'You don't mind?'

'Ask him what he thinks of it,' Willem suggested.

'Who?' snapped Steyn.

'This reporter we've got with us.'

'Ja, why not?' Oeloefse said, nudging Buchanan's arm with his elbow. 'Let's see what an outsider has to say. Willie's got a point there.'

'Well, what was on the news?' Buchanan asked, feeling a prickle of caution.

'Vorster's taken some more steps to come to a better understanding with the Black states to the north,' Oeloefse said. 'There's some big-wig coons coming down to visit Pretoria and talk about a loan.'

'You're asking the wrong man there,' Koos said quickly, heaping the mutton on Willem's plate.

'He doesn't approve of détente?' queried Oeloefse.

'Ach, no, he just never talks politics!'

'Hey?' said Willem, reaching over to take the plate. 'Since when? Time he was here last –'

Koos cut across: 'Was the time the BCP was in trouble and Ntsu Mokhele did his escape to Zambia. Hell, we were all talking politics then, Willie – even you were. All this trouble over a one-party state and the fighting.'

'Oh aye, police stations attacked here and God knows what else – did you by any chance read about it?'

Steyn shrugged as though the matter was of total indifference to him, and began to cut the fat from his meat.

'So what's the Lesotho position now?' Oeloefse asked. 'Is it turning one-party, in your opinion, *meneer*?'

'Opposition's agreed to a five-year political holiday that ends somewhere around June 1979. We'll have to wait and see. Mustard, anyone?'

'I never want to see another '74,' Koos said, still intent on keeping things uncontroversial. 'You must have heard about the tribal clashes on the mines? Ja? You know what happened when they sent those stupid bastards back to Lesotho? We lost twenty million rand. Ja, straight out of our tills, gone! Man what can you expect in a country that's got only twenty-five thousand jobs? Including hotel wash girls!'

'Talking of jobs,' said Buchanan, who knew a fair joke.

'The real question is,' Oeloefse interrupted, 'the question I want to put to you is this: do you think Vorster's making a big mistake siding with these people?'

'Against Rhodesia,' Tagg added, 'and Old Smithy?'

Koos sighed and sought solace in the gravy, which he poured like oil on troubled water until his green beans disappeared.

While Buchanan played for time with an overlarge mouthful.

'What's the alternative?' he asked finally. 'Mr Vorster has warned it's either détente or the future doesn't bear thinking about.'

'You think the terrorists could beat *us*?' Willem hooted.

'I think it's very important they don't, Willie.'

Then Dirk Steyn began to smile and the smile spread. It was taken up by everyone at the table, Buchanan included – his answer couldn't have been less committal.

'Ja, nor must we forget what Vorster has often reminded his new friends,' Oeloefse laughed. 'When he says he was among the first guerrillas to oppose imperialism on this continent.'

After that, the meal had continued almost boisterously, with Oeloefse and Willem vying with each other to tell the best hunting tales. It appeared then that Willem had spent a great number of his early years at Mapapeng exploring the surrounding terrain with a gun. Which was new to Buchanan, as were so many of the snippets he picked up, and he was careful not to allow his thoughts to wander for fear of missing anything.

The tension remained though, as it might at any dinner table where one of the guests had sat down in his sheep's clothing to eat mutton with wolves. It gave an edge to things that Buchanan really quite enjoyed, although the images seen in the darkroom kept recurring spontaneously in his mind's eye, spoiling the taste of the food. He'd also noticed that his every nuance was still under careful scrutiny, particularly from Oeloefse.

Who put down his coffee cup, stretched, and announced he had a couple of films to put through the developer.

'Can't you give it a miss tonight?' asked Koos, who'd started drinking brandy and had become quite convivial.

'I'd like to, man, but you know my routine.'

'But it's later than usual.'

'That's okay, I'm not going to do any printing. Half an hour will see me through.'

'Can Finbar help speed it up?'

'You can't help a man do his films,' Buchanan said, flopping into a deck chair on the front verandah. Tagg was already dozing off beside it.

'See? He knows.'

'And that's a promise about printing? You'll be back to join us?'

Oeloefse paused at the door and said: 'How can I print? The negs will still be wet, and I'm up to date on the others. You saw those village lifes from yesterday?'

Koos pressed his fist against a hiccup, and nodded.

When Oeloefse had gone, Willem dragged a chair over and sat down opposite Buchanan, rather like a watchdog Alsatian – a breed he now in some ways resembled. Steyn sat apart, drawing on a dead pipe, and staring; not blindly, but as if he was watching something a long way off.

For the next twenty minutes or so, Koos fired a steady stream of questions at Buchanan on subjects as varied as buying a cottage on the Natal south coast, and the price of mealie *stamp* in Maseru. He appeared genuinely interested in the answers, and so they had to be given carefully and as accurately as Buchanan could. Particularly as Willem was listening to every syllable with that suspicious tilt of the head he'd developed.

Then Koos asked Willem the time and said he wanted everyone to have a final nightcap together.

'Don't worry, man, Pik will be along soon,' Willem said, yawning. 'Hell, he's only got till Saturday.'

94

Steyn cleared his throat.

And Willem flinched, and went into a gabble: 'I tell you something, *meneer*, when Stoffel comes tomorrow I'm going to ask him just who the hell they've got flying planes who thinks he can –'

'Willie,' said Steyn from the shadows, 'is there any of that good snuff around?'

'Some in my bedroom. You want me to get it for you?'

'Please.'

Willem hastened away, looking round once at Buchanan.

Who suddenly had an idea which would possibly throw some light – in a strictly metaphorical sense – on Oeloefse's dark-room activities. The processing of two films and Willem's odd slip about having only until Saturday didn't combine well.

'You've got me interested now,' he said to Steyn. 'Anyone mind if I turn the news on?'

It was just after nine.

'Ach, no – go ahead.'

'Of course, Finbar! Do as you would in your own home,' Koos said, waving his hand at the doors into the dining-room.

'Buggered if I give a damn,' Tagg added good-humouredly.

Buchanan sauntered through and turned the radio on low, bending to get his ear near the speaker. He moved the tuner over to the English Programme; the news had already begun, but it was not what he was there for.

As the announcer started on the third item, Buchanan heard it: a click of static. He started counting. At three seconds, there was another fizzle. Half a minute passed, and then there was another pair of clicks, three seconds apart. Followed almost immediately by another pair and another and another.

Anyone listening to their radio when someone else in the house has switched on a light would have heard the same click as the spark of contact caused momentary interference. The sound was so common most people hardly ever noticed it.

The first click had been the enlarger going on. The second it being switched off. Thirty seconds later, Oeloefse had known his exposure was right, and had begun printing off the required number for simultaneous development.

Conjecture, of course, but a very reasonable assumption – especially as film processing didn't involve switches or lights.

'What's this?' Willem asked, prodding him in the back.

'The détente thing again – wanted to hear if there had been any comment. Not a sausage.'

'Huh! They're as bad as you, man.'

'You've changed, Willie. By the way, Father Waldo sends his blessings, and asks how the fiddling's coming on.'

'I gave that up long ago!'

'But he –'

'Hey! Where's my snuff?' Steyn demanded.

'Sorry, *boet* – I'm coming, man, I'm coming.'

Willem made hurriedly for the verandah. Oeloefse came out, wiping his hands on a towel, and accepted Koos's nightcap. His face was darkly brooding, and he said nothing at all before bidding everyone good night. Steyn rose almost immediately to follow him, and Tagg went soon after that. Buchanan, pretending mild intoxication, tarried for a while and listened to Koos being maudlin. Willem reverted slightly to character, and spilled some tobacco down his front.

'Tell me something, Willie,' Koos asked plaintively, his words a little slurred. 'Isn't it a fact that for years I've looked after you like a big brother? Like a big brother should? Am I not right?'

'*Kak,*' sneered Willem, with a laugh. 'Time you were in your bed, old man.'

Buchanan took himself off then, satisfied that no one had thought it important to keep a close watch on him, and heard whispering stop as he passed the first rondavel.

Tagg was out cold and snoring like a fatigued bush pig in the other hut, having not bothered to remove his clothes properly. He made a rather pathetic sight, as did most members of a master race when caught with their Sieg Heils down. His small face wore a small, sweet smile: perhaps he was dreaming, knowing he was dreaming, not wanting to wake up; dreaming of being big and black and unafraid.

All four members of the Mapapeng commando had shown signs of abnormal tiredness that night, even allowing for their age. Buchanan took off his boots and lay back to ponder this – among other things. There was so much he had to sort out, and besides, to sleep might be foolhardy, however confident he felt of having hoodwinked the lot of them.

Presently, the lighting plant coughed, choked and stopped. The mountain stood in darkness.

Chapter Seven

The sound was too constant and then too loud for an insect.

'Stoffel's on his way in!' announced Koos Brandsma, his relief evident, and raised the binoculars.

Buchanan looked round and saw a dark speck dancing against the sun. Never before had the sight of that jaunty wee deathtrap been as welcome – although, to give them their due, Oeloefse and his henchmen had behaved in a superior fashion all morning. Not one of them had come near him.

Being ignored wasn't without its tension, of course, and Koos, feeling very badly about Willie's manners in particular, had become restless and suggested a short stroll. This had taken the pair of them out to the edge of the Mapapeng shelf, where the dramatic setting imposed itself fairly literally. Buchanan had been amused to note the row of huge boulders arranged like the footlights on a gigantic stage, and a sky filled with creamy, voluptuous cloud, making it as baroque as the ceiling of any Italian opera house. Then again, looking back the other way, the bungalow, wool shed and trading store were just like flats stuck up against a Wagnerian backdrop, with exits and entrances possible only along the paths coming in at the wings. Waiting for Stoffel had been like waiting for a speciality act in which an acrobat landed on a nickel – and, considering the length of the strip, this was hardly hyperbole.

'May I borrow those things?' Buchanan asked.

'Just a sec, he's got someone with him,' Koos reported, 'could even be another in the back.'

'Oh aye?'

'No, not Basutes, I don't think. Yellowish hair.'

'Both?'

'One. You have a go.'

While apparently checking the focus on the binoculars,

Buchanan first made a check on the front verandah of the house. Good: Oeloefse was still tinkering about with the sound equipment for his 16mm gear, watched by the other three. Their plans had been to shoot some documentary stuff on the trading store, but Oeloefse had discovered that his camera had gone out of sync, and had been blinding and cursing ever since. No, wait: Tagg had now detached himself and was walking down through the garden.

Buchanan missed seeing anything in the plane, as it had swung away to begin its approach.

'Give me them again,' asked Koos, who seemed very unhappy at the prospect of further visitors. 'Man! Stoffel can't do this to me, hey?'

By then Buchanan's attention had returned to Tagg, who was putting a lot of effort into idle curiosity, and trying to amble at a fast walk with his hands in his pockets. He reached them and nodded affably.

'How's the repair work going?' Buchanan asked.

'Don't ask me!' Tagg answered, with a shrug. 'I'm just a mere water boffin alongside those chaps. Got company, have we? Up there?'

Three heads were now clearly visible as the plane swiftly lost height. Stoffel bounced the Piper once, braked in a zigzag of friction that brought him to a halt yards from the brink, and then taxied over. The propeller twitched to a stop, the right-hand door swung open, and Stoffel emerged; the shift of his great weight making the wings wag as he stepped backwards on to the ground.

'How goes it?' bellowed Stoffel, lugging Cassidy along with impatient jerks. 'Man, I'm bloody starving!'

Nancy Kitson slid out of the plane behind him, and stood smoothing the creases in her bright cotton dress. She hesitated demurely before giving Koos a quick, pretty smile.

'Who's the young lady?' Koos demanded.

'Hey, you dirty old bugger – hands off, you hear? That's company property, that is, specially entrusted to yours truly for the day. Miss Kitson, please to meet Koosie Brandsma, who is half-mad with love for you already.'

Koos screwed up with embarrassment. But Nancy didn't let

him suffer long, and was over in seconds to enchant him with her little-girl ways – those pigtails were killers, the devious bitch.

Buchanan would have found her something of a distraction himself, if the other passenger hadn't disembarked at that moment.

The likeness was so strong it struck like a fist: tall, strapping and Dirk Steyn to a T – except for the baleful brown eyes, and a nervous, diffident air. He was about twenty-five, dressed in khaki shorts, a yellow sports shirt, yellow socks and a pair of veld boots; he also wore a white straw hat – the kind bowlers favour – and carried a black canvas suitcase, a cheap camera, and a string bag containing pineapples and a bottle.

Tagg moved towards him, bulking his arms like a bouncer. Then he must have seen the likeness, too, because his advance faltered.

'Wolraad Steyn,' the young man said, putting down his suit-case to extend his hand.

Tagg looked shaken enough already, but took it and mumbled: '*Aangename kennis* – er, Johnny.'

His accent was horrible.

'Ach, you're English! I'm sorry, hey?'

'Just a minute,' Koos growled, coming across. 'I haven't been told any –'

'Meneer Brandsma?'

'Ja, but your –'

'You've got my pa staying with you; Dirk, Dirk Steyn. Ma said, "Go on Wolraad, you take the weekend off and here's some *pynappels* for him. If you're too many for the house, then surely they can find you –"'

When Koos interrupted again, he spoke in Afrikaans, but it was plain he was trying to be cordial and make up for his initial gruffness.

Then he said in English, pointing to Buchanan: 'Finbar's just going, so you're welcome to his bed, youngster. It's a pity you two won't be getting together, hey?'

'Aye, a shame,' agreed Buchanan. 'Pleased to meet you, Wolraad.'

The friendliness of his voice brought a shy smile to the young

100

Steyn's face, and for a moment their eyes locked in mutual assessment.

'Finbar's the photographer who Stoffel and me were telling you about,' Nancy chipped in. 'How well does he fit our description?'

Wolraad tried not to smile any wider.

'Oi,' said Tagg, 'oi, shouldn't we call Dirk over?'

He should have glanced behind him first.

'*Middag, Wolraad,*' said Steyn, striding up.

'*Middag, Pa – hoe gaan dit?*'

'*Maar nie te sleg nie.*'

Their greetings sounded strangely formal.

'Good to see you,' replied Wolraad, breaking into English for politeness' sake. 'You don't mind this? Me just dropping in? Ma sent these *pynappels.*'

He handed over the bag and his father gave the pineapples a couple of bobs to test their weight.

'*Kom, laat ons na die huis gaan – Pik wag op die stoep.*'

Dirk started for the house even before finishing his sentence, with Wolraad loping at his side, and Tagg not a shadow's length behind them.

'Phew!' said Nancy, and then whispered to Koos: 'Whatever did his father say? He seemed a bit riled there at first.'

'Ach, never; he was naturally a bit surprised. He said things weren't going badly, and that Pik would be waiting to see the boy on the stoep. You'll excuse me a minute, please – I'd best go and tell Solomon there's nine for lunch.'

'Chicken, I hope?' said Stoffel. 'You know I –'

'Only the one chicken so –'

'Let's go and see what we can fix up,' Stoffel urged cheerfully, throwing himself forward to gain impetus. 'Meantime, you two love-birds can bloody earn your keep and sort out the post for Koosie. Go on, it's all in the plane. I've got your number, hey? You bloody cheap-skate Scotchman!'

Buchanan grinned and turned back towards the Piper.

'Christ, you stupid bint, what the hell are you doing here?' he said to Nancy, who'd taken out her compact.

'Come to tell you you're fired,' she quipped.

'Oh aye?'

'Thought maybe you could do with some female intuition on your side.'

'Certainly; like I need castration.'

'Any time,' offered Nancy, pouting at herself in her little mirror. 'Actually, I'm here on orders, lover. These things can be pretty subjective, so the boss wanted me to cast an eye on our behalf, see if you were coming up with the right answers.'

'Pretext?'

'Didn't really need one. The story of our passionate relationship's all over town and, I guess, Stoffel just took pity on me. Why so jumpy? You've got something?'

'Did Louis –?'

'Look, this was practically half his buddy's idea, so relax! I talked it over with Stoffel right in front of him, and he said I was entitled to a free ride now and –'

'BOSS was in on this?' Buchanan sighed, bewildered.

'As Cupid, sure. Now what's the big deal?'

He told her about the photographs. It made a much nicer person of her. She looked sick.

'This – this is terrible.'

'On all levels,' Buchanan confirmed. 'It could blow the whole détente thing out the window, and the Republic's only chance of survival with it. You imagine what'll happen if the neighbours get to hear there's terrorism smack in the middle of them. They'll all be back into the laager, poking their guns through the spokes and shooting anything black that moves.'

'Vorster will be finished.'

'Oh aye, and you know who'll take over: the real hard-liners, the lads who just don't see that the right things done for the wrong reasons are all that'll save them. That's not to mention a world shift of power.'

'Maybe we'd better cool this, huh?' Nancy suggested quietly, opening the Piper's cargo hatch. 'Sort the mail and run through a nice, balanced assessment.'

She was right. The catastrophe would be no less than Buchanan had described it – not Macmillan's Winds of Change, but a bloody tornado, ripping up through Africa and into Europe and beyond. But nobody did their best thinking on that sort of scale.

A glance at the house showed everyone gathered around Wolraad.

'My reading?' Buchanan said.

'Shoot.'

'The uprising here in January put Lesotho on thin ice with Pretoria. Following month, a Bill was passed making it an offence to obtain money from abroad for guerrilla activity.'

'Appeasement.'

'Up to a point, lassie. Chief Jonathan also had to push an anti-South Africa line to pacify internal opposition.'

'Huh! He and Vorster met for a patch-up.'

'We could go on all night. But let's take it as common cause that Chief Joe swore on his granny's nightshirt there would be no nasty frightening things happening again to upset his white neighbours.'

'The apple cart!' she interposed.

'Oh aye. So what happens next time there's trouble?'

'Nobody gets to know about it,' she said very softly.

There was very little mail in the cargo hatch, and it was now sorted. They took the few envelopes for the store, put the rest back, and began to walk along the row of boulders.

'But somebody on the "outside", so to speak, *does* get to know about it,' Buchanan went on. 'Wee Willie Potgieter, way up here on this remote trading post. Willie who writes letters to his half-brother – Willie who writes a letter which he thinks will buy him that ticket home. And with honour.'

'Uhuh. And Dirk reports that Willie's stumbled on something?'

'Not just "something". Those uprisings weren't so much sinister as spontaneous. But here you have the genuine article; infiltration and consolidation by classical methods. Guerrillas in the mountains, busy building up a solid backing first from the people, and dealing in salutary fashion with the ones who won't play ball. Setting examples, while knowing damn well that only fools are going to leak it back to Maseru. And what does Maseru do? Sends in its men on the quiet, hoping they'll find a way of nipping this thing in the bud. The alternative's admitting . . .'

'Unthinkable,' said Nancy.

She and Buchanan stopped, turned around and began to walk back towards the house.

'At this stage, I agree,' Buchanan went on. 'But how does this sound to Dirk's friends in high places? They don't want any publicity either. They want to check this rumour for themselves and then see what to do. Lesotho's never going to be able to hold down anything big – that's for sure.'

Nancy stooped to pick a wild flower.

'They could have sent Louis up here,' she said, then corrected herself: 'No, he'd be too well known.'

'Exactly. The South Africans wanted these cards for themselves, to smack them down on the Chief's desk, scare the brown out of him, and say: "Right, now what do *we* do?" What's known as the whiphand. The easiest thing then would be for them to arrange some manoeuvres in the Maluti, make it a combined exercise with the Lesotho PMU, and do the necessary – without blanks.'

That earned him a light kiss and a flower in his buttonhole.

'Yug,' said Nancy, 'but I guess that looked good from afar. Can I carry for a while? Dirk is chosen to go in, because he's the man with the contact, and because his being here doesn't mean a thing. He brings in Oeloefse to actually make the cards which are going to be slapped down on the Chief's table. Irrefutable proof.'

'And Johnny Tagg?' Buchanan challenged.

'Ah.'

'Would it help if I told you he's got a pamphlet on terrorism beside his bed?'

'It would,' mumbled Nancy.

'And if I told you he's got a quiet confidence, doesn't say much, but is obviously part of the team?'

'You're also telling me that our data on Mr Tagg could be way out. Okay, I'll accept that. Or could it be he's just kidded them into thinking he's some kind of expert on insurgents?'

'Either way, he fits now.'

There were about two hundred yards to go.

'The darkroom doesn't – I just can't figure out the reason why,' she objected, giving a little skip.

'Not our job. Unless it's a certain check they've got the goodies before sneaking them out in a diplomatic bag.'

'And Louis? His partner? Why are they out on a limb?'

'In case their security isn't all that good. They're too near to the hub of things – check?'

That seemed to be all. They had already exceeded their brief by troubling to make sense of the situation, but there were some things a man was happy to do for free. And very soon now they'd be in earshot.

'Very concisely, Miss Kitson, how do you rate this latest arrival? A courier?'

'A clown,' she answered, laughing. 'Manages his pa's farm – I had the whole life history, brother died not long ago, was a cop in Rhodesia, and – well, concisely, I think he goofed coming here.'

'Hmmm,' said Buchanan.

At the last moment, Nancy added in a lover's whisper: 'Jesus, this is going to be like carrying a goddamn egg through Fun City rush-hour.'

'On a spoon, Miss Kitson,' he cautioned, 'so watch yourself.'

There was a buzz at that table which made chewing chicken something you had to think about. Nancy was aware of it, too, and so sparkled with vivacious inanity.

Buchanan was puzzled by this undercurrent until it occurred to him that these final minutes could be fairly tense for the South Africans themselves, especially as Willem had already shown his self-control was wanting. Willem was of course, by necessity, the one member of the group who hadn't been hand-picked for the job.

Koos kept the conversation going, mainly by questioning Nancy as an uncle might a favourite niece. He really was a good old soul, as people said to mask their disappointment when confronted by uncomplicated virtue.

Nancy had no other active admirers though. Stoffel was eating, Wolraad's glances were covert, uneasy and awed, suggesting that this contrast with the surly maidens of his acquaintanceship was making him think of Babylon. His father ignored her completely.

Tagg, who could have been expected to rise to the occasion, in any number of ways, had retreated into the shallow depths of himself. And Oeloefse, seated opposite her, had vigilant eyes only for Willem.

Who kept looking at his watch and squirming.

'And tell me, Juffrou Kitson, how long do you intend staying with us, here in Lesotho?' Koos asked, as Solomon came to clear away the plates of the main course.

'I guess Mom and Dad are really expecting me back this fall when Rhoda gets married – she's my kid sister, as you've probably all gathered by now, *and is she a brat*! My Mom says she's set on just a quiet little affair – y'know, St Peter's in Rome and the Waldorf when the jumbo gets back there. But that depends also on –'

And she gave Buchanan a flutter of eyelashes that even Stoffel caught the breeze of.

'Hark at these love-birds,' he said, wiping at his greasy chin with his shirt tail. 'Man, who would think they'd only been intercoursing for a matter of two weeks? What you call love at first –'

'Thank you!' Buchanan laughed, genuinely entertained by Dirk Steyn's thunderous look.

'Sorry?' queried Koos, who'd got himself lost.

'Two weeks only?' Willem said.

'Manfred is talking now, boss,' Solomon called up from the garden. 'I give him sugar like you say.'

'This you must see,' insisted Willem getting to his feet. 'There's this crazy kaffir who can just spout the Bible like you've never heard. Come on, man.'

'Ja, you must,' Koos said, getting up as well.

Stoffel, effectively gagged on a gargantuan piece of cold mutton – his was the one plate Solomon wouldn't have thought of removing – shook his head.

'But he's seen him before,' Willem pointed out, helping Nancy to get her chair back. 'Pik? Bring your camera, hey?'

'Ach, the tape's still to hell. I'll get him tomorrow; you can give him some money to stay around.'

'It is not blasphemy?' Dirk Steyn asked, already on his feet.

'How can it be? He just recites – but you must see it. And you, Finbar!'

Buchanan was not too happy at the thought of leaving Stoffel alone with Oeloefse. The pilot's lack of inhibition could easily lead to a little too much being said in reply to the right questions – he could, for example, drop a brick or two more with regard to the short-lived relationship with Nancy. Or recall questions that had previously been put to him.

Yet there was no way out of it, not with Koos at Buchanan's elbow, reminding him that Manfred had been the mad kaffir with the rabbit dung. And so he joined the party that went down into the garden and across to the gate, reassured by the size of the joint Stoffel still had to engorge. And the fact that nobody seemed much interested in himself any more – he'd been, in a tacit way, dismissed, and this could only be good.

How cool it had been on the granadilla-screened verandah. As they moved out of the shade, Buchanan felt the sun instantly prickle his scalp with sweat, and then come off the white glaze underfoot to do the same with his chin.

Now that he found very surprising: one of the main attractions at Mapapeng was the grey-haired, grizzled old Basotho who walked away the last days of his life in tight circles under the blue gums. This old man turned strips of wet hide into whip-lashes a dozen at a time, by tying one end of them to a branch and the other to a log, which he pushed round like a capstan bar. However, the twist of thongs and their deadweight hung as unattended as yesterday's lynching, and the old man – who'd not as much as looked up when the three stallions fought in the yard – was gone.

No, he wasn't. He'd joined a crowd just the other side of the trees. It seemed everyone had.

'Up there,' said Willem, pointing.

Manfred had somehow climbed part of the way up the cliff behind the store, and was striking a Mosaic pose with his staff held high. Most remarkable of all was the change in the colour of his beard from Afro-black to sagacious sugar-white.

'Oh aye, so that's –'

'Shhh,' said Nancy, 'listen!'

From the jutting rock above, came the lilt and boom of a deep baritone voice, reciting a passage from the Old Testament and, it seemed, word for word.

'How about that?' Koos whispered

'Impressive,' murmured Buchanan, and meant it.

For a few moments, he'd been lifted right out of context, as it were, and had forgotten the predicament he and Nancy faced until take-off.

Then Dirk Steyn grew restive, and pushed into the back of the crowd. The Basotho made way for him, hiding their giggles at Manfred behind cupped hands, or keeping their eyes fixed on him, absorbed by wonder.

'*Dirk, wat maak jy, man?*' Willem asked anxiously.

'It's all right,' Koos said, 'Manfred won't bite.'

'But – ach, doesn't matter.'

The challenge Dirk barked up at Manfred was direct enough: 'Who the hell do you think you are, hey? You think you're a prophet?'

Manfred looked down, lowering his staff as he did so.

'You just stop that – you hear? God is a boss who doesn't like this kind of nonsense! You're a Bantu, not a prophet – you understand?'

The crowd waited, every face turned upwards. But there was no answer.

'You know what a prophet is, boy?'

The staff was raised high and Manfred began addressing them again.

'For there shall arise false Christs,' he said without expression, 'and false prophets. Matthew Chapters Twenty and a Four. Behold, I have told you before. Wherefore if they shall say unto you, Behold he is in the desert; go not forth, behold he –'

'You know who I am, boy? Boy, do you hear me?'

'Please,' Koos urged, 'don't cause upset, Dirk – these people are all –'

Manfred, who had not ceased his recitation, began to speak over the disturbance that was growing beneath him.

'For as lightning cometh out of the east, and shineth even unto the west; so shall the coming of the Son of Man be. For

108

wheresoever the carcase is, there will the eagles be gathered together. Immediately after the tribulation of –'

'He's playing our tune,' Nancy said, nudging Buchanan.

It took him a moment to get what she meant.

'Coincidence,' he said, half-smiling.

'Yes, maybe we'd better go,' Koos agreed with Willem on
their left, and the party from the house made its way back.

Buchanan got himself in front, so he'd be able to have some
idea of what had happened at the table in their absence. Nancy
must have had similar thoughts, as she stuck at his side without
saying anything.

But Stoffel was alone at the table, when they came up the
steps, finishing off a small glass of something.

'They say you brought this peach brandy?' Stoffel said to
Wolraad, who nodded proudly.

'Ja, *meneer*, it comes from our farm – my ma is famous for it.
Often we take it to people as a little gift. It is her own recipe.'

'Then you must tell your ma that she must watch the pips,
hey?'

'You criticize my wife's making of peach brandy?' Dirk
Steyn said, turning on him angrily.

'No, no, please don't get me wrong! As peach brandy goes,
this is among the best *sluks* I've ever tasted. It's just peach
brandy is something I know about – ja, if I say so myself. And
I was only trying to give some helpful advice. You see, if you're
not careful, the inside of the pip can have a bitterness that –'

'So it's bitter is it?'

'Again you get me wrong. I'm talking about the very
slightest –'

'Koos Brandsma! This I will not have! You will tell this
insolent –'

'One minute, one minute, please,' Koos pleaded. 'Why not
let us all try a little for ourselves? I see Pik has poured the
other glasses now. Then we get a majority opinion!'

Oeloefse came out through the french doors, with Solomon
to help him carry a drink for everyone. He'd heard the *faux pas*
being made and was trying not to smile.

'I'll give you a refill, okay?' he said to Stoffel with a wink,
and brought the glass up to the brim.

The buzz had been overtaken by a crackle of tension Buchanan found disproportionate to the situation, although he had to concede that an outraged Dirk Steyn had the edge on most malcontents.

'Cheers!' Koos called out, and the drinks were solemnly sipped.

Stoffel raised a brow, and turned down his lip in grudging reappraisement.

'Not bad, very good in fact. Perhaps my mouth was still full of fat.'

'Of course!' Tagg agreed. 'One of the best ways to kill a good beer is to have a bit of grease of a ham sanny on y'lip.'

'Well, *I* think it's the most gorgeous, delicious thing I've ever tasted!' Nancy gushed, God bless her.

But only Koos really responded, and an awkward pause kept everyone on their feet. Stoffel pretended indifference, sipped the rest of his glass slowly, and took his time about getting up at the end of it.

'You're off now?' Willem asked, moving aside for him.

'Ja, better chop along – that cloud up there is getting pretty thick, not many gaps left. You ready, Finbar?'

'Oh aye, stuff's right here.'

Buchanan lifted up his two bags, and then turned to bid good-bye to Koos.

'I'll come out and see you off,' Koos said.

'Me too,' Willem offered, and went to the top of the steps.

Parting was sweet when it came to saying farewell to the Mapapeng commando and its latest volunteer; Nancy had nicer things said to her, and then Willem impatiently led the way to the plane.

Koos made several apologies for the peach brandy incident – which Stoffel cheerfully blamed on himself, but made no apology for – and the trader impressed upon both Buchanan and his lady friend that they'd be welcome back whenever they wished.

Willem almost danced with irritation when all this went on rather too long after all the seat belts had been done up, while Stoffel enjoyed every moment which added to the delay. Buchanan just wanted up and out.

'Koos, we mustn't keep these good people,' Willem growled, and pulled his companion back so the door could be closed. 'So long – have a good trip!'

Stoffel waited until the engine was running smoothly before he shouted through his side window: 'The food was *lekker*, Koos! And you, Willie – don't fall off too many horses, you hear?'

He heard. The Piper rolled forward. Buchanan twisted round to note the effect of this last gloating remark, and saw Koos had been quite right in his misgivings: little Willie looked murderous.

But what Buchanan would never be able to forget was how – in that final split-second before the runt disappeared from view – how Willem Steyn had burst out laughing. And he learned the reason for this all too soon.

Chapter Eight

When Stoffel died, some eight minutes after take-off, he did so with what appeared to be uncharacteristic politeness. This should have alerted Buchanan, but he, in turn, was uncharacteristically slow on the uptake; once off the ground, he'd deliberately severed every string of tension, to flop back, virtually inanimate, like a large, well-contented puppet. Nancy was doing the same on the rear seat.

'' 'Scuse me,' Stoffel seemed to say, ducking his head to one side, as a gentleman does who attempts to stifle a sneeze.

Buchanan naturally looked the other way, and then, lazily, down at the ragged-toothed ranges beneath them.

The plane flew on.

Leaving Mapapeng with the wind to the east had, as Stoffel warned, been like taking a standing jump out of a bloody great bucket with one leg tied behind you: they had barely made it over the brim. And the climb that followed had been long and steep, taken in a rush to gain height before being ambushed by the violent turbulence of a very hot day. But all that was over now; they had eased into level flight on a course due south, and soon Siwewe, the next mail drop, would appear like a thumb smudge on the tinted contours below.

Slight ear-ache caused Buchanan to turn and pick out the altimeter. They were at 10,000 feet; the Maluti at eight to nine. Stoffel was being very restrained for a man who usually enjoyed a good sneeze – perhaps it had been stillborn, as some were.

Buchanan glanced around.

Stoffel was dead.

The plane flew on. Its control column, grasped in the cadaveric spasm that complicates taking razor blades from suicides, was finding just the right amount of play in moribund arm muscle to simulate the relaxed yet firm grip of a living aviator.

This was the only explanation as there was no automatic pilot. Meanwhile, the engine went on draining the fuel-tanks of high-octane spirit, inserting its idiosyncratic hiccup into the rhythmic throb every few beats, and the invisible propeller continued its magic. All as if nothing had happened.

But for how much longer it would continue to do so was quite another thing. A fragile equilibrium, born of mere chance, existed between an infinity of conflicting factors. In the same way, mere chance could introduce, at any moment, a tiny gust, a puff of air lifting high a whirling dandelion seed as deadly as a missile, and upturn the applecart, bursting its fruit on the hard rock below.

Only seconds must have passed, because Nancy hadn't as yet noticed anything amiss.

Buchanan, using the old trick to enforce total concentration, closed his eyes. Whereupon his mind played an old trick of its own: it took him back another eternity to the loch, and to the canoe his father had given him on his fourth birthday – that canoe which, at first, capsized at his slightest movement, and made him crouch rigid on the lift and sag of the water. Buchanan opened his eyes and found his limbs were stiff with the same fear of precipitating catastrophe. He would have laughed, if this mightn't have brought Nancy in too soon.

Plainly, his only hope was to take the initiative; to act first, using a corpse for his tutor while the opportunity lasted – to learn how to fly straight and level would be something at least. All the same, it seemed a pity to tamper with things as they were.

Buchanan reached out and closed his fingers around the dual control column on his side, handling the curve of the half-wheel like a sleeping serpent and ready to whip his hands away instantly. They were the hands, Nancy had said at their first meeting, of a horse strangler – and yet he managed to be so gentle the plane gave no hint of his touch.

He tightened his grip by degrees until he held in it the transmitted rigor of the flesh at his side. Then he extended his toes with the caution of a blindfolded acrobat and made delicate contact with the pedals. So far, so good. He breathed out.

He felt Nancy breathe out, too, warm and long against the nape of his neck.

'Stoffel's sick?' she asked softly.

'Totally.'

'I can't believe it.'

'You'd better.'

'We're ...?

'Oh aye, somewhat in the poo,' he said. 'Or can you fly? I'm afraid I never asked.'

'I can work a radio.'

'No good. Just noticed some careless bugger's stood on the hand-piece.'

Gradually Buchanan began to get the feel of the thing, of the vibrant, jumpy sensitivity of the little plane, and made a very slight but positive attempt to change course.

The nose drifted to the left along the horizon – then dipped. Buchanan squeezed the controls hard, swore for having done so, and willed himself to correct the angle while he counted slowly up to ten. The nose lifted again with no more than a faint tremble from the wings, but now the plane was turning, and carrying on turning, to the right. Again he tried a correction. Apart from making the bucket seat beneath him appear to slip sideways, this had no obvious effect.

He heard a rattle and looked down: a pencil stub was rolling about on Stoffel's side.

'It's his leg,' Nancy said, her voice casual.

The body's right leg was twisted. How comfortingly logical: when the plane had dipped, gravity caused the dead weight to slide forward, and now it was pressing against one of the rudder pedals. Instantaneous rigor, Buchanan remembered from somewhere, may follow ingestion of cyanide – sweet Christ.

With extraordinary care, he removed one hand from the controls and took hold of Stoffel's right trouser leg. He pulled at it steadily in the hope of releasing the pressure. The fabric bunched up, but the limb stayed where it was, fixed like a log, with the knee locked.

The plane flinched and went on with its endless turn. He brought his hand back to the controls.

'I can try,' Nancy offered.

'For Christ's sake don't change sides – we're just balanced like this.'

She pulled at Stoffel's shoulders, but hadn't the purchase even if she'd had the strength.

'Is it Cassidy?'

'No, it's rigor. But don't get distracted by what that suggests. Keep thinking.'

Then Buchanan noticed the glint of a heavy wrench jittering about in the side pocket of his door.

'Nancy, wrench, please; on my left.'

'Coming up.'

She passed it round on his right side and he let go of the controls again with one hand to take it.

The tool made short work of the joint. Then, to prevent a further problem, Buchanan took a chance and leaned across to smash the hinge on the tin leg with a single, short chop. The plane shuddered and flew on. Buchanan pulled the legs out of the way. The plane began to veer to the left.

The time had come to go solo, Buchanan decided. Flying one-handed, hopefully for the last time, he prised Stoffel's grasp from the controls and the plane passed entirely into his keeping. It started to fluster.

'You've really got a way with dames,' Nancy said. 'What was it he called this crate?'

'Lulu.'

Buchanan was purposefully slow to react but quite firm. After a minimal amount of trial and error, he got the thing back where he wanted it: straight and level at what was, to his surprise, 11,000 ft. The extra height was like another thousand in the bank, a windfall – old Stoffel's secret legacy paying out.

'Come on, you bastard!' said Buchanan, tugging the plane to heel. It was just so much artfully arranged junk, and would have to learn to appreciate this.

The first of the down-draughts hit the plane a back-hander and it slewed wildly across the sky, tipped against a thermal, slipped sideways from nosedived.

The world was set spinning dizzily below, sucking his fixed gaze into its vortex. Buchanan realized he was heading earthwards faster than a fastidious *kamikaze* with bursting bladder

115

– and liking it. He chortled and snorted and then heard the plane screaming: this brought him up sharply. There was a first time for everything, even mild panic, but this was going too far.

Nancy had let go a moan.

Acting instinctively, Buchanan pulled the controls towards him and stamped hard on the foot brake.

For a second his eyes filled with black blood, and then they cleared to show beautiful blue sky – somehow he'd slipped the spin to drag them back out of the Maluti's jaws.

'Left spin, right rudder,' he shouted over his shoulder.

'Thank God it wasn't a right spin,' remarked Nancy.

A euphoria, in its way as dangerous as the fright of only moments before, tempted Buchanan as he continued the climb to safety. What a beautiful, truly beautiful blue sky.

'See that, you old bastard!' he grinned, swinging the nose away from a lone, soaring vulture, and was amused the plane seemed a little out of breath.

The nose dropped, making Nancy grab his shoulders.

However, Buchanan knew what to do. He had help now – a legion of hazy crazy airmen, who'd left their vapour trails across the printed skies of his youth, shouted as one man in his ear: *This is a stall – open up!* So he slammed down hard on the pedal, and the plane swung round like a cat on a string.

'Jesus!' exclaimed Nancy, tightening her hold.

Jumping Jehosaphat! bellowed the magnificent men in their flying machines.

Gott in Himmel! screeched the Red Baron, purpling his duelling scars: *Is not a geschlitzen motoring car, you Englisher domkopfen! Vy again gif ze right rudder?* Too right, he had; this time his foot had stamped down for an accelerator on the floorboard.

Buchanan groped for the hand throttle, seeing rock rushing up at them.

Pull her ze stall out! bellowed the Baron.

Right again, and not a moment too soon. The sky came and went; then came and stayed. Held there until it became the blue triangle between the converging slopes of two mountains dead ahead. Buchanan aimed for the middle, rather wishing he didn't have to look.

116

Then the All-American barnstormer in the seat behind him hissed: 'Step on the gas, Buke – we're gonna need it.'

'Et tu?' said Buchanan, taking the throttle knob deep in his hand.

The plane lifted away neatly, the peaks flashing by on either side, and this time there was power for the climb. Buchanan was pushed back in his seat – he felt Nancy's fingers slip from his shoulders.

A slow, emptying sigh came from Stoffel, as his lungs were depressed by the weight of his flab-heavy chest. The sigh smelled of peach brandy.

'I want to go home now,' Nancy murmured. 'You got any plans?'

'We take her up as high as we can go and practise a wee landing? On a cloud?'

'Sounds advisable. How's the fuel gauge?'

'Full. But it's been full every time I've seen it. We've at least an hour though.'

Talking had made a big difference. For a while there, everything had become a little too unreal. In fact, his hands had already learned a lot, and so had his feet. It was really not unlike trying to ride a bicycle, only the consequence of a beginner's accident was more severe. It was also a matter of sensing the machine's balance, mainly with the backside, and of making adjustments without getting too uptight about them. They rode two bumps successfully.

Buchanan began to watch the altimeter. The needle was back to the 10,000-mark and dithering on around. It reached 11,000 ft and started on twelve. There was a red line from the centre of the dial to where 13 was marked. A red line that, in a fleeting fantasy, seemed to score right through his name.

'What's the red line for?' he said to Nancy.

'Piper's ceiling, maybe? Oxygen warning?'

'That's a thought.'

'Don't worry, I'll slug you when you start acting slaphappy. Look, it's stuck.'

'Do you mind if I try a little higher?'

'It certainly feels a lot safer. Oh Jesus, Finbar, this poor bastard . . .'

And she touched the dead man lightly on the arm.

Buchanan now faced entering a danger zone without actually knowing when he'd crossed the line. Their luck had been good – it had been almost incredible, but now with every foot gained, it was stretching thinner and thinner like a length of elastic drawn back to zap a fly clean out of the sky.

He held the climb.

Pop! the small explosion occurred right behind him.

The sound was really no louder than a child's capgun, but – things being what they were – Buchanan started violently, and heard Nancy's own gasp of surprise.

The plane jumped, too, twisting to the left. Whether it did this in sympathy with his instinctive recoil, or because some vital part had ceased functioning, it was impossible to tell. Burst fuel lines spurted in Buchanan's brain, unfathomable devices sprayed their pieces into the slipstream of his fright, and he bloody well shook.

'See anything back there?'

'No.'

He brought the nose down very gradually. He listened and heard nothing. He moved the controls and felt nothing. But the sharp report had to mean something – that was obvious.

'Your turn for a suggestion, lassie. Do we try for a few rehearsals?'

'I think we ought –' and she paused, 'maybe we ought to go down.'

'While the going's good?'

'The lowlands might be easier, but . . .'

'Point taken,' he said, then added: 'Any idea how far we've come?'

They looked down, trying to find a mountain that would give them their bearings. Smoke pinpointed a couple of villages, but they saw nothing that was any help.

'I've got the feeling it hasn't been much of a journey,' Nancy said. 'With all due respect, Buchanan, we've been doing a pretty good Cry-cry Bird. You know the one, flies round in ever-diminishing circles until it disappears up its –'

'Cry-cry-Christ! It's dark in here! – one of the old bugger's favourites.'

118

They were having to talk about Stoffel; something just had to be said. But enough.

Buchanan put the plane into a shallow dive.

Nothing fell off.

It did not take long for the needle – which relented with a jerk at 12,000 ft – to return nervously to ten and then back on round the dial. Not after a mind-reeling down-draught that very nearly ended everything right there and then.

They plummeted. They hit currents of living air that struck back viciously. They swayed, shuddered, all but went end over tip, took glimpses of both space and eternity, and then, incredulously, trembled into a low zoom over a terrified family of goats picnicking on a local landmark.

Buchanan had to hand it to Lulu. The triumph of their recovery was entirely her own – all he'd done was hang on and try not to wet himself. Stoffel, flopping about over his seat belt, went right ahead and did so, posthumously. It could never have been otherwise.

There was a coughing sound behind him – Nancy had been sick.

'Pardon?'

'Screw you,' she replied gamely, and then was sick again.

As the plane tilted and swung round, juddering over a washboard of cloud, and slipped into a new valley.

'Christ, there she blows – Dumela!' Buchanan said, recognizing the folded-leg ridge. 'You were right, lassie, we can't have – and look, the bridle-path down to Gotsong! I'm going to try it.'

If Nancy thought he meant the path, she didn't say anything.

Buchanan struggled to keep the plane level but saw they were losing height every second. Up at twelve thousand, there had been the room for error, and nothing fixed against which to measure it. Here, the rush of reference points ahead and below showed up each blundering dip and waver, magnifying his realization that he'd simply prolonged a problem, not solved it.

There was a sudden blast of air from the window behind him. Glancing round, he saw Nancy throwing out the wrench and a few other tools she'd found lying about. She was stripping the cockpit of all its movable hazards, working quite coolly although her complexion was like flour, and this helped his confidence.

'Aye, that's a fair notion,' he said. 'When you're finished, strap in behind Stoffel and get your head down.'

'When are you –'

'A wee while yet, I trust.'

The plane sank down and down, towards a boulder-rough saddle. The bridle-path grew wider, and the sheep fanned out up the slopes on either side. Buchanan tried to lift the nose, thought he'd stall, and pressed it forward again. The eddies of rising air felt like flak bursting underneath. They were not going to make it.

They did. Suddenly there were hundreds of feet of spare space below as they brushed over the escarpment and burst through a small lost cloud.

And there, bleak but magnificent, in the lap of a great black mountain that cooled its feet in a river, was Gotsong. They were over it and climbing before Buchanan could see what the air sock was doing. In that light, the strip looked like a matchbox label.

Nancy slid shut the side window.

'Wake me when it's all over,' she whispered into his ear.

But Buchanan had only thoughts for Lulu, as she sang, struts strumming, up into a wide turn and back over the mission again. On this pass, he saw Cousteau and Motseki – two white coats – come out of the surgery and shield their eyes.

He swung away towards the sun, travelling with the wind, and finding it full of fight as he made his turn. Lulu fought back even harder, straining every square inch of her spare frame, and they made it. They lined up.

'Is this it?' Nancy said, from the depth of her knees.

'Oh aye, this is Gotsong.'

The approach began with a sickening sag.

The landing strip shivered on the slope, becoming a diminishing band of yellow as Buchanan gunned the engine in short, anxious bursts for fear of coming down too soon – or too fast. The leap and drag of this motion brought Stoffel's hand across in a series of grotesque hops, to lie leaden against Buchanan's thigh.

'Oh, Christ,' he said. 'Now the commercial.'

And saw, skimming ahead of them over the coarse grass, over the rocks, and over the heather, a headstone, a huge cross, a presage of shadow cast by the plane with the sun dead behind it.

Chapter Nine

A heavenly vision floated over to hover somewhere on his right. Ethereal things of this sort had been happening for an hour or more, and would have been tolerably convincing, Buchanan thought, had they not been preceded by a most ungodly smell.

This smell, sharp as scalpels, had insinuated itself into the silent, unsurfaced darkness long before the first rustle of nylon wings, or the boom of a self-complacent baritone.

Then, as his other senses cleared, Buchanan saw the celestial shrink down into focus and become the earthy Miss Kitson.

The wall behind her belonged to the guest room at Gotsong – he'd have known its pattern of cracks anywhere – and the smell was ether.

'What have I lost?' he asked, finding his mouth hurt.

'Nothing you needed,' she said, with a funny smile.

'I'm?'

'Still functioning.'

'You're a great comfort to me,' he muttered, trying to sit up. 'I know where I am – but when am I?'

'It's a quarter after five.'

'Friday?'

'Still Friday.'

Nancy was in borrowed clothing, a white smock of some kind, which had possibly been Madame Cousteau's, and a wrinkled pair of old-fashioned brown stockings. She still had her shoes.

'Where's the party?' Buchanan said, flopping back.

'You bled all over me, you bastard. Isn't Doc a honey? He turned out three boxes for these. The pop noise was the aerosol in my bag going –'

'Was Stoff – I mean, what happened to the plane? And that pigtail?'

'A burn-out. You made a real mess of it. Overshot half the strip and went bouncing up the heather. Doc reckons it's what saved us. Motseki grabbed me and the Doc got you by the tail, then up she blew. That tank must have been full.'

'How much is left though?'

'Some ash and a few bits of junk. Cassidy. Stoffel's like a roll of burnt newspapers.'

'But you're all right?'

'I bit myself in the leg, but otherwise, sure, I'm fine.'

She wasn't. However slight her physical injuries, Nancy Kitson had been hurt very badly. Her eyes showed it: they'd died a little, along with Stoffel.

'They tried to kill us,' Buchanan said, taking the cigarette she offered him.

'Uhuh. Seems somewhere down the line you boobed.'

'Obviously, but how the hell?'

Buchanan went back over his short stay at Mapapeng, but could find no reasonable precaution he hadn't taken. In fact, once he'd straightened out the darkroom, he hadn't done a damn thing to provoke anyone. And as hairy as Nancy's visit had seemed at the time, that had gone off without incident as well.

'Or could it have been coincidence?' he asked, catching a smoke ring on his little finger. 'An aneurism could've stopped Stoffel in his tracks like that. That's common enough.'

Nancy sat down on the edge of the bed, and lit a cigarette for herself.

'A question: any more of that peach brandy in the house?'

'I think I saw some on the sideboard, near the radio. Stuff Dirk had brought with him, maybe. Anyway, it's a favourite tipple among the *volk*.'

'Sure. But you think back to how neat it might have been. Willem was clock-watching all the way through the meal – right? Then we get pulled out to watch that cabaret round by the store. Meantime, Oeloefse's –'

'And when we get back, Stoffel's bitching about bitterness and then changes his mind on the second glass. Willem's jumpy and sees we get to the plane double quick and then –'

'They could have used the old brandy – the fact the kid brought some just helped it along,' added Nancy.

'And it wasn't just a case of Wee Willie's revenge, because he wasn't anywhere near those bottles. In fact, it took all of them to do it – bar Koos – and you noticed the tension. That had to be timed just right. You were thinking of pot cyanide?'

'Almond taste, so it figured. Stoffel had been eating a lot. It wouldn't work?'

'Certainly – but within seconds, food or no food. I thought of nicotine, with all that insect-spraying gear Koos has got for the garden, but there wouldn't have been that complete cut-off. I'd say a Bushman could tell us. Hell . . .'

Buchanan's bad head reeled for an instant, and he put the cigarette aside. Concussion still lurked.

'In Lesotho?' Nancy asked. 'But Bushmen quit the place years ago.'

'In the Caprivi Strip. Down the west coast – Oeloefse's stomping grounds. Knows the Bushmen so well he can even manage some of their click-talk. They've got arrow poisons for hunting that –'

'Don't they eat what they shoot?'

'Oh aye, but not many have stomach ulcers – the blood-stream, all that. And there're a lot of different kinds too.'

'Oeloefse's the sort who might keep some of this stuff by him?'

'You've seen the bastard. On an operation like this, I wouldn't be surprised he'd be in charge of contingency planning.'

'And so, you do think –'

'It's what my gut says. The perfect accident: knock out the pilot – Willem's heard I'm no flier – and no inquest ever does more than a nominal job on mountain crashes. From ten thousand feet, we'd have been a lot untidier than a roll of bumf, and, I can assure you, nobody'd check for toxins. Not after Willem said his piece about too much peach brandy.'

'Jesus! They're a bunch of –'

'Not at all: the end will always justify the means, that's basic to their philosophy, from ethnic labour camps up. And naturally, in a situation like this, they'll be playing for keeps.'

Nancy stubbed out her cigarette, and then his own; grinding them down hard in the ash tray, as if trying to extinguish a debilitating anger.

'So, as we can't be certain it was natural causes,' she said, mostly to herself, 'then we think the worst and act on the assumption they did try to kill us.'

'We must do. If they wanted us silenced, they still want us silenced.'

'And Mapapeng isn't that far off. How long did it take on horseback?'

'I went two sides of a triangle – Dumela's further north – and that was five hours, all told. Say roughly two and a half straight across. Oh aye, we're well in range.'

'And out on a limb base-wise.'

Buchanan raised himself on one elbow, and looked round for his clothes. They were over on the wash stand.

'No, Doc says you're to take it easy a while,' Nancy warned. 'He hasn't put through his radio report yet, so we've a bit of time before word gets out. We could have crashed anywhere.'

'He hasn't? Why's that?'

'You've slowed down, Buchanan. For a guy reputed not to know his ass from a G-turn, you did pretty well today. Sure, passengers have taken over from heart attacks before now, *Reader's Digest*'s full of them, but most often they're talked down. If I were Louis Fouché, for example, I'd say you were a lying bastard and your story stinks.'

'Could I have this in short?'

'From Louis's point of view? That – and you being at Mapapeng at this particular time – could be just one happy coincidence too many, and I know how *you* feel about them. I'd say your cover's blown, friend, whether you goofed it or not.'

'And yours with it?'

'Uhuh, we're finished in Lesotho. And so, I didn't see the harm in giving the Doc a little insight into our problem, only I slanted it to sound like Maseru paid our salary cheques.'

'How did he take it?' Buchanan asked, seeing the sense of all this, but not liking it much.

'Surprisingly. Just nodded, said okay, no radio till later, and got back to his surgery. Oh yes, and made some allusion to a patient he'd had in.'

'Christ.'

'You know which one?'

Buchanan shrugged, and said: 'Could do. But we mustn't involve innocent bystanders too deeply, lassie.'

'Fine, but I had to do something with you sleeping it off, you bum. So what's the plan? How do we get out of here?'

Buchanan almost started a reply, then paused. He said finally: 'Sorry, not firing on all four cylinders yet.'

'Were you ever?'

Both smiled and dismayed themselves a little.

'Give me a deadline,' he suggested, 'and one for yourself.'

'Let's make it six o'clock. I could do with a little walk up the hill a way.'

'Six then. Do I get anything for my fevered brow?'

'There's Band-Aids on the bedside table,' Nancy said, 'if that's what you had in mind.'

Then she limped stoically over to the door, gave an unkind laugh, and left him alone. She was becoming quite likeable.

The first thing Buchanan did, before any hard thinking, was to explore himself. He flexed each limb and tightened up what other muscles he had. His chest produced a sharp surface pain. Gingerly he lifted the edge of the crêpe bandage wrapped around him, and peered in under the gauze pad. No wonder he'd bled so: by a freakish mischance, he had lost one nipple.

At six o'clock, dressed in khaki trousers and a winter shirt from Cousteau's wardrobe, Buchanan was seated at the harmonium in the living-room, waiting for Nancy to get back.

Matilda, the Basotho housekeeper, who was still weeping for Boss Stoffel, letting the tears just run, and getting on with her chores, came in with some cutlery to lay on the table. She glanced over at the corner in which Buchanan was sitting.

'Why this happen?' she asked. 'He good, good man, too much. One time he bring home my son for free and no payment.'

'Oh aye?'

'Big son who go to university in Lowlands; he is sent there by Doctor.'

'You've got many children?'

Matilda held up three fingers and sniffed.

'Two girls also. Five.'

'All here?'

'Except big son. He must not go down mines same as his father. My husband is killed in Johannesburg the time many men die. I cannot bring back him to put in the ground. Why they not bring Boss Stoffel inside?'

'I think the police must see him first, Matilda. Tell me: you know that man who was brought here on a door? How's he getting on?'

She shrugged, put down the last knife and fork, and gave her face a wipe with a corner of her apron.

'You want for me to ask Motseki?'

'You don't know who I mean?'

'I work just in the house,' she said more cheerfully. 'The supper tonight is lentils – you like? Pilchards, also.'

'Aye, sounds grand.'

Nancy and Matilda passed each other in the doorway to the kitchen passage.

'Doc's coming across now, so have you formulated anything?' Nancy asked, yawning.

'You'd better watch that,' Buchanan warned. 'You could be still suffering shock.'

'But have you? My mind's a mess.'

'Perhaps there's a way that won't put Cousteau in any kind of compromise: we just tell the truth.'

'Oh, come on, this has got to go out tonight!'

The door clattered shut and Cousteau moved wearily over to his chair and flopped down into it. He rubbed the back of his hands into his eyes, shook his head, and looked up at Buchanan with a slight smile.

'And so, m'sieur? You are feeling better?'

'Much – and my thanks for all you've done.'

'What is next?'

'I was about to offer you a cognac, Doctor,' said Buchanan, opening the dresser cupboard. 'And then I wondered if we could hear what had happened to that patient you mentioned.'

'You recall my need for an excuse?' Cousteau remarked wryly, with a twinkle of his humour back. 'If we were better acquainted, m'sieur, I would be shortly on the road to ruin.

However, a cognac would be most acceptable, and perhaps Miss Kitson will join me. You, I fear . . .'

'Shouldn't, and I won't. But about this patient. He didn't turn out to be Chief Rasumaati, did he?'

'No! Why do you ask?'

'Why the surprise?'

'Only I saw Rasumaati one minute ago! The old devil came to be treated for damages his wives had inflicted with hot mealie meal!'

Buchanan laughed, and handed over the two glasses.

'You were saying, Doc – this man died?' Nancy reminded him.

'*Oui*, his injuries inside were too severe. Indeed, it was a miracle he survived for so long, for we discovered three bullets from a .22 in his abdomen. Naturally, it was my fault for not noticing this before, but his external wounds led me to mistake –'

Cousteau broke off to tip back his brandy glass. He shivered at the shock of the spirit.

'I don't think we should go too deeply into this mess,' Buchanan said, sitting down. 'There will be a proper time for that later. And I think, Dr Cousteau, that the less involved you are, the better.'

'Am I not involved already? For a week now I have been aware that my people are disturbed by something they cannot explain to me. And then I have this case, such as as I have never seen before, the man with the –'

'But you've your work to do, and we've got ours,' Buchanan interrupted, 'can we leave it at that?'

'And we share the same cause,' Nancy put in.

Cousteau fiddled with his stethoscope, then nodded briskly.

'Very well, M. Buchanan, but it makes it more difficult for me to trust you and your intentions.'

'No need to trust us – listen to what we'd like to propose, and try to find the harm in it. Judge on that.'

'Then explain them, please.'

Buchanan waited until Matilda, who'd come in with the hot plates, had left again.

'We have reason to suppose that if certain parties knew we

were at Gotsong tonight, there could be some – unpleasantness.'

'How can that be avoided?' Cousteau objected. 'You must not forget it is my duty to report the accident so that officials can fly up here in the morning. We have already delayed in this matter for longer than –'

'It's very simple: you make your report, but you limit your description of what has happened to "a fatal air crash". That'll bring the officials, and we'll cadge a lift back to Maseru with them.'

'But there will be questions asked, M. Buchanan!'

'Oh aye, but I'm not asking you to be untruthful on our behalf – I suggest a small technical hitch instead.'

'Sure, cutting it dead after "fatal crash"!' Nancy said, catching on.

This idea was given careful consideration by Cousteau, as he slowly drank what remained in his glass.

'That is possible,' he said at last, with a wag of his brows. 'I need not lie, nor consider I have failed in my duty. I merely flick a switch?'

'Fake it any way you like. Radio trouble would account for the delay as well, and everyone knows radios up here malfunction every five minutes. Or put it another way, can you see any harm in this?'

'No, no I cannot. The only alternative would be that you and Miss Kitson left immediately on horseback, but I must forbid that on medical grounds. Ah, you realize, of course, that these official aircraft will have policemen on board?'

'That's what we're rather hoping,' Buchanan said, hoping this would be the clincher.

It was. Cousteau pulled out his pocket watch, pursed his lips, and then scratched his right ear.

'I will come on the air,' he said, 'I will identify myself, ask for confirmation of my signal, and explain that there has been trouble with the apparatus, I will then report a fatal air accident on my strip and – cut off. Is that correct?'

'That's perfect!' Nancy assured him, raising her glass in a toast.

'But would you have any objection to this taking place after our meal? Matilda has already been very patient.'

'The later the better,' Buchanan affirmed.

'Then I will go and tell her, and change my jacket – you'll forgive me a moment.'

Cousteau left the room, almost his sprightly self again; as confusing as the old fellow was finding all this, he still was a hard man to shake.

'Not bad, Buchanan,' Nancy conceded, moving over to the long window, 'but I can't say I'm wild about those officials to-morrow.'

'They'll all be Basotho, and they know me. I've been to the odd crash with them before now. Anyhow, lassie, I can't say I fancy our chances trying to get out of the Maluti any other way. It's got to be by air and that's the soonest anyone's going to get here. We have to take our problems as they come.'

'Buchanan?' she said, mating her finger with its reflection in the pane in front of her, and drawing circles.

'Aye?'

'Cut out this "lassie" crap, will you? It makes me feel like I come on goddam heat twice a year.'

When supper was over, and Matilda had cleared away and retired to her kitchen, Cousteau rose and said that seven-fifteen was as good a time as any.

'Want one of us along?' Buchanan asked.

'Don't you trust me, m'sieur?' Cousteau replied, giving him one of those playful slaps he gave to horses. 'I promise you I am word perfect! You will listen: Gotsong transmitting, Gotsong transmitting, are you receiving me, Marija? Does anyone receive me? Please acknowledge.'

'That's grand – away with you then.'

'Ah! One moment. Then: Radio fault, I repeat, radio fault, so please acknowledge, this is most urgent. There was a fatal air crash here this afternoon, please inform authorities and – zzzzzzz. How is that?'

'Beautiful,' said Nancy. 'Your zzzzzzz is terrific!'

Cousteau beamed and went off to the radio room, which doubled as his office.

'I notice,' said Buchanan, stirring his coffee, 'that you've dropped the Marilyn bit – why's that?'

'It's all in the timing,' she sighed.

'Oh aye?'

'Gotsong's not the time, and it isn't the place. I've noticed you've not been too keen yourself to throw the bull around. Like Doc's not a guy you try it with.'

'Or need to,' added Buchanan.

The paraffin lamps hissed and there was a distant sound of Motseki calling a group of singing patients to order.

'And all the time,' Nancy murmured, back at the window again, 'Stoffel's stuck out there in the dark, under that blanket. Oh Jesus!'

'Shhhhh,' said Buchanan, motioning with his cup at the sampler.

Her mood changed; she held on to the window sill, like it was the barre in a dancing studio, and watched herself in the glass as she practised two knee-bends.

Buchanan was experiencing some fluctuations between a gut-gnawing depression and the elation of outwitting the enemy – if such they were – but had had longer to learn how to remain still, seemingly unaffected.

Then Cousteau came back into the room, and they both turned, eager to hear how it had gone.

The doctor's face was grim.

'Marija knows about the crash,' he disclosed. 'Will the consequences be as serious as you have implied to me?'

'But how the hell?' Buchanan asked, getting up.

'Before I was to begin my broadcast, I had naturally to make sure I was on the Maluti waveband. In doing so, I heard Mashai being called up to repeat its earlier message.'

'What's Mashai doing in on this?' Nancy asked, bewildered.

'It seems from what the trader there says, that a man – possibly a patient – was travelling through here when the crash occurred. He rode on to Mashai, where he was to spend the night, and told one of the clerks about it. And the clerk told Chris the trader and Chris – the rest you can say for yourselves.'

'But what's Mashai's full story? Do they know anyone survived?'

'I fear so. Marija's already trying to raise us, and the authorities are being informed.'

'Then that's it – right, Buchanan?'

Cousteau's laugh made them both turn in surprise.

'The exact message from Mashai may be misleading in those unspecified quarters of yours, my friends.'

'Oh aye?'

'You see,' said Cousteau, 'the traveller is certain that only one passenger died. The pilot and a young woman were the ones to escape the flames.'

Mapapeng came through. Koos Brandsma and Willem were both at the microphone, asking anxiously after their lunch-time guests. But Marija said it was unable to supply detailed information, and asked them to clear the waveband in case Gotsong was still to make contact.

'But Marija, this is important, hey?' Willem's voice insisted through the crackle.

'Good night, Mapapeng, please cease transmission.'

The amplifier started a low hum that Cousteau turned right down.

'I must say something soon,' he said, 'or there may be – shall we say – complications?'

'Of course, just give me a minute,' Buchanan answered him, and went through to the living room.

'Willem's a little too worried about us to be true,' he told Nancy, who was sprawled in an armchair. 'I've practically no doubt left about that lot. It's eight now, so they could be here around eleven – that's a full moon out there.'

'Doesn't the fact Marija knows there should be survivors make a difference? That's an angle we overlooked before. I mean, if –'

'If we're not here, where are we and all that? Aye, I've got it. All the same, I'd rather not rely on the commando's better judgement – and I wouldn't like to think what they might get up to if we resisted. Their position is pretty bloody desperate: we've got more than one tale to tell now.'

'Fine, so we don't want to chance any hassle here at Gotsong.'

'Doc's got a lot of sick people around.'

'That had occurred, Buchanan. Better safe than sorry is the platitude you're fumbling for. Right?'

She put out her hand and he gave her a hoist from the chair.

Her limp had worsened, now the bruised muscle had had time to stiffen. That was worrying.

'Right: we're just going to have to find somewhere else to spend the night. If they come, Doc Cousteau can say . . .'

'What?'

'We – nicked a couple of horses and pushed off?'

'Sure, that's not bad. That would fit with their picture. Is that what we do?'

'We stay close, and we don't use horses. Dawn is in about ten hours. By ten, those planes should be here, and we can come down.'

'I trust you do not mind that I have been listening?' Cousteau said, stepping properly into the room. 'Who is this I should expect?'

'If you don't know, then your surprise will be genuine,' Buchanan told him.

Cousteau thought that over and nodded.

'But are these men likely to cause . . .' and his voice dropped, as he glanced across at his gunrack. 'There are children in my huts, pregnant women.'

'No, that's out of the question. We are all they'll want, and want quickly.'

'If they come at all,' Nancy added seeing the grey touch Cousteau's cheeks. 'We're trying to avoid something that very likely won't even happen. We could be imagining things.'

'I know nothing about you,' Cousteau replied, 'but I cannot believe you are fools. And so, may I make a small suggestion, please?'

Buchanan nodded.

'Then I suggest I send the message as we planned – to clear my name, as you say. Having done so, I will ask Motseki to guide you from here to a place you should be quite safe. It is not far and – with this moonlight – very romantic.'

Without waiting for a response, Cousteau left once again for his radio room.

'In a sneaky way, I think the old guy's begun to enjoy this,' whispered Nancy, opening a window to tip the remains of her drink into the garden. 'And if nothing does happen, he's going to be pretty goddam cynical with us in the morning.

'Let's hope so,' said Buchanan, stopping her in time to point out the grave below.

They had to wait until ten for Matilda and her brood to be bedded down and uninterested in mysterious parties of three setting off on foot. By then the patients had quietened down as well, and the youngsters, assigned to keep the dogs away from Stoffel's corpse, had nodded off over their fire.

Reuben Motseki, wrapped deep in his blanket, and managing to move almost gracefully in laceless army boots, led the way up the slope behind the house, with Nancy right in his tracks and Buchanan a few paces behind, carrying the rifle Cousteau had pressed on him.

It should have been a fairly solemn procession, but Motseki hummed a very old pop song remembered, no doubt, from his Sharpeville days and Nancy kept grinning back at Buchanan, who had several attacks of the unreals that made him grin in return. And so it went, for the best part of a mile, with the moon shining brightly.

Then the effort of the climb began to tell. Motseki grunted when he found it difficult to find his footing among the rocks, and all of them breathed loud enough to hear each other. The sand was only loosely bonded by straggly grass, and the stones had a way of slipping down the moment any weight was put on them.

'Time?' Nancy asked, and they all paused.

'Almost half ten. Much farther to go, Motseki?'

The man was looking back at Gotsong, and Buchanan turned to look with him. They had travelled a good way: the mission was no more than a throw of black dice in the velvety dip far beneath them, and the only light was a faint glow from the watch fire. Cousteau, who'd been a little haggard when they'd parted, was probably already asleep from sheer exhaustion; his working day was long enough to make most men drop in their tracks at the end of it.

There wasn't a sound.

'Yes, it is still very far,' Motseki said, coming about slowly.

His face caught the moonlight like gun-metal, and his wide smile flashed white.

'Oh aye, what's funny?'

'We are here,' Motseki replied, pointing.

They had almost reached the point where the slope ended up against a castle wall of sheer rock. Buchanan scanned it, and then took in the battlements of loose boulders along the top. He peered again at the cliff ahead of them, but couldn't see anything that would afford them cover.

Motseki began to climb again, giving Nancy a helping arm as she was now having a good deal of trouble with her limp. They went about another twenty yards.

And then Buchanan saw it: a low cave with a mouth like a bull frog, that gaped no higher than three feet in the centre, and which was no more than nine feet wide. Even in daylight it would have been difficult to pick out through the tall grass – and impossible to see from below.

Nancy flopped down and asked if she could have the water. Buchanan passed the canteen over. Motseki unslung the rugs he'd been carrying on his back and thrust them into the cave.

'Let us go inside,' Motseki invited them. 'It is not a bad place, you will see.'

Nancy rolled over and went on all fours, with Buchanan crawling behind her. Once through the entrance, they found the cave roof was high enough for them to stand, and that, instead of the slimy great tongue so readily imagined, the floor was covered in soft, dry sand.

'Bloody marvellous,' said Buchanan, helping Motseki sort the rugs out. 'Can't even smell the usual goat.'

'Goats never allowed near to here,' Motseki said, laughing. 'The ignorant believe it is a place of evil spirits, and the boy who lets his father's goats come here would get a very big thrashing. It would never happen.'

'Oh aye? Any reason for this?'

'Maybe a big snake one time lived here. There are pictures also, that the Doctor brought me here to see. Maybe that is what they are afraid of. I will show you.'

Motseki took his matches out of his pocket and lit one, shielding the light carefully.

'Bushmen's paintings?' said Nancy. 'Are they? They're so faint.'

But Buchanan could make out a hunter with his bow and arrows, and he nodded.

'People keep chucking water on them to bring up the colour, and that's what happens,' he said. 'It worries me though – how well known are these, Motseki?'

'That I do not know, sir. There are many paintings across the other side, in that wrong-shaped mountain there.'

'Better ones?'

'Dear me, yes. Very clear. When the Doctor brings me here, he said I am the first person to see these things after his wife. It is a special place for him in some way.'

The match went out, and Buchanan sank back on his haunches, saddened by a sudden insight into what Cousteau had meant about moonlight. And then he was gladdened by it.

'Let's fix the rugs and find places to sit,' suggested Nancy. 'I'm sorry you're having to go through this crazy business, Motseki.'

'All part of the service, ma'am!' the Basotho said so unexpectedly that she and Buchanan laughed.

Chuckling again, and well pleased with himself, Motseki settled down comfortably, nearest to the back wall. Buchanan took up a position near the entrance in the hope of being able to see down to Gotsong. But he couldn't, and Nancy pillowed her head in his lap.

It was a very hard head, for all its cloud of yellow gossamer.

The night noises began again soon afterwards. Toads burped and crickets recovered their nerve, tuned up and started sawing away. Then a wind stirred, and rustled the dry blades of grass, bringing a sweetness of wild mint.

Buchanan spidered his fingers over the sand until they touched the trigger guard on the rifle, allowing no hint of this movement to reach Nancy. By the green glow of his watch face, he could see the time was now exactly eleven o'clock.

Chapter Ten

Dawn bled into the cave and woke Buchanan. Its garish red soaked the cloud visible above the tall grass, and there was an absolute stillness, as if the world waited on something with bated breath.

Motseki opened his eyes with the quiescence of a man who had not been asleep, simply resting. He and Buchanan smiled slightly and nodded to each other, then looked down at Nancy. She lay on her side, curled up like an opossum, with her slow, regular breathing lifting and dropping a wisp of hair that had fallen over her face.

Buchanan brought his finger to his lips, and then tapped his ear, raising his eyebrows inquiringly as he did so. Motseki shook his head.

He'd heard nothing.

Nor had Buchanan during his own watch. Either the commando had called and been turned away by Cousteau's story, or they had not come at all. In the chill beginnings of a new day, the latter seemed the more likely – especially as Motseki had been certain they'd catch the sound of a party of horsemen.

Buchanan's first sleep in over forty hours had much refreshed him; he found his thoughts had solidified and were no longer passing straight into his bloodstream, which allowed him to review the events of the past two days more objectively. In the end, however, nothing could negate the enormity of his discovery in the darkness, and this made all things possible. It also made any reduction in his vigilance – encouraged, perhaps by the night's uneventfulness – sheer folly. Even reaching Maseru wasn't going to solve more than the immediate problem, but at least it'd be a leap back into a frying pan that – with any luck – had only just begun to heat up.

These were now the problems they had to face: the inevitable encounter with Louis Fouché at the airport; and the transmission of their reports under conditions of intensified hazard.

A crow began to caw somewhere overhead.

Motseki motioned Buchanan to stay where he was – Nancy's head was still in contact – and moved as stealthily as a lean black cat over them both.

He was gone for only a few seconds, but in that time Nancy awoke, stretched, and sat up. A pattern of pebbles had been pressed into her right cheek, giving her what looked like tribal markings, and her eyes were puffy.

'It's okay,' Motseki said, crawling back in again. 'Basotho; going down the path for Siwewe. The boys still watch by the plane and all is quiet.'

'I'd like you to take another look,' Buchanan asked him. 'Give it a minute though.'

'Yes, chief. Then do we go down?'

'I don't know,' Nancy demurred. 'Wouldn't that be a bit mean? Maybe Doc's just gotten off to sleep now the sun's up, and we're going to do enough to mess his day, bringing the fuzz in. What time will the patients start arriving, Motseki?'

He looked at the sun which had just hooked one bright finger over the horizon and was drawing itself up rapidly.

'Maybe one hour, maybe a little bit more. They will be waiting by seven.'

'Then, hell, what difference to us? Anyway, won't we be able to tell when they're up?'

'Matilda will make smoke with the fire, and the Doctor will go through for his shaving water.'

'Okay, Buchanan?'

'Oh aye. But first –'

Motseki wriggled out again and was away a full minute. Then he backed in with a grin.

'The watch boys sleep now, too,' he said. 'The Basotho have gone down into the valley – right out of sight. They head for the river.'

'Grand, then we await Matilda's smoke signal,' Buchanan said, getting up on his knees to search for his Texans in his trouser pockets.

They each took one and smoked in companionable silence, watching the sky brighten quickly. It was going to be another scorcher.

The rifle lay muted between them, like an alarmist decently covered in shame.

'What the hell are we doing sitting here?' Buchanan asked suddenly. 'There's nothing to stop us going outside and warming ourselves up a bit. The dew's gone.'

'Sure – only would anyone mind if I first did the lady-like thing and went out by myself?' Nancy muttered, slipping over his legs. 'In another minute I'll –'

'Why, Miss Kitson!'

'Explode,' she added primly, making a face to show he had a filthy mind.

And so, in that context, the first violent blast from outside the cave should have been apt and rather funny.

Light travels faster than sound. Buchanan saw the front of the mission house lift up and out in a glitter of glass, before the bang sent its echo to chase the first, still clattering around the peaks.

The thatch blazed up and there was a further explosion, followed by gun shots.

Motseki opened his mouth to shout in horror – patients were stumbling out of the hospital huts and pitching forward.

Buchanan punched hard with his elbow, knocking the wind from him.

'They just *couldn't* . . .' Nancy gasped.

'They? Christ, woman, it's the bloody terrorists! Look! Black hoods!'

He left her to pick out the darting figures in the smoke, and dived back into the cave for the rifle. He'd taken it almost reluctantly and, like a bloody fool, had brought only a single clip with him, enough for the commando but hardly –

'I'm coming!'

'The hell you are! Stick with Motseki!'

Then Buchanan began a low sprint along the mountainside, heading for a dry water-course that would provide him with the quickest way down. As he ran, the surgery and dispensary blew

139

outwards and the thatch collapsed back into them, shooting up flames as high as the wind pump.

He actually saw Matilda go down with a child in her arms, and the hut behind her burst back into rocks.

He heard the horses screaming in the blazing stable.

He took his first lungful of the stench of destruction and sobbed.

Cursed, swore.

Threw himself into the *donga* and went down it scrambling, jumping, slithering and falling, ripping himself on aloes and thorn scrub, grazing and bloodying himself, noticing nothing in his desperate bid to bring the rifle within certain range.

Because he was going to *kill*.

For once, something was just as simple as that.

The *donga* narrowed, and the grass above almost closed over it, giving just the cover he needed – but he didn't really take this in. He just kept on plunging down, taking miscalculated turns on his shoulder and using the rebound to hurl him into the next zigzag. Pebbles showered past under his feet, and small stones bounced with them, making each step more treacherous and twice sending him tumbling. But each time he struggled up, twisted the rifle sling around his wrist again, and forged on.

Suddenly the gully ended above a dry streambed and Buchanan leapt his own height to land on the other side of it. He thudded down on his knees and tore his cheek on the rifle breech. His lungs heaving, he straightened up.

A blur of grey earth and roots.

The mission in sharp, awful detail, less than three hundred yards away.

Another grenade burst inside the house – which already could have nothing left alive in it.

Three figures in black hoods ducked around a corner and became obscured for a moment by a piece of remaining wall.

The bolt worked smoothly. The sights reconciled and wavered at the point where the three figures would reappear.

He took a deep, steadying breath.

Just then a clumsy flight of rock, dislodged by his descent and having gathered ponderous momentum, crossed the streambed and felled him from behind.

Buchanan lay sprawled, partly-conscious. It had not been much of a blow, but it had certainly stunned him. The after-effects of the plane crash couldn't have helped.

He wanted the water of a cool Highland burn to fill that dry gutter and carry him out to sea.

He wanted the noise to stop.

Very much.

It did.

Although how long this took to happen, he couldn't say. Suddenly it wasn't there any more: no screams or shrieks, no sharp crack of arms, no booms, no bangs, nothing.

The smoke was thick and turgid overhead and the stench even more horrible. He could smell man in it, and straw, and horse. Vietnam had been the same, only there it had been water buffalo.

There seemed little point in getting up.

But, after a while, when Buchanan remembered where his legs were, he pulled his feet in under him and used the exposed grass roots to lend some support.

Parts of Gotsong were still blazing fiercely, and the dispensary was producing some muffled detonations of its own. If anything moved, this was because a flame shook it, or because of the light breeze which had come to clear some of the mess away. On the back of the stable and on the side of the water tank, large white letters had been painted that read LOP.

Buchanan stooped and recovered the rifle, poked the dirt out of its muzzle with a stalk of grass, and looked up towards the cave. Neither Nancy nor Motseki was visible, and he couldn't be sure of their position. However, they must have seen it was all over, and were probably on their way down. There was a lot of the mountain slope blocked out by nearby vegetation.

Buchanan tossed the rifle up on to the bank on the mission side, and scrambled after it. He was bringing his head up when he saw a movement that didn't fit the scene: a shadow that stalked confidently and smoothly.

Keeping flat, Buchanan waited and watched so intently he had to blink hard to keep his eyes from stinging.

What he saw then was a mere glimpse, but it was enough: a figure in a black hood with some sort of weapon poised to give the *coup de grâce* to the hospital victims.

'I've got you, you bastard!' Buchanan hissed, clenching his hands to halt their tremble. 'You're *dead*, you son-of-a-bitch!'

There was no need for him to advance any closer. Three – one – oh yards, and the wind blowing almost up the barrel. He took his time; adjusted the range setting, and found a white stone to chalk up the foresight.

Then he spread his legs in the classical position, lifted the rifle, nicely balanced between his hands, and curled a light touch on the trigger.

The white spot took its place in the black notch of the backsight, and they moved across.

There were two main ways of killing: quickly and slowly. Buchanan had the choice.

Not that, under these conditions, there was much in it.

'Slowly,' he said: dying was what distressed men, not instant oblivion.

The hooded killer had still not fired a shot. He moved strangely hunched, with his weapon held high, dark and glinting. He had a good, broad stomach.

If he died slowly, he'd have time, perhaps, to repent, and so there were sound theological and charitable arguments in favour of a bullet in the belly, rather than in the neck.

This was getting a bit sick.

Buchanan squeezed the trigger.

And shot the man carefully between the ears.

The hood bulged.

Buchanan slapped at the bolt, pumping in a fresh round for the first bastard to pop his head up.

Only the dead man moved. The head dropped forward, the knees gave, and then the whole lot sank face down into a smouldering corner of the second hospital hut.

A small cloud of ash arose, and was whisked away by the breeze.

But Buchanan wasn't taking chances. He remained motion-less until he heard a heavy, stumbling tread behind him and swung his barrel round.

Nancy was riding pick-a-back on Motseki up from the streambed.

'Jesus, you stupid –'

'Hold it,' Nancy said, slipping to the ground and standing on one foot. 'He was the only one left – we saw the others clear off. What the hell was he doing?'

'Seeing dead men didn't tell tales. We'd better look, someone may be left –'

'But what went wrong? You could have taken them all!'

'How many did you see?'

'Six,' said Motseki; his voice with a croak in it.

'I made it three,' Nancy contradicted, 'but the smoke was all whirling around and –'

'I must go and look,' Motseki said. 'Just maybe ...'

'Sure, and thanks for the ride.'

Nancy took Buchanan's hand without any of her usual non-sense, and leaned her weight on him.

'LOP, for Chrissake?'

'The nearest I can get off-hand is the League of the Poor – a Communist organization started here in Lesotho a long time ago. Before the war.'

'But this?' she asked, as she might question the reason for a road accident.

Buchanan's own defence mechanism had taken over as well, assisted by the feeling of total unreality the aftermath had brought with it.

'What it looks like,' Buchanan said.

'That is overkill! I mean there was no need ...'

'An act of war.'

'Huh?'

'An overt act of war; an undeniable, obvious, total act of commitment. With the time and place being chosen for maxi mum impact on a group of officials known to be arriving here. Nobody's found a way of securing a waveband.'

'Jesus! A publicity stunt? But why now? What's precipitated this all-out, crazy –'

143

'For God's sake, sit,' Buchanan said, seeing her wince with pain.

'You're a real gentleman,' she sighed wearily, pulling him down beside her. 'So, the terrorists are opportunists. They want to come to the crunch. But how come they're strong enough? If the Nats caught them in the bud, it stands to reason –'

'Oh aye, and that's just what must have happened. Caught them in the bud, but got caught doing it. LOP's only hope was to take the initiative before Big Brother could organize. Suicidal, but look what they do on jumbo jets.'

'That I don't argue with. But.'

Cartridges exploded in the embers, making them turn sharply. Motseki had moved on from the house. He had a hand cupped behind an ear in a pathetic gesture of hope. Yet all he could hear with it, Buchanan felt sure, was the spit and crackle of fire, and the cawing of the gathering crows.

'Yeah, this is what I've been trying for,' Nancy said, clearing her throat, 'why hit Gotsong? Convents, mission stations are usually the first to get it, but Doc gave them their medicine straight. They, they . . .'

'Loved him? Pure and simple? Certainly! Then he was a dangerous man to have putting pressure the other side. They'll think of stories – like they've done before: he was experimenting, filling them with sterilizers. You know –'

'Where's the plane? *The plane?*'

'Easy, it's only just half-six.'

'Half-six?' Nancy repeated, and laughed like someone found drinking before breakfast. 'D'you think that's what has just struck Motseki as so goddam energy-making?'

Buchanan looked round. Motseki was storming towards them, his deep-set eyes bright with a terrible glare, and his mouth working without finding words.

The Basotho halted in front of them, grabbed them as they got up in alarm and screamed in their faces: 'You bloody pigs, come!'

Buchanan knocked the grasping hand aside, but did nothing else.

'You come and you see!' raged Motseki. 'You see!'

'Cool it,' Buchanan ordered.

144

'Motseki, what's the trouble? Fine, we'll come – you show us.'

The man hugged himself, weeping and snorting, fighting for control. Then he straightened up and turned on his heel.

He stopped first outside the house and pointed out a charred hand clutching Cousteau's pocket watch. It also wore his wedding ring.

He stopped next beside a pregnant woman who'd given birth posthumously, to no avail. Twins.

He swept his hand around what still stood of the walls of the first hospital hut. Brain still adhered to them, but weightier jams had left a smear and fallen to plop holes in the soft ash of the thatch.

'The *Anatomy*,' murmured Buchanan.

'Look, I can't –' Nancy started to say.

'Look, you bloody look!' Motseki spluttered, stumbling over to the second hut and grabbing the dead L O P man by the heels.

Although the body must have weighed close on two hundred pounds, Motseki jerked it clear over the rubble and right to where Buchanan and Nancy had halted. Then he kicked it savagely over on to its back, and the burned fragments of hood fell away.

'What colour?' rasped Motseki, shaking again.

Crimson and black, mostly. Pink where the bone was exposed by grilling.

But the Basotho's anguished demand was rhetorical rather than literal. For notwithstanding what else Pik Oeloefse might have been during his life time, he'd always regarded himself as a white man.

And this still somehow showed.

It was a dumbfounding discovery. The 16mm camera lying on the ground a few yards away did little to mitigate it. An age seemed to pass before Buchanan looked up at Nancy and said: 'Somebody must be holding his horse for him.'

'But this means they can't be Vorster's –'

'Not now! Hop it to the stream, both of you!'

The sharpness of his tone was like a slap across Motseki's cheek. The man sobered instantly and, grabbing up Nancy in

145

his long arms, loped off through the carnage. Buchanan crouched behind a remaining section of the hut wall, ready to give covering fire, and saw them drop to safety.

Another cartridge exploded in the ruins of the house, making him jump.

'Thank Christ for that,' he muttered, very aware now how these random bangs must have made his own shot sound unremarkable to any hidden listeners.

Unsighted listeners, Buchanan corrected himself, and this led him back to his first thought about horses: only trained animals could have tolerated being close to explosions as loud as the ones he'd heard. But if an untrained horse was placed a reasonable distance away, and below the level of the blast, with any luck, it'd mistake it for thunder.

Then instinct took over, and Buchanan moved with as little conscious thought as a jungle cat.

The point to head for was where the path to Siwewe dipped down to the river – the same path as had been taken by the supposed party of Basotho soon after dawn. He doubled low across to the wreckage of the plane, noticing in passing that the two lads on watch had had their throats cut, and threw himself flat to crawl the last twenty yards through the heather.

As he approached the edge of the drop, he angled slightly to the right to get his head in behind a pile of loose rock. Very cautiously, with his finger ready on the trigger, he looked around the rock and down.

And there, within fifty yards of him, Johnny Tagg was standing in a hollow, holding the reins of a black mare and a grey gelding. Tagg was also wearing a hood and dark gloves, but his distinctive physique was unmistakable. Moreover he had hooked the bottom of his hood over his nose to allow himself to smoke. He was watching the path, and seemed quite unconcerned.

So Buchanan began to note detail. There were obvious signs that at least another two horses had waited there, but a work party of dung beetles had already made sufficient inroads on the bounty to suggest that Tagg must have been alone some time. Then again, the man's boots were too clean to have trodden the mess around Gotsong, and so the conclusion was he'd ventured no further than where he stood. Probably he and Oeloefse had originally been left holding the horses, while the three Steyns made the raid – Willem with his homemade bombs; Dirk and Wolraad with their firearms.

Tagg glanced across to where Buchanan was hiding.

Buchanan froze.

Then Tagg looked to see what his watch said.

And Buchanan relaxed. The pity was that this time he oughtn't to kill if he could help it. Although, just for the sake of puerile satisfaction, he did allow his sights to dwell a moment on that bloody silly moustache.

Buchanan stood up.

The half-raised hood robbed him of very little pleasure when Tagg turned again and caught sight of him. The jaw slacked, closed and the lower lip quivered. The eye-holes went practically all white.

'Hold it right there, Johnny,' Buchanan said, and started down towards him.

'Hey, you guys!' Tagg called out ingeniously, in a very shrill voice.

'They've buggered off,' said Buchanan, keeping the rifle muzzle trained for a shot from the hip. 'So you just do what you're told, and that's to keep quite still.'

'Look, I warn you!'

'Oh aye?'

'Pik's here! Pik'll –'

'Pik'll do sod all, Johnny. I killed him.'

If that didn't put any sense into Tagg, at least it seemed to slow down his thinking. He stood rooted to the spot, doing his ventriloquist's doll act, while the distance between them was swiftly closed.

Then, just as Buchanan reached the flat of the hollow, Tagg made his break. He dropped the gelding's reins, barged it with his shoulder and tried to leap on the mare.

None of this held much promise, but the sudden movement startled an already very jittery horse to some effect: the gelding reared up, thudded down and fled the scene, forcing Buchanan to jump awkwardly to one side. For an instant his view of Tagg was blocked, and in that instant Tagg was mounted and off.

'Johnny!' Buchanan roared, bringing up the rifle.

But Tagg stuck his heels in and crouched low in the saddle.

Hating to do it, Buchanan squeezed off a round and removed the top of the mare's skull. The animal took another three flying strides on spinal reflex, snapped in the middle, and crashed down. Johnny Tagg gave a shriek and went headlong into an aloe clump.

Where he made other noises until Buchanan could catch up. Tagg's hood twisted round, blinding him, and making it impossible for him to know where to point the revolver he was brandishing.

Buchanan knocked it from his grasp with a blow of the rifle butt.

'Jesus! That hurt!'

Tagg should never have said that. It blew a vault open in Buchanan's mind, and this released everything he'd seen and heard and suppressed in the last half-hour.

'*Hurt?*' Buchanan repeated, ripping off Tagg's hood so savagely some scalp came with it. 'Hurt?'

He yanked Tagg up off the ground, smacked him about, and broke the man's thumbs when he tried to resist. Then he spun Tagg round in a daze of pain, jabbed the rifle into him and ordered him to run.

Tagg stumbled forward, gasping, and blanched with shock.

'What the hell have you done to him?' Nancy asked, as Buchanan helped her out of the streambed, and she saw Tagg standing tied to the windpump.

'Took a tumble off his gee-gee,' Buchanan replied. 'Then I've been showing him the sights – rubbing his nose in it, as you might say.'

That was exactly how it looked. Tagg's face was a bloody, ash-covered mess.

'Cool it,' Nancy said, keeping her hold on Buchanan's wrist. 'Cool it, for Chrissake! You're scaring me.'

Buchanan shook free, but made an effort to regain his self-control. Just for a moment, he'd come close to scaring himself, and that wasn't how wars were won.

'I've got something out of the bastard,' he said, giving

148

Motseki a hand-up. 'He and Oeloefse were the support group on this mission. Dirk and Willem have split and gone.'

'What about Wolraad?'

'That's a joke! Seems he wasn't much more welcome than we were. They got him to play cards until way past his farmer's bedtime, then he padded off for a kip and they hung about until three this morning for blast-off.'

Nancy tested her limp and Buchanan handed her the rifle to use for a support.

'One other thing,' he said, 'he's told me where the goof was made – could bloody kick myself!'

'Yes?'

'Oeloefse's sound gear. Just what a wild-life man would carry, one of those long-range directional mikes. While you and I were –'

'Oh God, then it was my fault: I got you talking and he was pointing that thing at us!'

'Aye, picking up our grunts and snuffles. But let's not go into whose fault it was, because –'

'My fault!' said Motseki bitterly. 'I saw men but I said they were Basotho!'

'Cut that crap,' Buchanan snapped. 'But if you want to help, I need you. That animal over there has decided he's said enough for one morning.'

'Ha!' exclaimed Motseki, cracking his knuckles.

'Like I said, cool it,' Nancy repeated. 'He won't take too much of that stuff before becoming no goddam use to us. Let me try.'

'Motseki will save us all time,' Buchanan said confidently.

'Which is? The time, I mean?'

'Rising seven. Patients will be arriving soon, so let's get a shift on.'

They went over to the windpump. Tagg had his hands lashed above his head to a crossbar, and was having to rise slightly on his toes every time he breathed in. He trembled with stress and exertion, and stank noticeably, very sweetly, but his eyes were defiant.

'Be sensible and help us, Mr Tagg,' said Nancy.

'You sodding whore! You Yankified –'

Nancy had her limits too. She hit Tagg across the shins with the rifle. His short, sagging body heaved up, twisted, and slumped. He whimpered.

'The facts, Johnny – the facts and we want them fast!' Buchanan said. 'Come on Motseki, it's your bloody turn!'

'You – you'd put a *kaffir* on to me?'

'Don't be ridiculous, Johnny. You of all people couldn't really mind Reuben doing my dirty work for me? I mean that's all they've ever been good for, isn't it?'

'*Hau*, and me very good torture boy!' Motseki complained indignantly, entering into the spirit of things with his salesman's flair for empathy.

'You could have hurt his feelings,' Nancy said.

Tagg looked from one face to another. His interrogators were all smiling at him. This wasn't intended to seem very real and it didn't. For a moment, he appeared to waver and then his eyes set hard. The man was a nutcase after all.

'Go on, hit me, *kaffir*!' he snarled. 'See what difference that makes! No *kaffir*'s ever made me –'

'Oops, no, don't hit him,' Buchanan said quickly, blocking the fist.

'Man, what is this?' Motseki asked.

'Just try a quick spit in his face.'

'*What?*' Tagg shouted, the manic gleam disappearing.

'And call him some names, if you like,' Buchanan added. 'I'm sure you'd rather not touch something like that.'

Motseki grasped the point of this and hooted with delight. He sucked in his cheeks and began accumulating saliva, waggling his eyebrows enthusiastically.

Tagg raved and struggled.

By sheer chance, he happened to duck right into Motseki's first, rather poorly aimed, attempt. And then, without the need for any further encouragement, he talked after all.

Chapter Eleven

There was an awful simplicity about the tale Tagg told. This gave it the weight of truth, but also underlined the horror implicit in each bragged disclosure, so plainly stated.

The scheme had been, of course, Tagg's scheme.

The objective had been the restoration of the white man's proper distrust of the black sub-species surrounding him. It would put a stop to Communist-inspired ideas such as détente, and allay not only anxieties with regard to racial purity, but also those concerning civilization's very survival on the continent.

That such an objective could be realized – taking into account the limited resources and manpower available – had become apparent during a long weekend spent together on the Steyn farm. And by the Sunday night, the three self-appointed saviours had decided that their modified plan should fall into four main phases.

The first phase involved masquerading as terrorists before the camera, and killing at least six Basotho in a manner which would be convincing to the eye – by blowing away parts of the head, for instance. In the event, they had killed seven.

The second phase, which partly overlapped, was the preparation of the photographs, each of which would carry a caption that revealed the exact location of the bodies, as an aid to their official recovery. This preparation was done *in situ*, as smuggling them to and fro across the border, under the nose of BOSS, had been considered too hazardous. The photographs were to be posted in Maseru, addressed to various aid agencies overseas, such as Oxfam, with impassioned pleas they should be given at once to the free press. The packages, sent by air mail, would also contain information concerning terrorist activity in the Maluti – and the claim that the suppression of this news was being done at the cost of hundreds of lives. Other photographs

151

were to be placed in pairs in ordinary envelopes and posted to South African and Rhodesian journals where, even if promptly banned from publication, they would have their effect.

The third phase involved a major attack on a major target, preferably a large mission station with a school hostel attached. Improvised handgrenades, modelled on those pictured in a book on the Rivonia Terrorist Trial in Johannesburg, were to be used. An act of overt aggression of this magnitude would be virtually impossible for the authorities to keep secret and, by using a 16mm camera, television coverage overseas would be fully exploited. Due to unforeseen circumstances, the target chosen for this phase had become Gotsong for the sake of expedience; or, as Tagg put it in as many words, to kill three birds with one stone.

The fourth phase was to have begun later that morning, when a light aircraft would have picked up the courier – Tagg himself – and taken him to Maseru. There he would have posted the paper bombshells, and then submitted himself to a Customs examination. As the 16mm film he carried was still in the camera, this would not have involved any risk. Tagg would then have flown to Johannesburg, and from there to London to assist the media response.

The timing of all this was crucial, as the full impact of the public outcry had been intended to coincide with a week-long Afrikaner festival that was being opened by the Prime Minister, Mr B. J. Vorster, the following day – Sunday.

Tomorrow, in fact.

'Hitting them at their weakest moment,' murmured Buchanan, leaving one of his prisoner's arms free, after retying the other at waist level.

He and Tagg were alone at the foot of the windpump; Nancy and Motseki had gone off to deal with the patients who'd begun to arrive. The breeze had dropped, the air was still and close, eerie with the sounds of lament, and Gotsong no more real than what it had become: a film set between takes. The Basotho would want pictures, too, if for very different reasons.

'Well, you know the *boets*,' Tagg said, smiling to show he understood any prejudice on Buchanan's part. 'Afrikaners are an emotional lot.'

'Oh aye. I can imagine them getting quite worked up when –'

'But, Christ, don't you see it was better it happened this way!'

'Hmm?'

'Better the people should get their scare from something that *wasn't* real! At least it gives them a chance to change their minds, to start thinking sense again about what's right for their children. It would only be a matter of time before genuine terrorists started here, and then there might not be the same chance, don't you see?'

'Jesus.'

'Oi, you mustn't start getting the wrong idea. Me and the boys aren't sadists, or whatever you call it – there wasn't any suffering, that I can promise. Didn't know what hit them! Man, you've had experience with coons, you've seen how slow they are. I mean, it was in our own interests to get a shift on, because don't think there weren't any risks inv –'

'Jesus!'

'No, listen: try and get it in perspective. Aren't we all fighting the same thing, the Basutes included? Is this too much for them to pay? Be honest! What's this against what could happen? That's how I see it personally. They don't want their race turning into a hotch-potch any more than you and me. Am I right? Ask any coon and he'll tell you. Ask him if he really wants to marry your daughter – see what he says!'

'Aye, and you think this'll save Rhodesia?'

'Of course! That's why I'm explaining, asking you to be reasonable. We mustn't let Vorster have any options, he's not so strong as he thinks. When the people realize –'

'And Dirk? What's his –'

'Dirk? His beliefs. And they killed his kiddie up on the border – didn't you know that? The Commies? His youngest it was. Then what happens? Vorster pulls the police back off the border and says Smithy better start talking nicely to these bloody murderers! What was Dirk to think? That his blood sacrifice had been for nothing? How would you feel? And then he reads they're planning in Cape Town to find room for the *boers* from Rhodesia – there's thirty thousand of them, remember. It was in the papers.'

Tagg paused as a spasm in his arm took his breath away. And then he gabbled on: 'It was obvious, wasn't it? The sell-out was

153

on its way. Vorster was reckoning that being big pals now with these tinpot nigger states was going to save his bacon, but he's been up in the clouds too long, hey? Has gone bloody soft! Just look around you and you can see it in the kaffirs' faces, the way they are beginning to laugh. Strength, that's what they respect! But every time you see Vorster in the paper, he's slooping up to some bloody Sambo. Dirk didn't understand what had happened to him, to Vorster, but Pik –'

'You're a wee dafty, Johnny. The harder the line gets down here, the better the Commies like it. Gives them something to plant their seeds in. Vorster's no –'

'What do you know? Hey? What's your real interest? This isn't your country, this is *my* country – like Dirk says, the only one we've got. Hell, where else do they understand this lingo? You tell me that!'

'In Patagonia – there's an Afrikaner community left over from the Boer War, ex-prisoners.'

'Oh, very clever! But I'm talking about us who love this country. Here, the one we're standing on! *Love* – do you understand what that means?'

'So this was done for love then, was it?'

'Naturally, what else would make men chance their necks like this? It wasn't money, my friend! It –'

'He's talking too much,' Nancy cut in, limping up at that moment. 'I think we ought to find out why.'

She was right. Buchanan realized he'd become caught up in the lunacy of the situation. Tagg's outline of the conspiracy had been delivered in a dull, sighing monotone; whereas now he was speaking, no less truthfully perhaps, but with forced vigour, piling sentence on sentence.

'Look,' said Tagg, urgently. 'I was just going to explain to our friend here that we didn't mean any harm in the sense –'

'He's stalling,' Nancy observed coldly.

'Oi! Why should I –'

But Tagg left it there, because Buchanan and Nancy had turned their backs on him and walked away.

'This is blowing our minds,' she said. 'I keep saying to myself: what *is* this we're in? Y'know?'

'I'd completely lost track –'

'That's a point,' Nancy muttered, catching his left wrist and looking at the watch strapped to it. 'Seven-forty. What time do you reckon they'll be expecting Tagg and the stiff back at the ranch?'

Buchanan winced.

'A point, as you say. A bloody good one. Where's Motseki? I don't really know the distance because I went two sides of a triangle.'

They beckoned to Motseki.

'Chief?'

'Mapapeng? How far is it direct?'

'Three hours; maybe a little this side.'

Buchanan did the simple calculation.

'The cunning bugger,' he said, turning for a look at Tagg who wasn't quick enough to hide a sly, lop-sided grin – or the watch he was consulting on his free arm. 'They must have some arrangement to hit the panic button if he and Oeloefse aren't back by about ten. He's kept on spilling the beans to hold us here long enough. Wonder what time that plane was due?'

'We'll ask him, but first –'

'Can you make it in less, Motseki?'

'There is a short way along the river, just for like three miles, but it's not easy, chief.'

'You want to try? Can you get horses?'

'There are patients with horses, yes.'

'Then move it, for God's sake!'

'Too late!' Tagg jeered, as he saw Motseki hasten off. 'You'll never do it, you bastards! Don't you think I – I – you ...'

Tagg collapsed.

'You know, I don't think he's fooling,' said Nancy, 'could even be dead.'

He was.

Tagg was dead. Dead the way Stoffel had been dead. Killed by a swift-acting poison, possibly of Bushman origin, self-administered in concentrated form. His tongue was brown.

'Very Nazi, so you score ten for it,' Buchanan said.

'Sure, these boys play for keeps. Haven't you met many fanatics or something?'

*

155

But it wasn't as straightforward as that. Like most suicides, Tagg hadn't just wanted out. It wasn't simply the fate that awaited him after the arrival of the police plane which had driven him to take that last, fatal step. Like most suicides, Tagg had used his death as a way of getting something of his own back.

For without Tagg, alive and talking, their only proof of the conspiracy had literally died on them. And nor was there any longer a way of finding out what to expect at Mapapeng.

The Halls of Hell had to be ringing with hollow laughter.

Nancy, who'd moved a little way from the windpump, was saying something. Buchanan broke off his blank stare and looked at her.

'– and he wouldn't have done this unless he thought their plan still had a chance.'

'Too right, it has! The bloody irony of it, woman. Remember us saying on the strip at Mapapeng what would happen if any of this leaked out? And here the buggers were, making damn sure it would!'

'Although I don't rightly see how we're going to stop them,' she said, glancing about her. 'I mean, how the hell do you *hide* this lot?'

'You'll think of a way.'

'Oh really?'

'Aye, I've decided. The ride's our one bloody hope. Even if the planes get here earlier than we expect, they won't be any good to us. Quite the opposite: the moment one pitches up at Mapapeng, they'll see who's aboard and we'll be right in the nasties. The Steyns will destroy the evidence – and then they could go one better and take a hostage to get them out.'

'Who?'

'Koos Brandsma.'

'God, I'd forgotten him!'

'All depends on the warning they get. Your job'll be to keep those planes away – and sort this lot out.'

'Those cops will go bananas.'

'Certainly. Send them on a wild goose down to Siwewe if you can't hold the situation, but for Christ's sake keep them until after ten. That's if they are early.'

156

'You're going to have to ride some.'

'Oh aye.'

'I don't like the shape you're in.'

'Have you ever?' Buchanan said, finding a smile for her.

And Motseki rode up on a sway-backed beast with a wicked eye, leading the grey gelding.

'Some boys caught this one,' he explained, his face dull with a new pain. 'All this was my fault, chief. I saw this very same horse when I looked out of the cave –'

'I said cut that crap,' Buchanan sighed, beginning immediately to lengthen its stirrup leathers. 'Maybe tomorrow there'll be a who's-to-blame party and you can come. Meantime, I need you. Can you use a rifle?'

'The gun? No, I am sorry, there has never been opportunity to learn.'

'Well, now's not the moment, so we'll leave it with Miss Kitson.'

'Gee, thanks. But what about you?'

'I've got Tagg's thirty-eight.'

'I see, lots of close work. And you're hoping to take prisoners, of course?'

'Naturally.'

'I've had an idea.'

'Oh aye?'

'We can fake it the plane hit the mission, just dump the wreck there on top and –'

'That's brilliant.'

'It is?'

Most farewells had a phony sound to them. But the flippancy which had entered their exchange made Buchanan glance keenly at Nancy. Her eyes met this glance and for a long moment they looked into each other.

'Some other time?' he said, hamming it.

'Sure,' she answered, 'some other place. Now get your ass out of here, Buchanan – it's all on you, baby.'

'Tchaaaaa!' yelled Motseki, and, with a jerk, they were off.

The bob of the pink beret ahead told Buchanan that they'd slowed to a trot. The gelding had been on automatic for a good

157

part of the way along the valley, while Buchanan tried to arrange his thoughts. But they bounced about inside his head like alphabet blocks in a bucket, and his efforts came to nothing. Not that this really mattered: now that he knew what the Mapapeng commando had done, he could guess what it might try to do – and the rest would have to be ad-libbed on the spot.

'We must swim this river over by that big rock,' Motseki called back, reining in. 'The ferry is a long way round where there's no white water.'

'Oh aye, after you then.'

'We're doing all right, chief?'

'Got an hour in hand.'

'That's not so good. Come, let us go more quickly.'

They covered the rest of the distance at a canter, and pulled up on a small beach of shale-like flakes. The horses, which always swam the rivers, ferry or no ferry, started to kick up a fuss, shying from the water and taking bites out of their bits.

Motseki jumped down, took off his boots and rolled his blanket up, secured them to the pommel rings, and then drove his animal into the current with a pelting of small stones. As it plunged in out of its depth, he dived and caught it by the tail, shouting encouragement. Buchanan, who'd tried this Basotho technique once before and had been kicked in the stomach, waded in and swam sidestroke downstream of the gelding which, like all of its kind, was now only concerned it wouldn't get left behind. They gained the far bank and struggled up through the reeds.

'God, that feels grand,' said Buchanan, as he recovered the gelding's reins from Motseki. 'Didn't think of it except as a bloody obstacle.'

'Cool, man,' laughed Motseki, 'real cool.'

That it had been. But the fast mountain flow had also sluiced away most of the dust and ash, making Buchanan realize just how clammy and uncomfortable he had been. Even his mind felt rinsed out and ready for what came next – with the usual reservations. While his toes relished the squelch in his boots, which he hadn't bothered to remove, and made him loath to mount up again.

But Motseki had already begun a groin-battering ascent

straight up the steep slope, and the countdown had started in earnest.

In less than an hour, they had to be at Mapapeng. Sixty-five minutes later, Buchanan was sure a mistake had been made. They were too high. The surrounding peaks were familiar but not the ones he had seen, standing out there beside Mapapeng's footlights.

As this conviction had grown in him, he'd allowed the gelding to drop back. The animal was blown and almost at the point of having the staggers. It had hardly a half-mile left in it. And, from the look of it, Motseki's swayback was no better, as it scrambled at an angle across the slope ahead.

His guide turned in the saddle and urged him on with a wave. Sixty-six minutes; the whole thing was a farce.

Buchanan dismounted and began to lead the gelding, jog-trotting along, holding its head in tight at his side. A sudden fury nipped his voice box, making his shout to Motseki a silly squeak.

'Christ, pull your bloody self together!' Buchanan said aloud. And then tried again: 'Hold it! Hold it! We're –'

Motseki signalled back frantically as Buchanan's yell echoed around them.

The reason for this became immediately plain when Buchanan reached his side. The long curve of the slope had deceived him into thinking it went on and over the other side. It didn't: it ended abruptly to drop away down to the back of the trading post.

Mapapeng! From a very different, far better angle.

'And there the bastards are,' Buchanan said softly, pointing with the revolver which had somehow come into his hand. 'Wolraad's walking with Koos into the store, and Willem's in the garden with the field glasses. Can you see anyone else?'

'There's a Basotho in the huts.'

'I see him. He's cleaning. But where the hell's Dirk? He looks like the other one we saw, walking with the old man.'

'There,' said Motseki, indicating that Buchanan should try farther to the right of the poplars. 'There's a tall one in the garden also.'

'My friend, you're a bloody wonder. And it seems we're just

159

in the nick of time. Can you get rid of the horses? See they don't pop up here?'

Motseki grunted and slipped away.

Buchanan lay flat and looked down. How abstract the scene below seemed suddenly. Those puny little figures could hold no possible threat to man or beast. And, if one wished, the buildings could be rearranged quite simply with a finger and thumb.

He shook his head and tried again.

Koos and Wolraad were now inside the store on his left. The hitching yard was fairly crowded with customers and their horses. A wide gap of nothing, and then Willem and Dirk in the garden of the house, just in front of the guest huts, talking together.

That gap was a gift. It allowed for a very simple strategy that was bound to work.

As Motseki landed in the grass beside him, Buchanan said: 'Mind lending me a hand with a diversion?'

'Anything you say, brother.'

'Then I want you down in that hitching yard, kicking up one hell of a fuss. If possible, right outside the entrance to the trader's office. Can you do that?'

Motseki nibbled the brim of his beret, which he'd wisely removed on account of its bright, unnatural colour, and then grinned.

'Consider it done,' he said.

'But you can be quick about it?'

'Yeah, man. Like a fork of lightning!'

'You'll what?'

'Make a pee on the produce.'

Both men laughed at that, and Buchanan knew it was now right to make their move. But first he had to give Motseki a quick fill-in.

'So you're going left – there's a goat path – and I'll try for a way down on the right. Must be one because the short-assed bastard down there arrived at this place from the back. I'm after the two on the grass. I'll get down as far as I can and wait where the poplars shield me until you start the fuss. That'll keep the ones in the store busy, and those two on the lawn'll be looking across. Keep it going as long as you can even when you see

160

me whip across. I've got to bag the other bugger, too. Okay?'

'I read you.'

'Fine.'

They lay there a moment or two longer.

Then, without another word, rolled over, got to their feet and went their separate ways.

Buchanan dropped behind the slope so he could move upright to where a downward path might conceivably begin. But the ground was uneven, and he had to abandon an attempt to sprint the distance for fear of twisting an ankle. The smallest mishap could now decide far more than his own fate, and he had to remember this.

'Oh balls,' he muttered, and broke out of his trot.

Running low, he reached the far side of the slope and found no trace of a path. He doubled back a little way, and took a look over the edge. By chance, he had happened on the very spot where the poplars would obstruct his descent for much of the climb. Pleased by the time saved, he started downwards, keeping an eye open for any sign of Motseki's progress.

The slope wasn't as steep as it'd been behind the gum trees where the crowd had gathered. Erosion had cut away much of the top soil, leaving ledges of rock which served as rough steps, with only the occasional gap in between. Buchanan took them sideways, leading with his right leg, so he faced the trading store and the goat path, and could keep a check on the guest huts at the same time.

Dirk and Willem were still in the garden, still using the glasses to search the conventional approaches for their missing comrades.

Then Buchanan saw Motseki rise out of a dip in the goat path, and start on his last two hundred yards or so to the hitching yard.

So far, so good.

The poplars drew closer and closer, and Buchanan lost sight of the two Steyns as the leaves became more dense lower down. But the obverse would apply, and he was going to be able to move in very near to them without any likelihood of being seen. Neither man had shown any indication of being about to leave the lawn.

161

A basking snake provided a tense moment.

Buchanan, promising treats to his gods, carried on, edging down past a large outcrop of black rock. But he barely noticed it, being too intent on reaching the bottom before Motseki did his thing on the store verandah.

Then Solomon presented a problem, by coming out of the kitchen to sun himself.

There was nothing for it but to freeze and wait.

Buchanan was so close to the back of the house he could read the detergent packets in the window above Solomon's head – and see the bees crowding the entrances to the hives. He moved his head very cautiously and, out of the corner of his right eye, caught a glimpse of two pairs of legs still standing on the lawn – the top halves were cut off by the lowest foliage on the trees. He looked back at Solomon; the old devil was still on his up-turned orange box, with its comfortable cushion of folded meal sacks.

Any second ...

Solomon stood up and tugged at a string of onions hanging from the rafters. He got a large one in his hand, inspected it at length for quality, and then went back inside.

As quickly as he could, Buchanan slipped down the last few feet until he was a bound away from landing in the backyard, and hidden by a bush that had grown out of something once thrown into the rubbish pit.

Dirk and Willem were in full view between the guest huts on his right, and he could hear loud, argumentative words being spoken.

To be sure, their deadline must have long since come and gone. They'd hung on in hope, most probably finding good reasons for a delay, but now they had been forced to accept something had gone seriously wrong. A hell of a moment for them – but nothing to what Buchanan had in mind. The moment they were distracted by the uproar, he'd be over the hedge, round the huts and –

There it was! Motseki had gone into action.

Dirk snatched the binoculars from Willem and raised them to his eyes. Willem went up on tiptoe, straining to make out what was going on.

Buchanan rose to his feet and poised himself for the jump.

'Woe to the Children of Israel!' cried out a deep voice behind him.

That was Buchanan's first mistake: he looked round and saw Manfred climbing the outcrop of black rock, and shaking his staff in the direction of the hitching yard.

And when he turned back to the Steyns, they had already seen him. There was, however, the natural hesitation of men who think they see a ghost.

Buchanan hurled himself over the hedge and dived behind the trunk of the nearest poplar.

'Woe!' wailed Manfred from the slope above.

'You stupid –' Buchanan whispered, realizing the maniac must have been resting unnoticed in the shade of the rocks.

The shots began from the guest hut window. Solomon charged out of his kitchen and charged back in again, slamming the door. A cat streaked across the path. A bullet whimpered off the tree above Buchanan's head.

What concerned him more was the fact only one gun was firing and he wondered where Dirk had got himself to – or perhaps Willem, which ever way round it was.

The final round in the magazine seemed as though it would never be fired. Then came the pause.

Buchanan brought his head up, saw nobody, took aim at the hut window – which was ajar on its catch – and ducked down again, leaving only his revolver and his hand exposed.

As the next shot was fired, he fired. There was a tinkle of glass and a scream. A splinter very often did what a bullet travelling in a straight line couldn't.

He fired again.

Then rolled away out of line of the window, jumped up and sprinted for cover behind a toppled wheelbarrow. He was now about twenty yards from the side of the hut and commanding both apertures although, because they were at right angles to him, he wasn't able to see into them. A rifle barrel poked out of the window on the left. It was withdrawn and reappeared seconds later through the doorway on the right.

The bastard was trapped and he knew it.

'Dirk!' Willem shouted from the hut. 'Dirk, man!'

Undoubtedly he found the answering silence as unnerving as Buchanan did.

'*Dirk!*'

A moment later Willem dived from the hut and threw himself flat. Then he sprang up, caught sight of Buchanan, and went down again, firing wildly and much too high. It was like watching a homicidal sea lion do the flops.

The .38 slug smashed Willem's right wrist as it worked the bolt. This was a safe shot, as the wooden butt ensured the thing would travel no further.

Buchanan rushed the wall of the hut, took a quick look and made it safely to the one nearer the house. Then he took off for the poplar trees again, with a very unpleasant suspicion he'd guessed where Dirk had got himself to. Even as he did so, a flash of shirt told him he was right – and a split second too late.

Dirk Steyn had got round the house and into the darkroom to destroy all incriminating evidence. The door had only just slammed shut.

The obvious response was a couple of low leg shots. But several objections to this arose immediately. Leg shots were all very well when there was a surgeon handy to deal with arterial bleeding – that was one of them. Another was the fact that nobody could vouch for a bullet maintaining a level course through an inch of wood that was stuffed full of iron screws which might cause a fatal deflection.

Buchanan wanted Dirk Steyn alive and he wanted the photographs intact. Which certainly appeared to be a have-your-cake-and-eat-it problem until a straightforward solution presented itself.

The bolt on the darkroom door shot home as Buchanan reached the stoep. He snatched a folded meal sack from Solomon's seat, shook it out and ran back to where the three beehives stood. He tugged the mouth of the sack down over the nearest hive, upturned the lot and twisted the sack closed. He thumped the sack on the ground until he heard the hive breaking up, and then ran for the darkroom window, bouncing his load as he went. The sound the incensed insects made was a good deal louder than a buzz.

Once outside the window, Buchanan took the neck of the

sack in both hands, swung it round like the hammer, and let go. The hive, with its combs and honey, must have weighed close on a hundred pounds, and there was some force behind it: the window frame splintered and the black curtains flapped open and closed.

True Afrikaners of pioneer stock have a campfire game, played in pairs, which is regarded as a test of manhood: they pinch small pieces from the inner thigh of their opponent, and the first to flinch concedes the round. President Paul Kruger created quite a name for himself at it.

The bees made a lethal, terrifying noise, like a spread of grenade fragments, as they exploded in fury from the sack. But, for upwards of ten seconds, there was not a sound from the man trapped in there with them. A gasp of surprise, the scrape of a match being hurriedly struck: that was all.

Then Dirk Steyn screamed. Just the once.

And burst open the door with his shoulder, to come reeling out of that hell with bees pinned to his ashen face and his hands cupped to protect his eyes. He began to run.

He ran straight past Buchanan and tripped over the casually extended foot, to go down so hard the wind was knocked from him. Buchanan hauled Dirk to his feet, manhandled him over to the rainwater tank, and heaved him into it.

Just as Koos Brandsma and young Wolraad rounded the corner and stopped dead in stunned amazement.

'Hold it right there,' Buchanan advised, drawing his revolver on them.

They gaped.

While he risked more stings by dodging on to the stoep for a moment. He had to be certain that whatever Dirk had been trying to do with that match hadn't succeeded. One quick glance through the darkroom doorway was enough to reassure him, and then he was back in the garden.

Wolraad froze in the step he'd taken.

'You try anything again and I'll blow your bloody head off,' said Buchanan, whose patience always gave a little when a crisis seemed over.

Chapter Twelve

Mountains are notorious for the way in which bad weather can descend suddenly and at any time. Although Buchanan, who was silently cursing his luck, had to admit that the first distant rumble of thunder came as no real surprise to him. The sunrise had carried an implicit warning, the morning had been abnormally hot, and he'd been marginally aware of the build-up of low, heavy cloud during his ride over with Motseki. All it meant, he told himself, was a few hours' delay before any plane could get through, and that the radio would be useless with static. As he now had the situation at Mapapeng well under control, this really made no odds.

'In there,' he said to Dirk Steyn, and motioned him into Koos's office.

The trading store, being the only place of plenty in roughly nine hundred square miles of very little, was built like a fortress, and the office – which held the safe – had thick bars over its window and three bolts on the door. It made an excellent cell.

Dirk hesitated, showing defiance again. His hands, arms and head were swollen, but he'd managed to save his eyes and they glared back steadily.

Then, with a shrug, he stepped into the office and Wolraad made to follow him.

'No, you wait where you are,' Buchanan ordered, changing his mind on a whim. 'Fine, now pull the door closed and put on the padlocks. Come on, move it!'

The young Steyn interested him. Perhaps Tagg had been telling the truth when he said the son was no part of the conspiracy, but Buchanan had an odd hunch there was more to it than that. When Koos had demanded an explanation for a world gone mad, and had been given a brief outline of events, Wolraad had reacted with what appeared to be genuinely horrified amazement. And yet he'd not sought a denial of the allegations from his father, as he should, by rights, have done. Instead he'd simply shaken his head and groaned softly, like someone who has seen a thing come to pass that he feared might happen. Nor had he said a word to anyone since then.

The last padlock snapped shut and Wolraad straightened up. Another curious thing about him was that he never seemed to look at the gun in Buchanan's hand.

Then Wolraad broke his silence to ask in his slow, uneasy English: 'I must know who you are, *meneer* – please will you tell me?'

'I've made that clear already: I'm in charge here.'

'But are you police?'

'Turn and go out the back way again.'

'Where to?'

'The house.'

Wolraad didn't move. For a moment Buchanan felt he'd made a mistake, and would be far better off locking him up, too. Then he saw that the man was preoccupied more than anything, and so tried repeating his instructions.

Wolraad lumbered forward and went out through the clerk's door, oblivious to their stares as they paused from shutting up shop. The dispersal of customers had been high on Buchanan's list of priorities, as they could so readily become an unmanageable mob if the news of the massacre reached them; but it'd all passed off smoothly enough because nobody had any reliable means, such as a watch, to tell them that closing time had come an hour earlier than usual this Saturday.

The sky was dark with bruise-coloured clouds that had sunk down over the surrounding peaks, making what landscape that remained eerily dim for just after eleven in the morning. Again the thunder rumbled, and far off, in the direction of Gotsong, sheet lightning glimmered behind the black ranges.

Buchanan and Wolraad crossed the gap to the blue gums apparently unnoticed by the few customers still in the hitching yard. The old whiplash maker ignored them completely and went on pushing the twisting stick, rheumy eyes fixed on his circle of footprints in the sand. The two men kept close to the slope and entered the back garden by way of the small gate

167

Solomon used, to find that the bees had swarmed in a small, stunted apple tree.

'Whoa there, stop on the stoep,' Buchanan said, as Wolraad was about to enter the house. 'Now go down to the end.'

He followed him to the darkroom door and saw a tartan travelling bag on the enlarger shelf.

'Get that for me,' he said.

Wolraad obeyed without demur, still rapt in his own thought, but gave Buchanan an odd look when he, too, caught the strong smell of paraffin from the bag he'd brought out. There was a broken bottle of the stuff – and a dead match – on the floor behind him.

'Your pa tried to set fire to it,' Buchanan explained.

'*Waarom?* Why?'

'You'll see. Inside, please.'

As they went into the house, Solomon peeped from his kitchen door and then slammed it again hurriedly. It was going to be a day for misunderstandings, Buchanan could see that.

It was also going to be one hell of a storm: the air had turned icy against his cheek.

The incapacitated Willem was where Buchanan had left him, stretched out on the settee in the living-room, and still making a production of being treated for his injuries by Motseki. This was typical of the man and yet, for once, fairly understandable, as Motseki had insisted that neat iodine was the only thing for bullet wounds – and there were several less drastic antiseptics available in Koos's medicine chest.

The moment Willem saw Buchanan, he spluttered abuse.

Then switched to English and said: 'Next time I kill you, you kaffir-lover bastard!'

'Oh aye?'

'I shoot you dead!'

'You couldn't hit a bull in the bum with a banjo,' said Buchanan wearily, and indicated that Wolraad should place the bag on the table.

'What you say?' snarled Willem, raising himself on his good elbow.

But Koos, hunched in wretched confusion at his side, pressed him gently down again and managed to quieten him with a

168

whisper. Then the trader sighed one of his deep, shuddering sighs, and looked across at Buchanan, making it plain without words they could never be friends again. Nor could any amount of talking ever change that.

Sad, thought Buchanan.

As the room darkened and shook in the grip of the storm.

There was a palpable shock in actually seeing the things which Tagg had described. However crude and horrible the plan might have been in its conception, and Willem had already pleaded Hobson's choice, it'd lacked little in the way of efficient execution.

Two piles of mail, recovered from the travelling bag, lay on the table top, looking totally innocuous.

The left-hand pile, which had been destined for aid agencies overseas, was made up of cheap A4 manilla envelopes stiffened by card inserts and sealed with Scotch tape. The fact that they were identical, and that the same typewriter had been employed for each block-lettered label, gave them an immediate look of junk mail. The audacity of the sticker *PHOTOS – DO NOT BEND* only made them that much more authentic in their appearance, more commonplace and even less worthy of sorting-house scrutiny. After all, once you've seen one institutional begging letter, backed up by glossies of starving kids with saucer eyes, you've seen them all. They would have been franked and tossed into the air sack with the rest of them.

The envelopes in the right-hand pile, intended for more local distribution, wouldn't have touched ground either. They were unremarkable by contrast, in their very individuality; each was a different colour, a variety of writing implements had been used, and the addresses skilfully rendered in a range of hands. But most ingenious of all was the choice of recipients: pen friend columns, children's corners, crossword puzzle contests – every one of which would have editors who actively solicited sizeable enclosures.

While the same careful preparation had gone into the photographs, captions and copy themselves.

Buchanan, eager for some diversion during the long wait, which was proving less easy to endure than he'd supposed, had opened one manilla envelope and spread out its contents.

The response was, however, disappointing. Although Wolraad hadn't been able to take his eyes off the pictures for a good ten minutes, he'd said nothing whatsoever. And Koos had refused point-blank to as much as glance at them.

During which time, Willem had passed out, and the conversation, desultory as it might well have been, had ceased altogether. Thanks largely to Motseki, who'd learned a fair bit from the late Jean Cousteau, but whose touch was still a trifle heavy.

'How are we doing?' Buchanan asked, from his chair over by the french windows.

'Easier now,' Motseki grunted, beginning to wind on the wide bandage. 'Can the master put his finger there?'

Koos obliged.

'And you, Wolraad? Anything to say?'

All that got him was a shake of the head.

'Not impressed by your uncle's boasting?'

'That's wrong of you!' Koos protested. 'Willie's a sick man, very sick! If you were sick, too, then you'd be saying foolish –'

Wolraad snapped at him in Afrikaans and there was silence again.

Motseki went on with his bandaging, overlapping each layer neatly and then slitting the end in the approved manner so he could tie it off. The finished job looked reassuringly professional, and Koos mellowed fractionally.

'Ta, boy,' he said.

'You are welcome,' grinned Motseki, getting to his feet and winking at Buchanan.

'Aye, a grand wee job.'

'A lot of blood he lost, brother.'

'He'll live. Tell you what: why not nip through to the kitchen and see if you can chat old Solomon into whistling up some tea?'

'Can do,' replied Motseki, who was somehow relishing the situation, and sauntered out with his beret tipped saucily over one eye.

The storm continued increasing in intensity, and some rain began to drip through the ceiling in one corner of the room.

This tiny sound brought Koos's head up. He arranged Willem more comfortably, drew a rug over him, and tucked it in all

170

round. He adjusted the position of the bandaged arm, and put a hand to the fevered brow. He sighed his sigh.

And then it was Wolraad's turn to sigh, but he did it quickly, impatiently.

'So it seems we must believe what you say, *meneer*,' he said to Buchanan, gathering together the set of photographs.

This brought another outburst of protest from Koos.

'*Ag nie, oupa!*' Wolraad retorted. '*Kyk!* See for yourself!'

Koos brushed the pictures aside.

'Leave him,' said Buchanan. 'It won't do any good. The funny thing is, though, that I thought you believed me from the start.'

Wolraad kept his eyes on the table.

'Didn't you?'

'I – I must fetch another blanket,' said Koos, getting up suddenly, very agitated. 'I'll fetch the sheepskin *kaross* from my room – that'll be best.'

Buchanan nodded; it suited him to have the young Steyn on his own again, now things had progressed a little further.

'Can I go?'

'Of course, it's your house.'

Koos didn't leave immediately, however, but dithered annoyingly, dropping swabs into the bucket beside the settee and having another go at the rug, as if unsure Willem would be safe in his absence. Finally he forced himself from the room, taking the bucket with him, just as lightning struck very close at hand.

Wolraad looked up involuntarily, and the flash revealed an agony of conflict on his face that was gone before the thunder crack which followed.

In that same split-second, Buchanan had a strong presentiment of danger. As he had yet to develop his sixth sense, if indeed there was such a thing, he knew this feeling had to have originated with something the first five had picked up. Something he'd seen or heard within the last minute or so.

Nothing came to him – unless it could have been that expression on Wolraad's face when he'd been caught off guard.

A look of conflict. The look of a man steeling himself for a make-or-break move – yes, that worked. A move calculated to take place when they were, to all intents and purposes, alone in

the room. When Buchanan had finally been lulled into thinking
– yes, that worked, too.

'Oh aye,' he said, and deliberately allowed the revolver to
slip from his fingers into his lap.

If there was going to be any more of the rough stuff, then he
wanted it over and done with before tea. Fatigue was beginning
to drag at him, and he'd suddenly tired of speculating endlessly
about this and that; a direct assault on his person would immediately clarify the issue.

'Sorry?' said Wolraad.

'Nothing really. Just that last one was a bit too near for my
liking.'

'Ja.'

'Want to come round and see if it hit anything?' Buchanan
asked, waving idly at the french windows.

But Wolraad stayed his side of the table, ignoring this open
invitation to try his luck, and staring out of the windows from
where he sat.

'You know,' he remarked, after a considerable pause, 'even
now I can't get this matter into my head.'

'Meaning?'

'Ach,' Wolraad said, smiling bitterly, as though at a loss for
words.

They listened to the storm for a while. Buchanan grew pro-
gressively more tense. The feeling was still in him, gnawing little
holes in his vitals, and yet now there seemed to be nothing to
account for it. He must have been wrong about Wolraad, although in what way he wasn't sure, and that meant –

Buchanan leapt up, gun in hand, at the sound of a peculiar
grunt from the passage. Then felt excessively sheepish when
Motseki came into the room carrying a large, heavy tea tray,
with Koos just behind him. The tray was loaded with enough
goodies to make any man grunt.

'That's the stuff!' said Buchanan, pocketing his revolver.
'You've got Solomon to do us proud!'

But Motseki didn't return the smile.

He had a shotgun in his back.

There had been nothing unduly subtle about the subliminal

172

impressions Buchanan had recorded. His ears had heard Koos pacify Willem with a single whispered sentence, and his eyes had seen Koos procrastinate like a man about to take a momentous, fateful step. If his mind hadn't been so content with its benign distortions of the obvious, all this might have reached him at the time it took place. Or at least soon enough to avert what had happened now.

'Why?' he said, already guessing the answer.

'It's what Willie wanted,' Koos replied, with a lift of his chin.

'Dirk is gone?'

'Ja, he's gone. You never asked me for my keys, you know that? Anyway, Willie had a spare set.'

'*Pa het –?*' gasped Wolraad.

'Quiet a minute, I will explain. And I think it's best we speak in English so everyone can understand.'

'*Maar –*'

'Please don't make it hard for me, Finbar. Put Johnny's gun on the table and stand back.'

Buchanan might have tried something desperate if Motseki hadn't been standing half an inch from destruction. As it was, he had no choice but to do as ordered.

'That's good,' said Koos.

'And now?'

'You can sit.'

Again Buchanan did as he was told. There was a tremble in Koos's voice that any sensible person would have heeded.

'I have to do this, Finbar, you understand?'

'Aye.'

'And it frightens me, I don't mind telling you that.'

'It's bound to, Koos.'

'You just sit still for a while and all will be all right. Okay?'

'Fine. But one question: is Dirk armed?'

'Whatever for?'

Koos slurred his words like a drunk. In a sense, he was intoxicated, high on a compulsion that would possibly destroy him when his reason tore itself away, aghast at what was being done in its name. And once that happened, all hell could break loose as total delusion took over. It might be a question of an hour, but more likely just a few minutes.

Then Wolraad grinned, animated at last by this turn of the tables.

'Where's Pa gone, *oupa*?' he asked, stretching his arms lazily.

'To hide. High in the mountains — where they will never find him.'

'How long will it take?'

'Sssssssh! We mustn't say! Aren't you pleased?'

'Ja, ja, of course. But can I say something?'

'Mmmm.'

'Send the boy across,' Wolraad suggested. 'It'll be safer with him on the other side. One shot will get them both if there's trouble.'

Koos laughed shrilly. The weapon was shaking in his wrinkled hands now, and the sweat running from his face.

'That's clever,' he said. 'Go on, boy, do like the boss says.'

Motseki walked stiff-gaited over to Buchanan and turned to face the twelve-bore with fascinated, terrified eyes.

'I must sit?' he whispered.

'Sit,' confirmed Wolraad.

Again Koos laughed.

'Hell, Steyntjie, you don't know how pleased I am to have you help me!' he chirruped. 'What Willie said about you was wrong, wrong, wrong – and, as true as God, I have already told him so!'

'*Wat was dit?*'

'English, English, remember? Or *Meneer* here gets nervous –'

'Oom Willie said what?'

'Ach, it doesn't matter now. Hey, you, don't look at me like that, you hear?'

Motseki trembled against Buchanan's calf.

Then Koos smiled kindly and said: 'I'm only doing this for Willie's sake – you realize? You won't hold it against me?'

'He's an old friend,' said Buchanan gravely, 'I can respect that.'

He could see no way of reaching the revolver without Motseki catching the first barrel.

'Good, good, I can tell you're being honest with me. I don't want you to have to lie.'

'Oom Willie is going to wake up soon,' Wolraad said, twisting round in his chair.

'That is good also. It is very important that he should know that Dirk was not let down, hey? That was his fear. That his brother would no more put trust in him. If that happened he wanted just to die. Now instead he and me can take food to your pa in the mountains. You're pleased?'

'Pleased, *oupa* – you've handled this well.'

Buchanan found that debatable. He could not see why Dirk hadn't returned to the house for the bag and its contents, if only to ensure their destruction. Nor could he understand how Dirk could think that becoming a fugitive would help. Holding hostages would have been a far better plan to pursue, as tough as the South African Government had shown itself to be in such matters. These thoughts must have made him frown slightly.

'What's the face for?' Koos demanded with nervous anger. 'I've just told your boy not to –'

'Oom Willie's waking up, *oupa*!'

Wolraad got out of his chair and looked down at Willem. 'Steyntjie, do me a favour, hey? Take that gun off the table so I can look.'

That was it. With the revolver now totally out of reach, Buchanan's last hope died.

'He doesn't look like it to me, son,' said Koos crossly.

'But he is! Look harder!'

Then a most surprising thing happened.

As Koos turned for another snatched glance at Willem, the young Steyn smacked up the barrel of the shotgun and wrenched it from his grasp. To top that, he tossed it across the room to Buchanan an instant before Koos attacked him.

It wasn't really a fight, and it didn't last long. Less than five minutes later, Buchanan helped Wolraad get the poor old bugger to bed, and there they force-fed him almost a tumblerful of brandy.

'Ay, he'll sleep a wee while on that,' said Buchanan, stepping out on to that section of the verandah.

His next most immediate concern was the weather. The rain had slowed to a drizzle, but the cloud lay as heavy as ever, without a single gap in it, and lightning still flickered all around them. He looked at his watch – incredibly, it was only twelve-twenty –

and then back at the sky. It would be an hour at least before the radio could function again, and twice as long before a plane could get through, unless a wind came up from somewhere. And in that time, God knew where Dirk Steyn could get himself to. Or what he might do.

Wolraad came out to stand beside Buchanan. There was now a strange, tacit alliance between them; a fragile thing, born of the moment, too brittle to be questioned.

'I must go after my pa,' said Wolraad.

'You'll need help.'

'The boys on our farm are Basotho. I can speak the *taal*, ask which way he has gone.'

'You'll still need help.'

Wolraad smiled slightly, and murmured: 'Why do you say that, *meneer*?'

'Your father's no coward.'

'And so?'

'There's a limit to what one man can do.'

'But I am his son.'

This was spoken so softly it had an ambiguity that made Buchanan turn. Wolraad had changed again: he was standing tall and taut like his sire, no longer the plodding, lead-limbed bumpkin who had huddled inside himself, bemused by the shattering events of the morning, or the wistful, bitter young man who had sat at the living-room table. He had made some adjustment which chilled the sentiment in his remark, giving it the connotation, not of filial trust but of a claim to parity – perhaps even something colder than that.

Wolraad, aware of Buchanan's sharp appraisal, shrugged and said in an ordinary voice: 'It is my duty.'

And Buchanan replied lightly: 'Oh aye.'

But wasn't too sure what to make of that either, and turned it over in his mind until he realized that none of this was directly relevant to what had to be done.

'I'd best make my meaning clearer,' he said, tugging a leaf off the granadilla vine. 'Your father isn't a man to run from trouble.'

'And you think?'

'The same as you do, I'd imagine. Pa isn't through yet. He's been thwarted, but he hasn't given up the fight. What's happened already involved a total committal.'

'Sorry?'

'Your father didn't run away. He ran on.'

That slight smile returned.

'Do you just bluff you don't know Afrikaans?' asked Wolraad. *'Speel jy die gek met my?'*

Buchanan shook his head.

'Then I'll tell you something. Remember when Willie was in the room there, boasting at you in my language? You know what he said?'

'Not a word.'

'That Pa had made a covenant.'

Rain fell in a quick splatter, and then the drizzle went on drifting down again.

'Do you know what that means, *meneer*?'

'Aye: like when the Voortrekkers promised the Good Lord a kirk if they beat the Zulus at Blood River.'

'And you know how serious a covenant is with my people? When they promise God something?'

There was no need for Buchanan to answer that: his face must have said it all. Wolraad nodded, and they turned, walking slowly down to the end of the verandah where the steps were.

'You'll get the horses?' said Buchanan, as Wolraad went down into the garden. 'I'd better leave a note.'

They rode hard for the first five miles, anxious for confirmation they were on the right path, because their only reason for choosing it rested on Solomon's assertion that all the others would have been cut off temporarily by storm-swollen torrents. They rode unarmed. Then a Basotho herdboy, shivering under an overhanging rock, told them that a white man had passed by. The strangest-looking white man he'd ever seen, with a puffed-up face like an udder, who travelled very fast and had taken the right turn in the fork up ahead.

'Sticking to the bridleways for speed,' Buchanan remarked, urging his horse forward. 'But for how much longer, I wonder?'

'Do you know where this path leads?'

'Didn't the boy say?'

'He's a *malkop* – just that it went to the west.'

'Too small to be on the map, but I'd say it runs towards the Catholic mission.'

A mile down the turn-off they came to a spring and saw hoof-prints in the fresh mud on the far bank.

'Ja, look at the *spoor*,' Wolraad said, making his mount keep to the edge of the path. 'He's slowed down. Why's that?'

'Conserving energy – maybe he's got a long way to go.'

'Or he's got sick.'

'Aye, that's not unlikely. Let's push on as quick as we can – we could still make it.'

The pursuit was proving much easier than Buchanan had expected. For a moment, back there in the hitching yard, as he'd swung up into the saddle, his whole being had protested at the idea of having one more demand made upon it – in fact, he'd very nearly dismounted and called it a day. But Motseki, despite a sudden rage over his beloved doctor's fate, had promised to act responsibly until the plane arrived, and, with the travelling bag secure in the store's safe, there had been really no justification for opting out. Not when the fourth rider of the Apocalypse was still on the loose.

They met a man, going the other way, who had seen Dirk, but he was not sure when this had been. Some miles back.

Buchanan let his horse have its head and thought for a while about Nancy, and then, for some odd reason, about Louis Fouché. She seemed real still; he didn't. When it came to that, very little had substance any longer. Even Wolraad, leading the way down yet another slope, had lost any particular meaning, and was just something that moved along, drawing him with it.

Slopes, crags, ravines; short grass, tall grass, tumbleweed and aloes; crows and finches, widow birds trailing their tails of mourning ribbon, crying weep-weep-weep; sheep grazing, goats bleating, children begging for pennies; widow birds crying weep-weep-weep.

He closed his eyes, just to rest them, and must have nearly dozed off, when his horse suddenly jogged into a trot.

Wolraad was way out ahead, going like the clappers.

With a rake of his heels, Buchanan gave chase, feeling an exhilaration in the surge of power drub-drubbing beneath him.

178

And realizing, when he saw the silhouette of a lone horseman drop down behind the next ridge, what this was all about.

Although it seemed too easy – too easy by far.

When he had recovered sufficiently from his fright, the Basotho pot mender told them that a white man had stopped to question him not long before. So it had not been entirely a wasted effort on their part.

'Pa asked the way to a place called Soai,' Wolraad interpreted. 'This man says there's nothing at Soai except a small village.'

'Oh aye?'

'Over to the west even further, right in the *bundu*. You take a right at the next river, and follow the path that leads highest each time.'

'High in the mountains, like Koos said.'

'Ja, but that . . .'

Wolraad returned to his interrogation, speaking the language fluently and using hand gestures. The pot mender had a screw of wild mint in each nostril; a common if arresting practice in the Maluti.

'He says it's a long ride and he didn't think Pa could get there before nightfall.'

'What are our chances of catching up?'

'Not so bad maybe. This man noticed the horse was very tired. Also Pa looked sick; he was shaking. I asked him if he was told to say Soai – you know, like it was a trick? – but I don't think so.'

'It's three now. Four hours of daylight left.'

The Basotho added something.

'What was that?'

'Ach, he says a big witchdoctor lives at Soai,' Wolraad replied, smiling wryly. 'So this could be the reason my pa wanted to go there.'

They thanked the man and rode on, given fresh impetus by knowing exactly where to go. But each was so perplexed by Dirk Steyn's extraordinary destination, that hardly two sentences were exchanged between them until sunset.

When they halted at a stream to water the horses, and looked back across the vast panorama spread out beneath them. It seemed hours since they had passed the last village, and no-where, in all that immensity of space, could they see any sign of human habitation. It was enormously peaceful, dreamy even, and very still.

'Empty,' Wolraad said, 'man, I've never seen any place so empty.'

'Aye, and we've climbed a good height.'

'Or so far away from anywhere,' Wolraad added.

'It's that too.'

'Why? Why travel so far?'

'To the ends of the Earth, you mean?' Buchanan murmured.

Wolraad handed him his reins and they pressed onwards and upwards, silent once more and subdued. Their quest no longer needed rhyme or reason, or any thought at all, it had become an obsession. Which drove them ruthlessly for another half hour before their goal came in sight: Soai, a tiny village as the Baso-tho had said, almost invisible in the fading twilight if it had not been for its cooking fires, which made apricot holes in the mountainside.

Buchanan and Wolraad hobbled their horses and went in on foot. Their stealth startled the villagers.

Who told them that they'd not seen a white man that day, nor for as long as some of them could remember.

Chapter Thirteen

A rat woke Buchanan. Or perhaps, his waking disturbed the rat. There were a couple of thumps over in a corner of the hut, a skitter, a squeak and then the only sound was Wolraad's soft, uneven snoring.

He tried to get back to sleep. But his mind was busy with its scrapbooks, which it rifled through under the glare of a 200-watt bulb in the vault of his skull. Cousteau; Stoffel; Koos; Dirk. Tagg; Dirk. Dirk. The twins between their mother's knees. The hot buttered toast Solomon had made, curling cold on its plate. The aerosol can. Mint.

He opened his eyes.

The luminous face of his watch said it was a quarter to six.

The hut was pitch dark. He breathed in deeply, enjoying the aroma of wood smoke that permeated the sooty thatch, and thought again of the kindness of the villagers, who'd killed them a chicken and served it with black tea in jam tins. Served it like a banquet, and that's how it had tasted. And then had given them a thin blanket apiece, a sleeping mat and a snug place to bed down. Where, without bothering to discuss anything, they'd toppled like trees, slept like logs, zizzed their little piles of sawdust.

He wondered why the witch-doctor had not appeared.

Buchanan heard the rat again and knew that its plump blunderings could hardly have aroused him so suddenly. He'd been elbowed by his workaday self which, sufficiently recovered, was impatient to get the show on the road again. What show: that was the question. And what road? It could get stuffed.

Presently, however, he began to feel the hardness of the floor, and his blanket lost its muzzy cosiness. The odd ache started up. Dawn etched a grey outline around the door and, not far off, a cockerel sounded its rusty cliché. Then there was nothing for it but to rise quietly, slip on his boots, and go outside for a bit of a wander to relieve his stiffness.

The sharp mountain air made him sneeze and cleared his head like a pinch of snuff. He could think again, with detachment and clarity, probably for the first time since leaving Mapapeng on that long, muddled ride.

Buchanan shuddered, recoiling as from a fevered childhood dream, and climbed the knoll behind the village. A wind was shaking out its sheets in his ears and generally busying itself about the place with sky-broom and duster; he hunched his shoulders against its bustle and fuss, and trudged on up the narrow terraces of coarse grass. The sheep already grazing here – if, indeed, they ever stopped – skipped aside in their clumsy, half-hearted fashion, and then carried on with their breakfast. Otherwise, he was quite alone.

'The cold light of day,' he murmured to himself, as he reached the top and selected a rock to stand on, out of the wet.

But Buchanan wasn't ready yet to review the situation.

From there, the mountains stretching away before him looked like the wind pattern in a soft, sandy dune and, at most, a mere two strides across to the whipped-cream horizon. Then the true scale reasserted itself, and he saw elevations of five, six hundred feet, set not a mile apart, all to be endured again under a huge, vacant sky.

Oppressed by the sheer immensity of it all, he crouched to take a close look at a small spider which had spun its web between two blades of grass; remembering, as he did so, the legendary Bruce. But this wee fellow had everything well under control, and was plainly in no mood to offer cheap comfort as he suckled on a fat, ugly fly. After a while, the dew drops of moisture on the web held even tinier suns in suspension, and began to grow smaller as the dots of light grew brighter.

Buchanan became so absorbed in watching this that Wolraad, wrapped in a blanket, was half-way up the slope before he noticed him.

'Have a decent kip?' Buchanan inquired.

Wolraad made no reply. He came and stood beside him, glowering back over the route which led, ultimately, to Mapapeng.

182

'When do we start?' he asked Buchanan.

'Soon as you like.'

Neither made a move to leave the rock. The wind buffeted them, and swirled away the smoke which was rising now from various points on the other side of the huts. Then it hurried off somewhere else.

In the calm, Wolraad said: 'He fooled us nicely, hey?'

'Possibly.'

'No. Pa fooled us.'

'By laying a false trail?'

'Ja; this Soai rubbish. Willie must have told him the name, told him to say it to all the coons so that when we came along, we'd go the wrong way.'

Buchanan followed the logic, but only so far.

'Not sure you're right,' he said. 'Your idea presumes Pa expected to have someone on his tail a lot sooner than he'd got reason to.'

'Then where is he?'

'Probably ducked sideways along one of the paths farther back, circled away in that direction where it's also pretty desolate. You couldn't pick a better place to lie low than in these mountains.'

Wolraad said very quietly: 'They'll hunt him down like a *kaffir* dog.'

'That'll depend on –'

'They will, man!'

'Your pa took that chance when he rode off.'

'Like a dog – do you understand what I mean?'

Buchanan did, all of a sudden, understand precisely: Wolraad was appealing to him to continue the search then and there, instead of making the return journey to Mapapeng. That way there might not be a dog hunt, one which would reduce its quarry to a limping, snivelling tat of bones, ready to lick the first black boot that offered it water.

'We don't stand a hope in hell, old son,' he told him. 'And anyway –'

'Can I go on my own?'

That was a good question. Strictly speaking, an agent of Her Majesty's Government had no power of arrest in the Kingdom

183

of Lesotho. Under these particular circumstances, however, he was probably welcome to shoot the young bugger if he wanted to.

'I wouldn't advise it,' Buchanan replied, still unsure of who or what he was dealing with.

'I see.'

'Shall we make a start then?'

Wolraad didn't move. He stood staring out over the terrain that lay between them and the interior, apparently absorbed in making up his own mind as to what the next step should be.

'To the ends of the Earth,' he said at last, his mouth twisting wryly. 'Man, but it seems even further than when we first got here. See how far it stretches ...'

'Well, the lighting's changed with the sun moving round,' Buchanan suggested, looking over his shoulder at the peaks behind them.

'Ja, that would make the difference.'

Then the penny dropped, heavily.

'Wolraad,' he said, his voice tight, 'it just could be that you're facing in the wrong direction altogether.'

'Hey?'

'Turn round. Where are we? At the edge of nothing – or is that just in terms of the trip we've made from the middle?'

Wolraad turned, catching Buchanan's arm to keep his balance, and the penny dropped for him, too. On the other side of that final range was the vast and teeming Republic of South Africa.

There had to be a reason for their extraordinary oversight, and Wolraad spoke for them both when he raised an immediate, scornful objection.

'No, never!' he said. 'Pa couldn't have gone there! You can't hide in South Africa – not from Security, that's impossible.'

'If you have the right friends?'

Wolraad's laugh was bitter.

'Pa will have no friends now,' he said.

'He might try –'

'He's not a fool! Lesotho's his only –'

'How long could he last over there? A week? Long enough to make his way north and –'

184

'Never! They'd get him in a day. Sooner, if he did try to find friends. I tell you, Buchanan, we didn't think of that because Pa wouldn't have thought of it either. Or is that a place you'd try to escape in?'

It wasn't. But perhaps escape was the wrong word – perhaps they had misjudged the man's motive in making his break from Mapapeng. And once doubt had freed the situation from the bounds of the obvious, it brought a chilling realization.

'One day could be all he needs,' Buchanan said softly. 'One man in the right place at the right time could still achieve what he and the others set out to do – not as subtly maybe, but with much the same effect.'

Wolraad frowned.

'What I'm saying is that your father by-passed Soai and *went on.* Down into Natal, where today in Pietermaritzburg the Prime Minister is going to open a Voortrekker festival.'

'*Nie*, Buchanan! You can't think things like that, man!'

'We've got to, Wolraad. Vorster is their bogy man, and when needs must the Devil drives.'

'That would be – be stupid!'

'Not when you consider who might take over then, in the wake of official reports that I doubt will mention your pa's name. He'll get his way, all right.'

'I can't accept!'

'Then let's hope I'm wrong,' said Buchanan, jumping down from the rock. 'The one thing in our favour is that I don't think he would tackle a mountain pass after dark. He'd have too much at stake to risk a silly accident. Wouldn't he?'

Their guide, a lanky youth from the village, trotted just ahead of them on a shaggy pony, plainly feeling his importance. He'd taken them about two miles north of Soai along a series of sheep tracks, with the Drakensberg mountains defining the border on their right, and had just begun a new tack.

'Ask him how much longer before we reach this pass of his,' requested Buchanan.

There was a short exchange between Wolraad and the youth.

'Soon, he says.'

It would have to be. Doubts of a negative kind had started to

185

niggle Buchanan. A better plan might have been to have hired fresh mounts and ridden hell-for-leather to the nearest mission with a radio. An even better plan might have been to have stayed at Mapapeng to explain the situation – something only Nancy could do besides himself, and God knew what had happened to her in the interim. And, of course, Dirk Steyn might be somewhere near Soai, but asleep in a cosy cave, way back in one of the empty valleys. Time was really the critical factor involved: if he was wrong about Steyn, then he'd botched everything; if he was right, then he might be able to raise the alarm before anyone else realized the danger. That left the odds at fifty-fifty – and a sinking feeling in Buchanan's gut.

Which disappeared the instant Steyn's gelding came trotting round a bend in the sheep track, whinnying with delight at rejoining its stable mates, whose harrumphs had obviously attracted it.

The gelding wore its bridle but the saddle was missing.

'Bingo,' said Buchanan, with deliberate self-restraint.

And Wolraad yelled at the youth to travel faster, but he shook his head and pointed to where pieces of the track had slid away into the ravine beneath them. So they proceeded at the same infuriatingly slow pace, with the riderless horse attaching itself to the end of the procession, until a few minutes after seven.

Then they arrived in a hollow which looked, from that angle, as if it led up to a pass, and found the camp where Steyn had spent the night.

It was a discovery to be dwelt upon. Steyn had built himself a small fire, and had slept beside it wrapped in the horse's blanket, with his head cushioned on the saddle. But what made Buchanan damn near whoop was the fact that the man's imprint was dry and innocent of any dew.

'He can't have been gone all that long,' he said, straightening up after feeling the blanket to make sure.

'The boy says we can't take the horses any further if we want to go over the pass,' Wolraad said, dismounting. 'What shall we do with them?'

'Oh Christ, give him the bloody things!'

It was not a moment to be delayed by trifles.

Wolraad led the scramble up the gully, but Buchanan was

only a pace behind and so they dropped together for a cautious look over the top.

The pass below was a steep jumble of rocks, boulders, stones and other debris left by a mountainslide that must have happened a million years before. Climbing down it would take time but, if they were careful, it wouldn't present any real problems.

They raised their sights a little.

There, on the near side of the first foothills, was a neat pattern of huts, divided by gravel paths and rockeries, and to the left of it was a car park and a tin-roofed bungalow with a hedge around it.

'Rest camp,' said Wolraad. 'Giant's Castle?'

'Maybe – I don't know any of the Natal game reserves. The point is that he could have got down there by now.'

'Ja, no question of it. Look, there's a Land-Rover going out towards the gate – it's stopping!'

'Just the usual check,' Buchanan grunted.

The black game guard snapped off a salute and opened the camp gate; the Land-Rover accelerated away down the twisting dirt road.

'Do you think –?' began Wolraad, and left it at that.

Even since finding his father's camp in the hollow, he'd changed his approach somewhat – which was as close as Buchanan could come to defining the curious look in his eye.

'I think, old son, it's high time we got a real shift on and reached that phone down there. Are you coming?'

'Of course!'

'Here we go then,' said Buchanan, dropping to the first ledge, and adding in a mutter: 'The things I'll do for Balthazar V – I only hope he's grateful, the bastard.'

The climb took nearly an hour. Buchanan reached the bottom first and looked up to see how his companion was doing, just as the man lost his footing on a slippery tuft of grass and fell. As Wolraad pitched forward, his raised his arms instinctively to protect his head, and landed heavily on an outcrop of orange rock, before rolling the rest of the way. He got to his feet immediately and gave an ashamed laugh – then Buchanan noticed that the left arm was hanging strangely.

'You're all right?'

'Fine, man! Just thought it would be the quickest.'

'Isn't that arm of yours –?'

'Ach, it's nothing. Let's hurry, hey? We're already miles behind.'

Thank God for the Steyn Stoicism, thought Buchanan, who really didn't have time right then for attending to lesser matters, and he turned to lead the way. A few yards off he came across a worn path which led round a rock the size of the dome of St Paul's past a cave that the bilingual sign said had Bushman paintings in it, and then down to a river.

There was a small shock in seeing sweet papers and cigarette cartons in the grass on either side of the path – the dawning of civilization, no doubt, after an aeon spent in a primitive, litterless landscape. This sense of transition was very strong at first, and made Buchanan, with his two-day beard and torn clothing, feel like an actor who'd left by the stagedoor in full make-up and costume. Wolraad, he noticed, was far more presentable.

Once they had forded the river, the path took them out of sight of the camp and up to a stile of sorts in a barbed-wire fence. There was a wooden bench beside the stile, provided for the less vigorous visitor who wished to enjoy the view, and the pair of them sat down to collect themselves.

'You'd better do the talking,' Buchanan said. 'Go in there and see if they know what you're on about. I'll keep an eye on any sudden moves he may make.'

'And if he isn't still here?'

'Then we pitch in together and sound the alarm.'

'But I don't see exactly –'

'Good God Almighty,' exclaimed a deep, very English voice, 'not *another* two!'

They spun round.

On the other side of the stile stood a big, bony man of about fifty, wearing the green beret and khaki uniform of a Natal Parks Board game ranger. He was loading his pipe from an ostrich-skin pouch, and grinning beneath a flat moustache.

'I'm Travers, o/c camp,' the ranger said breezily. 'Saw you hobbling up from the river. He might have said there'd be more!'

188

'Who might've?' Buchanan asked.

'You're not part of his outfit? The old cove who ran into wild bees? From the stings on your –'

'So you've seen my Pa?' Wolraad cut in urgently, stepping forward.

'Seen him? Lord above, I've had him turning the camp upside down. That family from Durban didn't like it a bit! Not cut out for this sort of thing. Never fear, never fear. Care for a brandy?'

Buchanan needed a few seconds to adjust, and the same went for Wolraad, who had turned very pale. They watched the camp superintendent suck a match flame into his bowl, spit, and put his pouch away.

'All's taken care of, me hearties,' he went on, beckoning for them to cross to his side of the fence. 'Mark you, I couldn't get a sensible word out of the old bugger. Except that he'd been camping somewhere and the little sods had pounced on him. Damn fool, not allowed, camping. Sent him off with my Number Two. Bad things, wild bees.'

'Sent him off where?' inquired Buchanan, as the three of them began to walk up a stone-edged gravel path.

'Estcourt, as a matter of fact – to see the quack there. A bit delirious, wouldn't you say?'

'I'd say very,' Buchanan agreed in anxious tones. 'He went raving off in the middle of the night and we –'

'Or is it a little early for brandy?' asked Travers, who was the sort of man who lost interest if anyone else spoke. 'Course not! Not after what you must have been through! Don't like the look of that arm – bees?'

Wolraad's arm had swollen quite a bit already, suggesting a nasty fracture; it had to be hurting like hell, but he hadn't made a murmur.

'Ja, bees,' he lied – and Buchanan winked his approval.

'We'd better see what can be done about getting you to Estcourt as well then. I can't leave here, but someone's bound to –'

'I'm more worried about my dad, actually.'

'Worried? Perfect right to be! Known a fella take one sting and, bing-bong, off he went! Tragic. Lovely girl his wife. We'll give that quack a tinkle and see what's what. In we go!'

As they entered the bungalow through its back verandah, Wolraad whispered to Buchanan: 'Can you understand him? What's happening, hey?'

'Relax and we'll be all right.'

There was very little in that living-room. Two leather arm-chairs, a divan, a skin rug, a shelf of reference works on flora and fauna, a radio, a pipe rack on the stone mantelshelf, and a water-colour of the scene outside the window, presumably for somewhere to rest the eyes after dark.

'Park yourselves,' Travers invited them. 'Feel at home. I'll go and rustle up some tea.'

'Actually, what we'd be most grateful for would be the use of your phone – and then if possible, a lift into Estcourt,' said Buchanan.

'Really. Quite sure? Then I'll go and ferret among the guests, see if any are leaving early. Damn unlikely, mark you. Sunday morning. Still. Contraption's in the hall. Can't take you myself, can't promise anything. Well, that's settled then.'

And off he went, stepping straight out over the window sill, and striding energetically away towards the huts.

'Good man,' said Buchanan to Wolraad. 'It was best leaving him to think he knew all the answers. If we'd tried it any other way, he'd probably never let us near the phone until everything had been explained to him.'

'You're going to ring the authorities now?'

'Right,' said Buchanan, knowing this was the moment when a lot could go wrong.

But Wolraad simply nodded and went over to the window.

One glance at the telephone on the hall table told Buchanan that life still had its complications in store. The thing had no dial, just a handle you cranked: it was on a rural party line, which meant that any number he requested would be duly recorded by the operator. This immediately ruled out the buck-passing call made mandatory by his orders, and left him no alternative but to contact the South African Police directly.

The exchange in Estcourt answered within seconds, showing surprising efficiency for a Sunday morning, and connected him in as many seconds again with the offices of the Security Branch in Pietermaritzburg.

That was when the problems began. The duty officer was cordial at first, and then started, quite politely, to quibble. This led to longer and longer qualifications of everything Buchanan put to him, which somehow made them only seem more and more absurd. And the duty officer, a man chosen for the job because of his highly suspicious nature, sat there in the real world and plainly didn't believe a word. Finally he thanked Buchanan for ringing, but said he had other hoax calls to attend to. None of which, he hastened to add, would be half as interesting, because who else would think up a story about a former O B man wanting to kill Vorster?

'You don't know what happened yesterday at Gotsong?' Buchanan demanded.

'Ja, ja, a plane hit it, sir, just a plane – like on the news. And that was the day before yesterday, hey? You'd better get your facts right. Now will you please promise not to ring me back?'

'Would any of this sound better to you coming from his son? I've got Wolraad here with me.'

'Oh ja?' snapped the officer. 'I only heard about a "son" that got killed with us but, okay, put him on.'

Wolraad must have been eavesdropping on the conversation, because he sidled into the hall without being called.

Buchanan, cupping his hand over the mouthpiece, said: 'I'm getting nowhere with this bastard, so for Christ's sake get him to –'

'I'll try,' said Wolraad. 'Hello? This is Wolraad Steyn speaking. Ja, Boet was my brother. What this man was telling you is true – honest. Proof? On the telephone?'

And then Wolraad started speaking earnestly in Afrikaans, turning to Buchanan when he mentioned place names, and nodding, to show that something was getting through.

He switched back to English and said: 'That's right, we believe he's already on his way down there. If you want to check this, ring the camp superintendent at Giant's Castle. This is his phone we're using. You've got to catch him, please, man he's sick, my pa, very sick.'

Wolraad kept his cool until he'd replaced the receiver, then he coughed to disguise a sob, and pushed past to get back into the living-room.

'Well, old son?' Buchanan said gently.

'It's done. What's done is done.'

'Aye.'

For no particular reason, Buchanan looked at his watch; he did not even note the time on it.

'Let's see now, the next thing is to get that arm put into plaster.'

'I want to go there.'

'Where? Pietermaritzburg?'

'Maybe – you know, maybe they could have a use for me.'

'Is that what the officer said?'

'No.'

It would have been so easy to say 'yes'.

Buchanan was tempted: he had blown his cover, he was an illegal immigrant in the Republic, and he was dog-tired – yet he had personal reasons for wanting to be in at the kill, if it came to that.

He waited for the phone to ring. Nothing happened.

'All right,' he said. 'But how? And that's assuming old what's-his-name can fix us a lift to Estcourt.'

Wolraad tried flexing the fingers of his left hand, and blanched with the pain this caused.

'If I can get a car, will you drive me, *meneer*? This isn't any good for gears.'

'You've got some cash on you?'

'No, but I'll –'

'You're in luck!' boomed Travers, crashing in through the hall, pursued by two mastiffs which were attempting, in a good-natured way, to maul him. 'Bloody Catholics, no less. Caught them at it. Just off. Off to Mass first thing – say they like to have their Sundays free. Down, boys! Incredible humbugs, Catholics, always said so. No need to ring the quack, have you there in a trice, drop you at his gate. Brass plate. Got the address. Splendid.'

And that, as they said, seemed to be that – and all in what had been a gratifying short space of time since their descent from Lesotho.

It was inevitable some sort of reaction should set in sooner or later. There was still a lot which could go wrong, and besides, Buchanan had an inborn distrust of any sudden upward turn in his fortunes. But the feeling which began to press in on him, as he travelled towards Estcourt on the back seat of the church-goers' Cortina, was fairly specific. Somewhere along the line, this feeling said, he'd again taken too much for granted. Perhaps it was debatable, now he had passed on the baton to the South Africans to finish the race, whether such an oversight still had any importance to anyone but himself, yet his uneasiness was worth pinning down, if nothing else.

The Cortina dipped and growled its way out of the foothills, following a dirt road which soon levelled off and wove between the barbed-wire fences and telegraph poles of an otherwise featureless landscape.

Nor were the Catholic couple a distraction. Their stomachs grumbled about the fast they were keeping, but they said nothing themselves. From the look of it, they'd had about fifty years of this easy, companionable silence, and must have felt it was something their passengers similarly valued.

As for Wolraad, he was hunched in the other corner of the back seat, nursing his arm and saying nothing either.

But Buchanan got nowhere with his critical analysis of the situation. The lack of distraction became a distraction in itself. He fidgeted with the ash tray and then took an auto club year-book out of the door pocket, turning to the section with Pieter-maritzburg in it.

He was just putting the book away again, having memorized the map, when the thought struck him.

'Wolraad, did you tell the SB your father was taken to an Estcourt doctor – or just to Estcourt?'

'I didn't say about the doctor, I expected –'

'Exactly! Neither did I. Anything could have happened to him there: the doc might have insisted on him going in for special shots or whatever, and he could've been delayed. He could still be in Estcourt for all we know! We'd better tell them.'

'Something wrong?' asked the driver.

'Aye, please would you stop for a moment if you see a telephone anywhere?'

'All right – although I doubt that we'll find one along this stretch.'

'What about at that little store?' his wife suggested.

'Keep your eyes peeled, dear.'

The Cortina picked up speed.

'But look,' Wolraad objected, loud enough for only Buchanan to hear him, 'if Pa didn't want to be delayed, then nothing could've delayed him.'

'You're forgetting he had a Parks Board bloke breathing benevolently down his neck, bent on seeing he got the right treatment.'

'Even so, if Pa wanted to, he could –'

'No, he wouldn't try anything drastic in case it resulted in his being chased the rest of the way.'

'Ja, that's possible.'

'It's a fact,' said Buchanan, leaning forward to see how the speedometer was doing. 'If Pa wasn't playing this one very cool, he'd have just stolen a vehicle at the rest camp and the hell with the consequences.'

'And you could be wrong in the first place, *meneer*! Pa could be only interested in getting medical help.'

Buchanan wanted to tell him he was an optimist, but left it at that.

'There's the store!' the old lady exclaimed.

'No phone though,' her husband replied, 'I can't see that it has any wires leading off to it.'

Buchanan had already established as much. The general dealers, which sat like a cement shoe box on the next bend coming up, probably didn't even have a proper address. Then he saw a Land-Rover parked outside it and facing their way.

'If that's the Parks Board, will you pull over?' he asked, his hand moving on to the car door handle.

It was the Land-Rover from the camp, and the youngster driving it – who had stopped for some tobacco he'd meant to buy in Estcourt – told Buchanan what had happened to poor old Steyn.

'You look as if you could do with an antihistamine shot yourself,' he said, scratching under his green beret. 'What did you lot get up to with those bees?'

'But after the doctor treated him – where did he go? That's his son over there in the car, and he's doing his nut.'

'Really? His boy? Must've been worse than I thought, but he seemed lucid enough when we were –'

'Please, if you can hurry it. This is much more important than you realize.'

'Simple enough, man. Steyn just said he wanted to get home to his place in Pietermaritzburg, and asked if I knew anybody going down there to this thing on today. I said no, but if he liked I'd take him out on the national road to hitch a lift. I nearly lent him money for the train, as a matter of fact, only he said –'

'And that's what you did? How long ago?'

'Bloody hours. I dropped him near my chick's farm and said I'd look out for him on my way back, in case he hadn't been lucky and we'd try something else. He was gone though.'

'Christ.'

'You're not trying to tell me I've done something wrong, are you?' the youngster demanded, starting to flush beneath his tan. 'I'm not paid to be everybody's nursemaid! And Travers just said, get rid of the old bugger, Terry, and I think what I did was a lot more than –'

'You've taken a load off my mind,' Buchanan cut in, shaking him by the hand and hurrying back to the Cortina.

'Where's he?' asked Wolraad eagerly.

'In Maritzburg already, by the sound of it. We're going to need that car of yours after all.'

Estcourt was Ladysmith on a reduced scale and without the surrounding hills; if you'd seen one, you hardly noticed the other.

Buchanan and Wolraad asked to be dropped off in the main street, as their benefactors were running late for Mass, having waited for them twice, and the surgery couldn't be all that far to walk. This was done gladly – if with a touch of Christian guilt.

'And now?' he said to Wolraad. 'Where do we go from here? Perhaps the cops would arrange a lift for you.'

Wolraad surveyed the garages and service stations which seemed to fill the street, and pointed to one the neon sign said was *Venter's* – and, in smaller letters, *we never close*. Then, without saying anything, he crossed over to it and went inside.

After a minute or so, Buchanan followed in his wake, keeping him in sight all the time through the huge glass windows. From the number of long-distance travellers about, despite the no-petrol laws at the weekend, it was obvious the place did the bulk of its business on a Sunday, specializing in towing and quick repairs. And that would mean there was a good chance the boss was about too. Interesting.

What must have been Meneer Venter himself, who resembled evolution's attempt at a tank on a human substructure, presently emerged with Wolraad and pointed to a Fiat sports coupé on the forecourt. Then he pointed to Wolraad's arm, and Wolraad pointed to Buchanan, and some sort of a deal was struck. Venter removed the price from the Fiat's windscreen, tossed over the keys, and went into his office with a wave.

'How did we manage that so effortlessly?' asked Buchanan, checking the tread on the tyres. 'Venter isn't a relation of yours, is he – by some uncanny coincidence?'

'Ach, not really.'

'Brotherly love then?' Buchanan murmured, knowing damn well what sort of brotherhood he was alluding to.

'Maybe. I just took a chance; plenty of other places to try in this road.'

Wolraad's smile was slight and preoccupied.

'We must hurry,' he added.

As if the day, which had really only just begun, hadn't a harrowing momentum all of its own.

Chapter Fourteen

The city of Pietermaritzburg lay in a hollow at the foot of a misty escarpment; travelling from the hinterland, you came upon it suddenly, two thousand feet below and with its own Table Mountain in the background.

This was how the Voortrekkers had themselves approached the site of their first real settlement, and its lush promise had made them lock their waggon wheels and go straight down the steep slopes. This had left deep ruts in the rocky outcrops beneath where the radio mast now stood, and people went there to drip ice cream on them. They also went there because it was a vantage point the English had dubbed World's View, and from it you could see, in the centre of the capital, a neat grid of streets which had been laid out with the problems of turning an ox-waggon in mind. And almost in the middle of this grid was a small white church, with gabled ends, that marked where the original Church of the Covenant had once stood. It was ironic then that Pietermaritzburg, which owed its name to two Voortrekker martyrs, should have been regarded for more than half a century as the country's most British town, and that its Afrikaner population should have been long far outnumbered. But things were changing.

The dual carriageway swung north of the line the trekkers had taken, and went down the escarpment in a series of fast, clean curves, before flattening out to by-pass the city. Pietermaritzburg could be reached, however, along several sliproads, all of which were clearly sign-posted.

Buchanan and Wolraad reached the capital with forty-five minutes to spare before the march-past outside the Church of the Covenant was due to begin. Apart from commenting on the weather once or twice, which improved steadily until they drove

197

in under a cloudless sky, neither of them had speculated about what they might find there, and each had remained engrossed in his own thoughts. Uppermost in Buchanan's mind had been the fact of the duty officer's ignorance of the true situation in Lesotho; it dismayed him to think he'd been forced to reveal a trump card, the full potential of which was still being gleefully assessed by Maseru, but took comfort from how satisfying it must have been to merely issue a confirmation of the Mapapeng conspiracy. And then for a time he had dwelt pleasurably, somewhat to his surprise, on Nancy.

After passing through the outskirts of Pietermaritzburg, they went straight to police headquarters in Loop Street and, as was inevitable on such a day, couldn't find parking. This brought Buchanan back into the present with a shrug and a weary sigh. He tried farther down.

'Everything seems so normal,' Wolraad said, breaking a long silence.

'Aye.'

'Why's that?'

'Oh, they'd not cancel the whole caboose, laddie. This thing's had too big a build-up.'

'Or else, *meneer*, it's more obvious.'

'Hmmm?'

'They've – you know, they've got Pa already.'

Perhaps they had. Everything did seem quite normal in the town, and there had not been a single road block on the way in. But then again, it wasn't Security Branch style to start a hoo-ha when this might, with the mass media present in force, detract from the State's much vaunted stability. Buchanan felt he would need to see how they were skinning this particular cat – which could, of course, be done several ways – before he indulged in any sense of anticlimax. Suspending that moment for just a few minutes longer could only make it sweeter, after all.

They cruised another row of rear bumpers.

'Pa has been caught,' Wolraad said dogmatically, as if affirming this as a fact to see how it felt. 'They've got my pa – now what happens to him? Must it be me who tells ma?'

'I think I'd better drop you off, old son.'

'No!'

198

'I'll do a U-turn,' Buchanan suggested, glancing sideways.

'No, please! Give us a chance to think first!'

Wolraad was cracking. The smell of his sweat was sharp, and his breathing had become audible. The fingers of his good hand were teasing painfully back and forth along the line of his eyebrows, plucking at the skin, pinching it.

Buchanan started back towards police headquarters, eager to end the alliance before it met with too much tangible reality.

'Or maybe,' Wolraad said, with a weak snigger, 'maybe that wasn't the Security we spoke with. Have you thought of that, Mister Clever Dick?'

'They got the message all right.'

'And I betrayed my pa!'

'Not at the time, Steyn,' Buchanan said quietly.

Wolraad nodded and wiped a sleeve over his mouth.

There were a couple of riot vans double-parked outside the entrance to the main building, so Buchanan stopped short of them and then leaned over to open the passenger door.

'Out you get,' he said. 'Go down and ask one of those buggers which way to go.'

'Who?'

'The cops by the vans. Say you want the duty officer, and tell him I'll be along pretty shortly.'

'Okay, I'll tell him,' Wolraad agreed blankly, wincing as his injured arm was bumped. 'How's the time now?'

'Roughly thirty minutes, but I –'

Wolraad had slammed the door. Buchanan watched him approach a group of policemen, receive his directions, and then walk slowly up the steps and into the building.

And with him went the odd feeling which had nagged Buchanan so incessantly all morning, and he was at last able to recognize it for what it was: a subliminal response to someone so unnaturally uptight that their tension seemed to become your own. The same feeling store detectives and gamblers relied upon to help them pick their marks – as did intelligence officers, for that matter, who were wary of a double-cross. But the tension in this instance had to be of a deeper, more personal kind, because Buchanan had no cause to suspect treachery – there had never been any evidence of the son sharing his father's obsessions; if anything, the reverse had been uncomfortably clear from the start. In fact, this could be the basis of the thing. And anyway, once the authorities had been put in the picture, there had been no way Wolraad might have cheated on him, whatever the motivation. Nobody could've unsaid what Buchanan himself had said, not in a thousand words in any bloody language.

For several reeling and irrational seconds, things had looked very nasty – just as they did on a bad jump, before the 'chute finally snapped open. Even so, Buchanan found himself hurrying back to police headquarters, from where he had left the car in an hotel yard. He had to be sure he was on firm ground at last.

In the event, it proved to be a quicksand, but there was no hint of this after some minutes after he, too, had asked the way to the duty officer in the Security Branch.

'What do you want with Security?' the uniformed constable inquired, picking at something on his protruding gun butt. 'They don't do shaves, you know.'

For a funny man, and he looked like Mort Sahl, he had a bloody awful sense of timing.

'I'm with Wolraad Steyn,' Buchanan said reaching the top step.

'Oh ja?'

'Look –'

'Look? What's this "look"? Now you better explain properly to me what you want here, or there'll be trouble, understand?'

'Let's say they sent for me,' Buchanan tendered, knowing the type fairly well.

'Ach, well, that's different. Come.'

And, as they went up the wide staircase inside, the constable asked for both his name and the name of the officer who had sent for him.

'It was the duty officer.'

'Captain Geldenhuis?'

'Must've been. But wasn't Steyn asking for him only a little while back?'

'Who knows?' the constable answered with a grin, glorying in professional mystique. 'Here's the door, only you best wait first.'

'Certainly.'

Buchanan read a few lines from a well-known fire extinguisher, and the heavy door opened again.

'Inside!' snapped the constable.

'Thank you, laddie.'

The office was an exact square like a position on a chessboard. Bars covered the windows, and there were three filing cabinets against the opposite wall; while across the far corner of the room was a broad desk supporting a small switchboard, a radio transmitter, and the elbows of a heavily-built man. Just above his head was a large clock.

Geldenhuis did, in fact, seem to have all the bulk and menace of a Cape buffalo, but his keenly intelligent eyes and his hand-knitted pullover made his humanity plain. As did the sticking plaster over a snick in his cleft chin.

'So you are Finbar Buchanan?' he asked, nibbling at a thumbnail. 'The one who phoned this morning? Who had the tip-off about Dirk Steyn's attempt on the Prime Minister?'

'Oh aye, in person.'

Then Buchanan noticed two things which seemed strange. The first was that the constable had closed the door and yet stayed on in the room. The other was that Geldenhuis appeared to be holding on to that thumbnail with his teeth, as though restraining his fist. It was a large fist, with a significantly prominent second knuckle.

'Captain?' he said politely.

The fist was moved into the safekeeping of the other hand, and taken down under the desk top.

'I have one question only, *meneer*: what gives you the cheek to come into my office?'

The floor did an odd thing beneath Buchanan's feet.

'Christ, to see if Wolraad was with you and to –'

'*Yirra!*' Geldenhuis exploded. 'Did you hear that, Du Toit? This – this degenerate just comes straight out with it! Maybe you should fetch the district surgeon to take a look – this man can't be normal. How does he strike you?'

Buchanan was standing, for the first time in his life, completely stunned.

'Er, well sort of like a hobo, sir. There's cuts on his *kop* from falling down in the gutter.'

'Ja, and it smells like he doesn't bath too often either, but that's not the point I'm making. There's plenty of tramps in this town who never give trouble.'

Du Toit fingered his gun lanyard, apparently at a loss to know how to respond.

'Let's hear your point, Captain Geldenhuis,' Buchanan heard himself say. 'You've had your fun.'

'Ach, but you haven't had yours, correct? It's a big shame, but you overdid it – that's twice you overdid it. You want me to tell you how?'

Buchanan stared at him with brow raised.

'Okay, for instance, when Wolraad Steyn rang me a few minutes ago, and said he'd been told by you to report to me, I was able to reassure him such a step wasn't necessary. Ja, and I also told him if he and his pa had any more trouble with you, they must come to see us about it.'

'What's this, sir?' asked Du Toit.

'Ach!'

'Hell, how am I supposed to know what to do? All you said was bring him in for a look-see, then chuck him in the cells.'

Geldenhuis checked his switchboard, and then said in an impatient tone: 'You can tell by looking, can't you? This animal has got a grudge against some folk from the Transvaal called Steyn, and so he does all sorts of mad things to cause them embarrassment. The son was explaining to me just now that this whatever-you-call-it got the sack off the Steyns' farm for messing around with Bantu females. You know these immigrant types, hey? And then he got the sack again for the same thing and must have come down here where it's warmer to lie in the sun. And so what happens? The Steyns are here for Voortrekker Week and by chance he sees them and – ach, I told them to forget about the whole business. And then what? He comes marching in, right here!'

So that was how the long silence in the car had been spent. The bastard was, in his crude way, an inventive genius. Only Wolraad Steyn could have made that call, and it must have been while the car was being parked. Keep it simple, Buchanan warned himself, or you will sink right into this.

'Malicious phone call, sir?' asked Du Toit, showing his earnest wish to be useful. 'Is that the charge?'

But Buchanan cut across with: 'I've got to know whether you at least reacted to my warning this morning?'

The laugh was richly appreciative.

'There you had me worried to begin with,' Geldenhuis admitted, rising to scratch behind him. 'All that stuff about this *ou* Dirk Steyn coming down to *donner* the Prime Minister, and whites dressing up as terrorists, and people getting killed by the bucketful – and what else was it?'

'*Hey?*' Du Toit gasped, delighted.

'Difficult to believe at first, I agree. And on a day like this, with every crank in the place trying to make life hard for us, I came close to dismissing it. Then this mate of yours, who talks such terrible Afrikaans, put me right in the picture. We had Mr Vorster locked up in a bank safe and put armed guards all around. So it's really to him we owe our thanks, you see, Meneer Buchanan. You just can't take chances when there's Martians on the attack.'

Martians. Just one word – and there was no need to ask him to repeat it. But by now Geldenhuis, who had probably seen to everything, was giving a small performance to win easy laughs off his subordinate.

'*Martians?*' echoed Du Toit right on cue, and who could blame him.

'You should get up to date, constable! You should also not believe everything you hear on the radio or see in the newspapers. Can you tell me what happened to a mission in Lesotho on Friday?'

'Ja, just a sec – isn't that the place which got hit by a plane?'

'Go to the top of the class. Only it wasn't a plane, I'm sorry to say, it was a flying saucer from outer space. Inside were these green shadows that could enter into a man's brain and make them follow their orders. The big idea was to attack Mr Vorster because they were afraid of his détente plans with them, especially as they are green and he has this belief in apartheid. Of course, you must realize it doesn't sound so good coming from my lips, my friend – I can't seem to talk so sincerely of matters like these.'

'You may surprise yourself yet,' Buchanan said grimly, sick to the stomach. 'What I told you is true, and you have just over twenty minutes in which to make up your mind about that. Possibly far less time, depending on when Mr Vorster is appearing to take the salute.'

That got a laugh from both of them.

'You can breathe easy, *meneer*, I'm glad to say. You see these gadgets of mine? At any second I like I can have the whole shooting match stopped like that, and Mr Vorster removed from the scene.'

'Then will you let me –'

'Ach, sorry, I'm a busy man and I've wasted enough time on this little matter already. You can make your statement later when we charge you for interfering. *Trek hom weg, man.*'

For a fleeting moment, Buchanan weakened his grip on the immediate – by trying to see what lay behind it – and felt he'd suffered an attack of the green shadows himself. It didn't seem likely he had a hope in hell of talking his way out of this, and every word he uttered lost another second, but nobody was ever going to say he didn't try.

'And I have one question for you, Captain, which I put to you as a British intelligence agent based in –'

'Can you prove that?'

'Not quickly enough for –'

'Quick, man! Your question?'

'If my story happened to be true, then what sense –'

'Sense?' shouted Geldenhuis, understandably giving way to his own exasperation. 'Who's talking about sense? I'm talking about *nonsense*, man! Criminal bloody nonsense that bastards like you think is funny! Why should I try to make sense of bloody madness? Of every loony story and crackpot I've heard in this office today? My job is to dismiss nonsense, that's all!'

The worst of it was that Buchanan could see exactly what the man meant, having dealt under similar circumstances with the lunatic fringe, and knowing how obscene they were when real risks faced every politician who stood up in public. The trick would be to find some ground outside the context of the telephone calls.

The clock gave him nineteen minutes to do it in.

'There are some quick checks you could make,' he said, taking a pace forward. 'Ring the game reserve we were at. Ring Louis Fouché of BOSS in Maseru and ask him to –'

'What do you know about him, may I ask?'

'A bloody sight more than he does about me, but he'll do in the circumstances.'

Geldenhuis opened a file and ran his finger down a list of names.

'Ja, just as I thought: Fouché is here on a special-duty detachment with the rest of the extras we've brought in. Have you been getting drinks off him then?'

'Bring him here and ask him,' Buchanan answered, fighting to keep calm. 'Or quicker still, ring his oppo in Maseru. For your own sake, as much as anyone's, get your bloody finger out!'

'What will he tell me?'

'Well, at least he should know that I was in the flying –'

'*Out*! Du Toit, I want this madman out! Out of here!'

Buchanan couldn't help a smile at that slip of his tongue, which had been forced on him by Wolraad's bizarre ploy, and which – ordinarily – could have been so easily explained away. But that seemed to be the end of the road, unless, of course, he could find a means of also exerting some pressure. Hearsay and logic alone only compounded the nightmare – as the little sod had cunningly calculated.

'Come on, the officer's finished with you, *malkop*,' grunted Du Toit, giving him a shove towards the door. 'Can't you see that?'

This decided Buchanan that a change of attitude was needed – plus a little pressure, of a subtle kind. So he turned on his escort and slapped him across the face to the right.

And then, as Du Toit spun to keep his balance, Buchanan grabbed him clumsily from behind. It was important that his movement should seem inept, because it was intended to bring Geldenhuis forward to the rescue – and out of reach of any alarm buttons. It was also important that the left hand going for Du Toit's throat should, like a conjurer's feint, distract the eye from the right hand, which was doing a pickpocket's job on the holster.

205

Geldenhuis moved quickly, clearing his desk and leaping to his colleague's defence.

Buchanan then did three things almost at once: he used his left hand to render Du Toit unconscious, with a snuffing action on his throat, and his right to snap the lanyard and bring the automatic to bear. The buffalo braked.

'Hands on your head, Captain, taking them up well out from your sides.'

Geldenhuis obliged rather than obeyed; his expression was thoughtful, and his eyes totally without fear.

'You mustn't ask me to do anything else, you understand?' he said. 'Because, I am afraid, I will not.'

'You won't listen again to what I have to say?'

'*Nie.*'

'Didn't think you would. Do you know what this is? It's the only gun I've got that hasn't been bloody spiked – how does it look in my hand?'

There was a faint smile on Geldenhuis's face as he replied: 'It proves you are a madman.'

'Mad? Beyond a doubt?'

'Ja.'

'Which was your first impression of me?'

'Sadly that is so.'

'You're good at judging character then?'

'It is not always difficult.'

'Then what would you make of a man who now did this?' Buchanan asked lightly. 'I'd like you to give it your serious consideration, but not for too long. Sane or insane?'

And he tossed the pistol over to Geldenhuis, who caught it on reflex before realizing what had happened, stood stockstill for a while, and then looked up.

Buchanan met his gaze and smiled. They probably had quite a way to go yet, and possibly this, too, had been overdoing things a little, but beggars couldn't be choosers.

'Seventeen minutes and counting,' he said.

Chapter Fifteen

Wolraad Steyn, his throat very dry, waited in the shadow of the Church of the Covenant, nervously clasping and unclasping his right hand.

If he wasn't so sure that the man Buchanan had been wrong about Pa's intentions, having believed some terrible lies about him, then he would, of course, be feeling a lot worse. As it was, though, the most dreadful thing which could still happen was that Pa would get a chance to make a fool of himself in front of all these people, and he was there to prevent that. And then, once he had found Pa, he would take him to a good hiding place for a while, until there had been enough time for this misunderstanding to be sorted out. He had himself needed nearly the whole night to see that Pa was in some way the victim of Oom Willie's craziness, just as had occurred before in the past. Pa would naturally be grateful for some help, and so, in the end, perhaps good could come of it. In fact, there had been plenty of proof that God was on their side – you didn't get ideas for stories like that yourself, you had to have inspiration, the same as when you made up a new tune. And there had been proof, too, that God wouldn't let you do a wrong thing if there was another way. Take, for instance, that moment when he'd been about to drop a rock on Buchanan's head to stop him chasing Pa for the natives – and had slipped because God made Buchanan glance up then, almost catching him at it ...

Wolraad shuddered and looked around again.

This seemed the best place to be, as a few yards away on the paved area in front of the very modern church – the gabled one beside him was now the Voortrekker Museum – newsreel cameramen were unpacking their equipment. There was a dais, too, wrapped in the Republic's flag, from where the dignitaries could view the procession. A few of them were already seated;

207

the men in black suits and waistcoats, with white shirts and white ties, and the women in dark frocks and broad-brimmed hats.

His eyes searched the crowd that was building up on the pavements on either side of the very wide road. Many of the onlookers were plainly members of the *volk*, but there were English-speakers among them, too, and a sprinkling of cautious blacks. He could always tell the English-speakers on these occasions, and not just by their clothes: they kept very grave faces to show their respect, but every now and then would twitch a small smile and whisper together. Gradually the blacks were being elbowed back, or people simply moved to stand in front of them. The front row was where Pa would place himself.

Wolraad felt sure of it.

'Hey, you!' said a sharp voice, and a beefy, purple-nosed police sergeant appeared from behind him. 'You can't stand here, you know! For VIPs only.'

'Sorry, uncle,' said Wolraad, and moved on to the pavement.

'No, no, go right to the side. You will still see all there is to see. Go on.'

Wolraad obeyed him, bumping into a bewildered black who was trying to get through the press with his suitcases, and nearly hitting the buffoon in his rage at being distracted. Then he found himself a gap on the kerb and made a quick check Pa had still not shown up. Wolraad took a step into the road to make sure this was true of his side as well, and then stepped back.

He was breathing heavily, struggling to subdue the guilt, panicky and craven, injected into him by that sudden bark of critical authority. But this was sheer weakness: what he was doing had to be right, and there was, besides, plenty of time left.

The city hall clock, high in its red-brick tower, two-thirds of a block away, struck the quarter hour.

Bringing another surge of dread and doubt, but Wolraad was able to quell it with a prayer for strength, and his pulse steadied. Belief, not thought, that was the important thing, and belief in himself, paramount: for the rest, he would have guidance.

Wolraad looked calmly about him.

No Pa. If he didn't come soon, he might find it impossible to get anywhere near the dais and the thicket of microphones. Then what would he do . . .

The street emptied of traffic. The blink of faces on the other side of the broad strip of grey tarmac thickened, and now even the toddlers were finding it hard to squeeze through with their little paper flags. Although, here and there, some men had taken up positions which must have been yielded grudgingly. One had a face that looked faintly familiar – or may have been just the hairstyle.

An ox bellowed a complaint in the old market square beside the city hall, where the procession was assembling, and the crowd laughed.

Wolraad had another look at his side of the street, and was hooted at by a traffic cop, cruising the route on a motor-cycle. This didn't bother him, and he stayed out in the road until satisfied the check had been properly made. All it revealed was that two trucks had drawn up some distance away to offload a police guard of honour and their rifles. A company of soldiers was also forming up.

Back on the kerbstone again, Wolraad knew he was being stared at and realized that the hoot had made him conspicuous. He shrugged: the crowd was getting restless, and had seized upon any novelty.

Pa would have to come soon.

If Pa didn't come soon, he would have to tell them. The shame would be enormous.

He was still being stared at. By that face which rang a bell somewhere – by a lanky, sallow young man with a clever mouth, and a black cap of longish hair, cut in a fringe.

Panic returned for an instant, as Wolraad allowed himself a glimpse of the puny hopelessness of his endeavour.

But he was not alone; never was he alone. That had been part of the bargain.

Wolraad stared back boldly, and saw the young man, who was looking very thoughtful, bring a cigarette to his lips. He saw the flash of rings on every finger.

'Maseru!' Wolraad gasped under his breath, and found himself forcing his way back into the crowd.

He hurried along the fringe on the inside of the pavement, not knowing quite why he felt so threatened, nor where he was going – except that it was away from the dais and the film crews. He was jostled and cursed, and twice indignant people grabbed his arm, but nothing could halt his frantic progress.

He came to a break in the fence on his left and looked up. He had reached the old market square where the oxen were being inspanned; there were at least twenty waggons, and a great number of people dressed in historical costume. They seemed very excited at the prospect of shortly parading in front of –

Providence! What had seemed a bitter reversal was in fact, Wolraad realized, the help he'd been promised. And then he also realized what a fool he'd been to think that Pa could do anything from behind a line of policemen. Whereas, hidden in a waggon, say, where his swollen face wouldn't show and make people notice him, he could get right to the dais and carry out whatever foolishness it was he'd planned.

Wolraad walked, as casually as he could, towards the throng. The womenfolk were wearing long dresses with long sleeves and lacy collars, and large sun bonnets – some had chosen to look stupid in sunglasses as well, while men had put on mole-skin trousers, leather jackets and bush hats. The children, who were running everywhere, wore the same as their parents, and the little black *voorleiers* who led the oxen were naked except for their *moochis*. With all the final adjustments being made to how each other looked, no notice was being taken of the waggons themselves.

He circled round, intending to come up on the waggons from behind. Beyond this first collection of people, he found a whole Boer commando trying to get itself organized. There had been no need for these participants in the pageant to make special costumes, as ordinary farming clothes were real enough, although they had dug out the proper bandoliers to hang criss-crossed on their chests, and some were waving Martini Henrys. They were not mounted yet, and their boys waited with the horses in rows. There seemed to be some sort of argument going on.

This only made it easier for Wolraad to slip in among them and make for the first waggon.

'Just a minute,' one of the commando said, blocking his way. 'Where have you sprung up from, man?'

'Hey?' said Wolraad, very surprised.

'Ach, it's this thing,' the man chuckled pulling off a false beard which had wire hooks like spectacles. 'Not bad, is it? Old Fanie bought out the whole shop for us in Jo'burg!'

And Wolraad saw it was Nik Claasens, who'd been at his initiation.

'Nik!' he said, trying to sound pleased. 'How goes it?'

'Not too badly. But your pa didn't say you were here, you know. There's been enough trouble talking the young one into giving up his gun.'

'*Gun?*' echoed Wolraad, putting a hand on a horse's neck quickly.

'Oh ja; gun, bandolier, bullets – the lot. Dirk wanted to ride with us, but there wasn't the extra. Still, little Japie has said he doesn't mind too much, and he'll still come with us on a pony we found. Sort of as a boy messenger, you know?'

'Beard, too?'

'Beard – everything!' laughed Nik, as if amused by the old man's childish insistence on being fully one of the boys. 'And you know Japie's only thirteen, so that's no loss; to be honest, I was worried him in that fluff could make the kaffirs laugh at us. But don't tell me you want to join now? Because I'm sorry, it's not on.'

Wolraad gazed at him blankly.

'No hard feelings, hey?' said Nik, hitching his beard on again, and virtually hiding his face. 'Thought I'd better explain before you talked to the others. Japie's dad is –'

'I was just looking for my pa,' Wolraad broke in, bringing his hands down.

'Oh ja?'

'Just looking. Where is he?'

'Man, his horse is that spotty one, so he can't be far away. We move in about five minutes – hell, I've forgotten something. See you later, okay?'

Nik Classens hurried off, beckoning to an official with an armband, and Wolraad was able to turn about and look at the horse with spots. Pa was nowhere near it. Pa wasn't in sight.

'Boy, where's the boss?' he asked the black groom.

'He go that way.'

'Which?'

'By that side.'

'He means the public lavatories,' said a stranger standing nearby, polishing up a bullet's nose on his sleeve.

Wolraad forced himself to keep to a fast walk as he made the approach. He was half-way there when a man with a rifle and a big beard stepped out of the doorway, freezing him in his tracks. But the man was too stocky.

'My pa? Have you seen him?'

'Who?'

'Steyn – Dirk Steyn.'

'Old Dirk! He's your pa, hey? There's a character!'

'But have you seen him?'

'In there, you mean?'

'*Anywhere*, man!'

'He could have been in a cubicle.'

'Look,' began Wolraad, and then gagged.

Pa had just sauntered out of the lavatory, with a magazine carbine slung across his back and the gleam of six rounds missing from his bandolier.

The stocky commando went on his way. The two men stood there. One trembling; the other astonished.

Then Pa began to run and, a few seconds later, having taken note of this with dull indifference, Wolraad came to life and chased after him.

'Help me!' he shouted, as they pelted down behind the lavatory block and the city hall.

But the black loungers in this alleyway, who sat against the walls and murmured to one another, merely grinned at the playfulness of white men on a day of celebrations. They even drew back their legs to avoid tripping anyone.

'Pa!' cried Wolraad. 'For God's sake, Pa!'

But his father ducked around the corner of the city hall, and when Wolraad got there, it was to see him already clattering up a fire escape.

Wolraad tried to take too many steps at a time and fell, tearing open his shin. Then he went up it two at a time, his ears filled with the beat of the iron-shod boots above him but catching distant sounds of a brass band on the march. He fell again, over a fire bucket that came rolling down from the top landing, and cut open his forehead on the edge of a step.

'Pa, I'm hurt!' he shouted.

There was a crash of glass and the thud of a rifle butt against woodwork.

When Wolraad staggered on to the top landing, he found the door there had been smashed open, and reeled his way down a narrow passage into a wide corridor. Blood was getting into his eyes and he had to pause to staunch it in the crook of an elbow.

His father must have gone towards the street side of the building.

'Help!' he shouted again, but knew everyone would be out, watching the procession.

'Help me,' he said softly.

With renewed strength, Wolraad went down the wide corridor, around the corner past the head of the marble stairs, and along the west wing. A brass doorknob and some wood splinters on the brown linoleum showed him which room to enter.

It was the office of a scrupulously neat official. One of those men who change into a thin black jacket when they reach work, and who can't go home on Friday evening before they've arranged their pens, pencils, paperknife and ruler with precision around their unstained blotter. Pale, squeaky men who value above everything their peace and order.

Pa, haggard and flushed, crouched beyond the desk at an open window, his carbine held ready, watching the street below. He glanced round and nodded casually. Then continued his vigil.

'Hello, Wolraad,' he said.

'Hello, Pa.'

They could have been meeting after a long, hard day on the land. Reality faltered for a second.

'I've come to –'

'Please, I would prefer not to talk.'

'B-but you're –'

'Don't stammer, boy!'

213

'You're not well, Pa. It isn't just me – everyone says so! You're sick. Please listen.'

Pa cocked his head. Not, however, in response to Wolraad's plea. The blare of the band had grown suddenly louder: it must have turned the corner into Church Street.

'When a man isn't well, he must allow himself to be helped.'

'Thank you, Mr Music-maker – only I can't believe your concern is truly for me. Don't let us start lying to each other after all these years, not now.'

'*You* lied to me, Pa! Right at the start you lied about going into the mountains! I would have come to you sooner, only I believed what –'

'It was necessary. In the same way this is necessary. Part of my duty.'

'No, Pa! Can't you see? This is treason!'

His father laughed. He seldom laughed, and the sound was frightening in itself.

'If it's treason we're talking about,' Pa said, slipping his finger through the trigger guard, 'you'll soon get a look down there at the greatest traitor of them all! Ja, he'll be on that box, standing with the rest of the soft bellies who'd betray the people to –'

'Pa, how many times has this been explained to you? What choice is there? Better we swallow a little pride and make friends with the kaffirs or we're finished. Russia and China are just waiting to be on their side. And what about our own natives? Can't they come into our army and fight with us? Ach, can't you see? Maybe it's something God has always wanted us to do!'

'Coward's talk! Friends, you say? What about our friends, our kin in Rhodesia? Are we to show weakness to the kaffir, just so as to keep him from –'

'Mr Vorster isn't showing weakness! It's real strength, Pa – the same strength the Boer generals showed when they made peace with the English, and then took the country back afterwards. He knows his duty as well as you do! He knows you can't stick with the ideas of the past!'

Pa turned at a roar from the crowd; he looked down the street and then back at Wolraad.

'He is arriving now, and so I must end our small conversation.

But first I must ask you: is God's will a thing of the past also? Are the holy oaths that him and me took things of the past? We must stand alone — have you never understood that? We must remain unsullied, strong, true to our mission, or the Almighty will no longer protect us from the world, and—'

'Pa, to kill a Prime Minister is still treason.'

All this talk. Very soon, unless Wolraad took some action, he knew it would be too late. Yet the wild urgency had gone from him, to be replaced by a dreamy, abstracted feeling, in which nothing seemed to matter very much. While his mind insisted that none of this was true and really happening.

Then he remembered the young man in the crowd and, jarred by his instincts, knew he had to act at once.

'Pa, *please*, I am your son.'

'No.'

'Then I will take it from you.'

'I would shoot you,' said his father.

Cheering rose from the street and Wolraad knew that the parade was going down towards where the saluting-box stood. There was only time for a final appeal.

'Pa, *please*, I am your son.'

'No, I don't think so,' Dirk Steyn murmured, raising his carbine and resting it on the window sill. 'A man may leave his lands to be divided among many who bear his name, but it is not often he has a son. A true son who knows what is right, and who doesn't hesitate to lay down his life for it. Little Boet was such a one.'

And he turned his back contemptuously on Wolraad, to lean forward and take careful aim.

This was betrayal, the son thought.

Then, out of nowhere, it came: the power and the freedom. The words Kroen had spoken, assuring him that, whatever was demanded of him, he would never fail his people. His movements would be swift, and they would be sure. So it had been promised. So it had been ordained from the beginning.

Wolraad lifted the paperknife from the desk and crossed the gap.

And when he had done what had to be done, he raised his eyes, blinked away the tears, and looked through the window down to where the carbine had pointed. Then he understood why his father had been so slow to pull the trigger: for some unaccountable reason, the Prime Minister must have suddenly left the scene at the very last second.